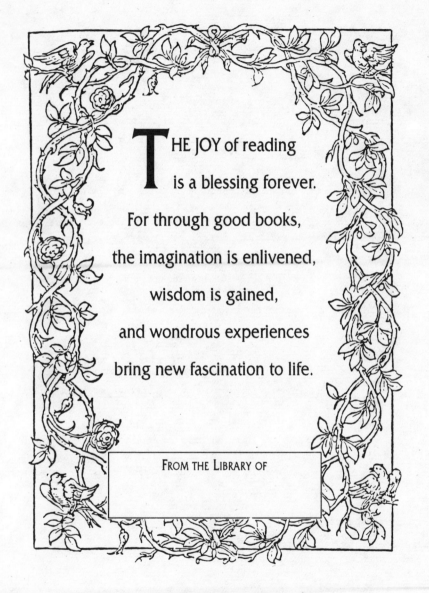

THE JOY of reading
is a blessing forever.
For through good books,
the imagination is enlivened,
wisdom is gained,
and wondrous experiences
bring new fascination to life.

FROM THE LIBRARY OF

EXCLUSIVE CHRISTIAN FAMILY BOOK CLUB EDITION

Mercy & Eagleflight

MICHAEL
PHILLIPS

COMPLETE AND UNABRIDGED

Since 1948, The Book Club You Can Trust

Cover illustration copyright © 1996 by Peter Fiore
Front cover photo copyright © 1996 by Brian MacDonald
Interior map copyright © 1996 by Kirk Caldwell
Author photo copyright © 1996 by Bill Bilsley
Design by Andrea Gjeldum

Scripture quotations are taken from the *Holy Bible,* King James Version.

Library of Congress Cataloging-in-Publication Data

Phillips, Michael R., date
  Mercy and Eagleflight / Michael R. Phillips.
    p. cm. — (Mercy and Eagleflight ; v. 1)
  ISBN 0-8423-3920-5 (alk. paper)
  I. Title. II. Series: Phillips, Michael R., date Mercy and Eagleflight ; v. 1.
PS3566.H492M47 1996
813′.54 — dc20   96-9793

Printed in the United States of America

04 03 02 01 00 99 98 97 96
9 8 7 6 5 4 3 2 1

First Hardcover Edition for Christian Family Book Club: 1997

To Fran Shoemaker

Faithful coworker and dear friend to both Judy and me, without whose encouragement this book may not have reached publication. Thank you, Fran, for being part of our lives! There are many things, as the saying goes, that ... we couldn't do without you, and we thank God for you.

CONTENTS

1

REVIVAL IN
BLUE GAP

"Won't you listen as the Lord Jesus urges your
heart to turn from its sinful ways? Oh, brothers and sisters,
now is the time to come to him, and he will give you the
peace your hearts have been longing for."

The attractive young lady gazed upon her listeners
around the tent, her eyes filled with earnest compassion
and hope for their souls.

1

No one stirred.

The congregation, sitting on folding wooden chairs she herself had set up three hours earlier, was comprised chiefly of women. Most of them sat prudishly wondering what such a young unmarried *woman* was doing this far from civilization. They were willing to put up with their irreverent suspicions, however, if her presence got their husbands into the revival tent.

To judge from the men in tow, the rumor of a pretty young evangelist's assistant had accomplished precisely that. While she had been setting up the chairs, the evangelist himself had been passing leaflets throughout Blue Gap promising "healing of body and mind, music to lighten the heart, and a message of salvation to the soul" to all who came and gathered under the tent just south of town, about fifty yards from the livery stable.

Some of the men in the Blue Kansan Saloon joked among themselves, wondering which direction the wind would be blowing.

"Just you doin' the preachin', Reverend?" asked a cowhand standing at the bar, shoving his wide-brimmed hat back on his head and looking over the paper he'd just been handed.

"Not on your life, young man. You don't think anybody'd come just to see *this* ugly face, do you?" The words carried a knowing expression and the slightest hint of a smile.

"What exactly do ya mean, Preacher?" asked another.

"You'll have to come tonight to find out!" answered the minister, turning toward the second man with a grin.

"Who's that pretty young thing that rode in with you on the wagon this morning?" now asked a third.

"You get the same answer as the rest," he said. "You'll have to come to the meeting to find out."

Then, distributing leaflets to the remainder of the occupants of the saloon, the minister strode through the double swinging doors and was gone.

It was a well-designed evangelistic strategy guaranteed to stimulate curiosity. Entertainment in out-of-the-way places like western Kansas was ordinarily limited to a tornado, a stampede, a new family moving in, a new business opening up, or someone getting shot. A revival meeting was at least sufficient to get tongues wagging.

The first night's attendance was usually limited to wives and whatever handful of husbands they could drag along. The rest of the men would wait to find out what it was like. If all went well, as it always did, the second night's gathering would require twice as many chairs as the first. By the third, the tent would be bulging.

Music, entertainment, lively preaching, promises of healing or other manifestations of the miraculous offered to the public free of charge by the charismatic evangelist and his demure assistant—it was a combination scarce a community west of Kansas City or Fort Smith could resist. It was better than the occasional medicine man with his sideshow of tricks to sell his concoctions of worthless elixir.

And they seemed to get that for which they came, for the souls that made tearful professions at the altar of Reverend Joseph Mertree's Tent of Meeting and Healing numbered in the many hundreds.

"Won't you pray, my friends, while we sing, and ask the Holy Ghost to stir your hearts in preparation for the words Brother Mertree will bring to us," the evangelist's assistant now concluded.

The young lady walked to the small pump organ on the section of the wagon constituting the platform from which she had been addressing her skeptical listeners, sat down, played a few bars of introduction, then began singing in a high, clear-pitched, but tremulous voice. Gradually the women in the audience joined in the familiar chorus, followed by about half the men.

> *Bringing in the sheaves, bringing in the sheaves,*
> *We will come rejoicing, bringing in the sheaves.*

She led them through two verses and two more choruses.

The organ fell silent as the final strains of the hymn died away into the evening stillness.

She rose. "Now, brothers and sisters, I want to introduce to you Brother Joseph, who will bring the Lord's Word to us."

4

BROTHER
JOSEPH

The moment the words left her lips, the boisterous

evangelist leapt to his feet and bounded onto the platform

from where he had been sitting in the front row.

"Thank you . . . thank you, Sister Mercy," he said, "for

your inspiring and challenging words, the wonderful sing-

ing, and that introduction!"

As he spoke, Sister Mercy stepped down off the back of the wagon and took the seat he had just left.

"And now, brothers and sisters," the evangelist went on, "before I begin, won't you please join me in prayer."

He paused momentarily while his countenance took on a solemnity of expression, looked upward, and folded the fingers of his hands across his chest.

"Our great almighty God," he began in a heavy baritone of reverence, "we thank thee for the abundance of thy blessings which thou hast showered upon us, thy sinful servants. And now we ask for thy Spirit to descend upon us in this tent of healing and meeting and to descend upon this town, that thy work here might be great, that many souls would repent of their waywardness from thee, that the miracle of thy healing touch would fall upon those whom in thy providence thou hast ordained to make whole, and that a great revival would spread throughout this community as a result of thy work, which thou wilt begin among those of thy faithful servants who have come this evening. We pray all these things in the name of thy Son, *Amen.*"

He took a deep breath, then slowly glanced over the twenty-five or thirty present.

"Ah, my friends," he said, "I feel such a moving of God's Spirit about to descend upon the town of Blue Gap! As I was praying, my heart sensed that great revival is in store for this community—a mighty spiritual awakening among souls burdened with sin. I implore those of you faithful ones who have answered the call tonight to pray with me that many more of your friends and neighbors will join us during the next two nights. Tomorrow I will speak on the healing power of God's touch. You will not want to miss it!

"Bring your friends, your children, your neighbors. Bring

the sick, the lame. God's power will be poured out before your very eyes, and many will be saved!"

The evangelist paused, then began again. "Now, my friends, let us turn our attention to the subject of this evening's message. I have chosen for my topic 'Holiness in the Midst of Sin.'"

A few of his listeners shifted in their seats, then settled in for the duration of the sermon, which lasted some forty minutes.

At the conclusion of that time, Sister Mercy again took her place at the organ for three verses of "The Old Rugged Cross," between which Brother Joseph made several impassioned pleas for a profession of salvation on the part of any of the congregation who might still be numbered among the lost.

An elderly man with a crippled leg limped forward, weeping and apparently disconsolate. Brother Joseph took him to one side, arm around his shoulder.

"Please sing with me one more chorus," said Sister Mercy, as she held out the song's final tones on the organ, "and let us be in prayer while Brother Joseph ministers to our brother in need."

Immediately she began again with the first verse, singing loudly as the congregation joined her.

Halfway through the chorus, the evangelist returned to the front, arm still around the old man, whose moist face now beamed with a smile. He held up his free hand to stop the singing. The organ and the high soprano voice of Sister Mercy fell silent.

"Hallelujah, my friends!" he said. "I want to tell you that our dear brother here has just confessed his years of waywardness. He has asked the Savior to forgive him and has dedicated his life to the service of the Master!"

"Hallelujah!" repeated Sister Mercy.

"Praise the Lord!" said one or two of the women in the congregation.

"What a wonderful night this has been!" added the preacher exuberantly. "A stray lamb has been brought back into the fold! Let us sing that final chorus again, that we might each go our way this evening with the rejoicing of angels in our hearts. And remember, come back tomorrow, and bring your friends and neighbors. God's Spirit will move again . . . in even greater ways!"

He turned toward the organ, and Sister Mercy led the congregation again, with voice and organ, joined by Brother Joseph and the new lamb at his side. "So I'll cherish the old rugged cross, till my trophies at last I lay down. . . ."

3

RIPE MISSION FIELD
OF A
YOUNG NATION

The small rough-and-tumble town where the traveling

missionaries found themselves was not so different from

hundreds of others in the American West in the final quarter

of the nineteenth century. It was filled with men who drank

more than was good for them and with a few women who

hoped better things would come before long to these out-

posts of civilization where they had—some willingly, others

unwillingly—made their homes. These women knew well enough that it was a region of sore spiritual need and was a ripe mission field full of men who needed the gentling influence of religion.

Despite the puritanical roots of its founding and the spiritual motives by which the proponents of its nationhood sought to undergird their revolution, the United States of America was hardly a thoroughly Christian nation in 1789. Atheistic societies were widespread throughout the northern states, and the skepticism of European philosophers was in vogue among students and the upper classes. A relatively small percentage of the new nation's populace professed themselves to be Christians at the close of the eighteenth century.

A great revival swept through the young country, however, in the early years of the nineteenth century. Frontier camp meetings pushed the spirit of this Second Great Awakening across the Appalachians into unchurched settlements in Kentucky and Ohio. Heavy emphasis on dramatic conversion experience led to rousing hellfire sermons by the often fanatical preachers at the vanguard of the movement.

The young nation emerged out of its infancy and grew. Settlements became villages, villages grew into towns, some of the towns became cities. Roads connected them. Stagecoach lines lengthened. Travel over greater distances slowly became less intimidating. People migrated farther and farther from the eastern seaboard.

Statehood came to Ohio, Indiana, Illinois, Michigan, and the South, extending the nation by midcentury to Texas and Iowa. A bloody war in the 1860s tested the fiber of the nation's fortitude, after which its western expansion once more resumed. By the 1880s an unprecedented era of growth and opportunity had come to the American West.

The war between the North and the South faded into memory, and the nation flexed its expansionary muscles more than ever before. Easterners flocked west in record numbers. The transcontinental rail lines linking the Atlantic and the Pacific made the huge land mass—formerly daunting to all but the most rugged pioneer spirits—one that could be traversed by women and families, businessmen, bankers, cattlemen, doctors, ranchers, lawyers, and farmers. Hundreds more miles of track were laid down every year, connecting once-remote outposts with the rest of the burgeoning nation.

Having begun at Sutter's Mill, east of Sacramento, the railroad now took to new heights—the subduing and settling of a continent. The gold rush brought statehood to California, but the rest of the West was not far behind. By 1890, eleven more western states had been admitted to the Union.

Though the western wilderness was shrinking, its frontier character remained robust and violent. Colonization was coming, but the decade of the 1880s more than any other earned Texas and Kansas, Colorado and Wyoming, Montana and the Dakotas the reputation of *the Wild West*. Indians still fought to maintain their lands. Buffalo hunters traveled west with their repeating rifles to enjoy the sport of slaughter. Saloons were the center of life in western towns, where lawlessness was often the only dependable law. Men wore guns on their hips and were not afraid to use them. Churches were few, cemeteries numerous.

The changing times brought many who sought to profit by them, for greed always accompanies opportunity. Civilization and settlement meant people with money, and the increase in train travel afforded endless opportunity for murdering gangs of robbers, such as the James gang, led by

Jesse and Frank James and Cole and Frank Younger, the Hole-in-the-Wall gang, and many others. It was an era when reputations were built, whose personalities—Wild Bill Hickok, Wyatt Earp, Doc Holliday, and George Custer—and the places of whose exploits—Tombstone, Dodge City, Boot Hill, and the Little Big Horn—would in time become both the famous and the infamous names of legend.

As the American West thus expanded, so did the frontiers of evangelism. The interest in Christianity begun by the Second Great Awakening continued through the nineteenth century, and the Industrial Revolution made possible the spread of its message via many new means.

Revival in the great cities of the East, led first by the preaching of Charles Finney and later in the century by D. L. Moody, fanned rapid growth of the Christian enterprise. The Salvation Army established its first work in the United States in 1880. Moody founded his Chicago Evangelization Society in Chicago in 1887. New denominations and organizations were formed. Schools, colleges, and Bible training institutes sprang up in every state of the Union.

The widespread hunger for spiritual knowledge led to a new literature of practical Christian faith. Bibles were printed in record numbers. Hundreds of thousands of books rolled off the presses and were eagerly consumed by an enthusiastic Christian populace. The sermons of Henry Ward Beecher and Phillips Brooks and the written studies of Moody and other biblical expositors were read widely. Topical and devotional treatises were produced on every subject imaginable, science and prophecy among the most popular. Darwin's theory of evolution was vigorously refuted with the former, the masses prepared for the imminent return of Christ with the latter. Commentaries, concordances, biblical encyclopedias, systematic theologies, and a wide variety of noted reference works were printed by a growing circle of religious publishing houses. Much of the fiction of the time carried heavy spiritual content.

This spiritual activity sparked a missionary zeal that led many to the harvest of the untamed lands across the far shores of the Mississippi. Revival came west with the railroad and the six-gun, bringing prairie preachers, women among them, who saw the possibilities presented by the growth of the nation in its spiritual context. It was not the prospect of gold or land or adventure that drove them but passion for the souls of men.

The prairie evangelists, however, would not tame the frontier. In many respects the West would remain wild and reckless for another twenty years. For the spirit of those who ventured here would always be that of the pioneer. Yet among them, even in the most out-of-the-way places, could one occasionally find a gentleman.

MANIFESTATIONS AND WONDERS

4

At nine-thirty on the morning following the service,

evangelist Mertree and his assistant met in the lobby of the

Blue Gap hotel.

"Good morning, Sister Mercy. Did you sleep well?"

"Yes, thank you, Brother Joseph."

"Are you ready for breakfast?"

She nodded.

The preacher led her through the lobby toward the hotel's dining room, where he had already secured a table and ordered their breakfast. They sat down.

"It was a wonderful service last evening," she said, taking a sip of the coffee that had been brought. "Have you seen Mr. Mohr yet today?"

"Yes, Sister Mercy. I called upon him at his home outside of town an hour ago. His face still beamed with joy."

"Praise the Lord! That is wonderful. There are men such as he in every town, it seems, hungrily waiting to hear the Word of God."

"The Lord has blessed and prospered our ministry, has he not, Sister Mercy?"

"Might I be able to call on Brother Mohr?"

"For what reason, Sister?"

"To . . . why, to offer him encouragement," she answered, "and speak words of faith to him."

"I think it best, Sister, that during these first hours and days of his new life, we not confuse him with varying points of view on matters of the gospel. The time will come, Sister. But you are yet young, and I think it best for now that I shepherd the new converts myself."

"I understand, Brother Joseph."

Their breakfast was served. They continued to talk about the day's plans.

"You will pass out our leaflets in the stores and shops, Sister. I will visit the saloons again. I have faith that a great many more will be in attendance tonight at the healing service."

A pause followed. Sister Mercy stared down at the table. Her mentor noticed her nervous silence.

"What is it, Sister Mercy?" he asked.

She looked up timidly. "I found myself wondering if we couldn't let Beula have a room in the hotel too."

"Certainly not, Sister. It wouldn't do for her to be seen."

"I'd be happy to let her share my room."

"No, it just would not do. People would not understand. The war may have made them free, but it cannot change the color of a Negro's skin. I harbor nothing but love for Beula, as you well know, and will take care of her all my life."

"She has been with you longer than I. It seems only fair that—"

"Please, Sister," interrupted Brother Joseph with a hint of sharpness in his tone, "you must trust that I know best. For the sake of the ministry, this is how it must be. She understands her place and is very comfortable in the wagon."

Sister Mercy said no more.

That afternoon they passed out leaflets as planned. Sister Mercy did not see Brother Joseph for most of the afternoon, though she herself was seen and noticed by every man and woman in Blue Gap as she walked the boardwalks and visited every shop, smiling and inviting all she saw to the meeting that evening.

In consequence of her efforts, by seven o'clock, the tent past the livery stable was filled with more than forty.

Nor were any of those in attendance disappointed.

The singing seemed louder and more enthusiastic, the confessions of saving faith more tearful and heartrending. Even the stoic wives from the previous evening entered into the spirit of the evening joyfully. How could they not but rejoice to witness several of the more raucous men of their town fall on their knees as the evangelist laid hands on them to pray for their eternal salvation?

There were manifestations of the miraculous too, just as

Brother Joseph had predicted. Mr. Mohr, whom nobody knew but who was taken into the fellowship of the community just like he'd been in Blue Gap for years, limped to the altar for prayer and returned to his seat, full of *Hallelujahs* and *Praise the Lords* and walking as straight as the rest.

Hank Jeffries, whom everybody did know and who'd broken his arm breaking a horse the day before, came into the meeting with the arm in a sling. Before the service was over he yanked the sling off and threw it to the ground and dared any of his friends to slug him right where the bone was broken. Finally several took him up on his dare, but Hank just laughed and said all the pain was gone.

When the collection plate came around at the end of the service, Hank stood up and made a show of throwing in a whole ten-dollar bill. After his example and the excitement that spread through the tent, most of the rest of those present liberally opened their wallets and purses.

By the third day, as Sister Mercy walked through town extending invitations for the third and final night's meeting, half of Blue Gap greeted her by name. Most promised they'd see her that evening. More than fifty did, with even greater results and miracles and outpourings and offerings and salvation prayers than before.

All the wives in Blue Gap declared they'd never seen anything like it. Indeed, spiritual revival seemed to have accompanied the tent meetings of Brother Joseph Mertree to their little community, just as the evangelist had predicted would happen.

5

THE
ITINERANT BAND

Three days later the evangelistic wagon bounced slowly

along, its Tent of Meeting and Healing neatly folded and

tucked away until it would be needed again, which would be

four days from now in the next town on Brother Joseph's

evangelistic itinerary.

The minister guided the team of two horses along the

dusty road across the Kansas plain, reins in hand, staring ahead with blank expression.

What was going through his head would have been diffi-cult to tell from his countenance. Sister Mercy had tried to read his mind on several occasions. The good brother never allowed her efforts to succeed, however, hiding behind the veneer of what was called a poker face when not preaching to a tent of listeners.

The young sister now sat in back with the aging black woman called Beula. Neither would it have been clear what either of them was thinking as they rumbled slowly along. Each carried her own reasons for being part of Brother Joseph Mertree's traveling ministry of evangelism, healing, and revival, but none of the three talked much about their pasts. In the territories west of Kansas City in the early 1890s, most folks weren't interested.

An hour later, the wagon slowed to a stop near a small grove of trees kept green by a creek flowing through them.

"This looks like a good spot," called out the minister. "We'll make camp here for the night."

Beula and Sister Mercy climbed out the back of the wagon while Brother Joseph unhitched the horses.

"Go fetch some water for the horses, Beula."

"Jus' lemme git da buckets down an' da fire started, then I'll give 'em all the water they want."

"Don't argue with me, Beula," the evangelist said sharply. "They're thirsty, and I want them watered now."

"We still got us half a bucket back here from da las' stop."

"I want fresh water since we've got it. Are you going to do as I say or not?"

"Lan' sakes, Joseph, if yo ma could hear da way you talk to me, she'd—"

"I know, Beula, for crying out loud. You tell me that once a week. And how many times do I have to remind you to call me *Brother* Joseph? Now go and get that water like I told you!"

The black woman pulled down two large empty buckets from the side of the wagon, then ambled toward the stream.

"Do you see what I mean, Sister Mercy?" the minister said. "It simply would not do for her to be seen with us in public. She can barely obey, cannot speak clearly, and as well as I treat her, she does not show me the respect due my office."

Sister Mercy said nothing. There was plenty of work to be done in setting up camp and fixing supper without getting into an unpleasant discussion. In spite of herself, however, the next words out of her mouth pointed to a silent annoyance in a different direction.

"When will you let me talk with the new converts we make?" she asked.

"As I've told you many times, Sister Mercy, as soon as you are ready. Evangelism is not a gift given overnight, you know."

"But it was to bring people to the Lord that I joined you."

"And bringing people to the Lord you are, Sister!" rejoined Brother Joseph. "We are a team, coworkers in a delicate work that cannot be rushed. You are yet young and inexperienced, only months away from your home in the East. You are on the mission field, exactly as you said you wanted to be when you came to me after the meeting in Evansville. You must trust me, Sister. Converts must be counseled with great care."

"You . . . you never allow me so much as a word with any of them," said Sister Mercy timidly.

"Are you complaining, Sister Mercy?"

"I'm sorry. It's only that sometimes I . . . I wonder if I am doing the Lord's work that I always wanted to do. Forgive me."

"Say nothing more, Sister! Of course you are doing the Lord's work. Did you see the wonderful response in Blue Gap? Souls were saved, bodies made whole. Why, Sister, we collected $105 in just two offerings! I've already wired it to the orphanage."

The conversation was interrupted by the sound of approaching horses, just as Beula returned with the water.

Reverend Mertree looked up. Two horsemen cantered toward them, pulled up, and stopped.

"Evening," said one of them, touching his hat.

"Good evening to you, gentlemen," replied Brother Joseph with a smile.

"You folks, uh . . . need any help?" said the other of the two, glancing around and taking in the incongruous scene of a middle-aged man, a stout elderly black woman holding two water buckets, and a pretty young lady who appeared to be in her midtwenties in the process of emptying some things from an oversized wagon unlike anything he'd ever seen before. Both Sister Mercy and Beula eyed the two riders skeptically. In these parts, not every man they ran into was one whose intentions they could trust.

"No, no, we're fine," replied the minister. "We only just stopped to make camp for the night."

"Kinda far out in the middle of nowhere, aren't you, mister?"

"We're on our way to Sweetriver. I'm Reverend Joseph Mertree."

"This your daughter, Reverend?" said the first man, nodding his head toward the wagon.

"No, this is my coworker in God's field of harvest, Sister Mercy Randolph."

"Well, I'm pleased to meet you, ma'am," he said, smiling and tipping his hat.

Sister Mercy nodded and returned his smile.

"My name's Jeremiah Eagleflight. This here's my nephew and partner in crime, Jess Forbes."

"You don't look a day younger than him, Mr. Forbes. Is this man actually your uncle?" asked the evangelist in surprise.

"Sometimes it happens that way, Reverend," Forbes explained. "His folks was pretty old when he was born. He was the last of their litter, and I was the first of mine. But if I had my way, we'd forget that we were kin altogether."

"Why's that?" asked Brother Joseph.

"Because Jeremiah's always holding it over my head, trying to tell me it's his duty to take care of me."

Eagleflight laughed. "It's only because of all the trouble you get yourself in, Jess," he added. "If it weren't for my cool head and quick wit, you'd have spent time in half the jails between Montana and Texas!"

"See what I mean, Reverend?" said Forbes with a grin of mock annoyance. "Just on account of his being two years older'n me, he thinks that gives him the right to treat me like a kid!"

"You can't deny that you can get into more trouble with a deck of cards in your hand than any ten ordinary men."

Before Forbes could reply, another voice entered the conversation.

"What do you mean by calling yourselves partners in crime?" asked Sister Mercy with a worried look on her face.

Now both young men laughed.

"Nothing you should be troubled about, ma'am," replied Eagleflight. "Just a way of saying we stick together through thick and thin."

"Where are you men bound, if I may inquire?" asked Brother Joseph.

"Just so happens we're on our way to Sweetriver too."

"You don't say," put in Brother Joseph. "Do you gentlemen have business there?"

"In a manner of speaking, you might say that, Reverend. We thought we'd play a little poker."

"Oh, gentlemen, wiles of the devil, that game is! I can't imagine what a fine-looking young man like you with a good biblical name like *Jeremiah* would find in poker."

"I don't know about the name, Reverend. My ma and pa gave it to me, and I never asked their reasons. Hard enough for a kid to grow up with a name like Jeremiah without having to worry about it coming from the Good Book. But as to the poker, I'm sorry, Reverend, but Jess and I happen to like poker, and sometimes we even make money at it."

"Well then, I won't hold it against you. You like to join us for dinner? Beula, you got the coffee on yet?" he said sharply, turning to his black servant.

"I ain't even got da fire started, Joseph, on account o' you sendin' me after dat der water."

A look of exasperation came over Brother Joseph's face, but he managed to keep from saying anything.

The rider called Forbes laughed, then dismounted. "Maybe you do need some help after all, Reverend!" he said. "At least let me help the woman make the fire."

"So you will join us?"

"Well, maybe just for the coffee," answered Eagleflight. "We were hoping to make Sweetriver before dark."

"That'll take some riding."

"We figured to push our horses all the way. You see, we got wind of a big game at the Silver Ox tomorrow. We're going to try to get into it."

6

SWEETRIVER

After arriving in town a day in advance of the first
scheduled meeting, as was his custom, Brother Joseph
went out alone into the town and community.

Beula and Sister Mercy used the occasion to set up all but
the heaviest portions of the tent and to unload what they
would need from the wagon. Beula made ready her sleeping
arrangements in the back half of the large converted medi-

cine-show wagon. The front half opened into the tent itself and served as platform and podium for the services that were held under the canvas cover.

This first day—in private and alone, according to Brother Joseph's testimony—was the most important component of the entire stay in any community, providing the foundation for whatever evangelistic impact the services would later have. It was at such times, he had explained to Sister Mercy, that he prayed fervently for the town, seeking the Lord's guidance and wisdom for how specifically to direct his preaching.

"Sometimes, Sister," he told her, "the Lord will speak a word to me about a particular sin in which a town is bound, which I must come against with the Word of God in order to loose the spirit of salvation to flow freely. At other times the Spirit will fall upon me, and I will discern in advance a need of a man or woman who will be in attendance."

"Is that why you are able to speak prophetically about those in the congregation before they come for prayer?" she had asked.

"Yes, Sister Mercy. I often know ahead of time what the need is that I will pray healing for. Walking the streets and byways of a community while in prayer enables the Spirit of God to come upon me so that God's power will be in evidence during the services."

"As well as your times alone before we leave a town?"

"Exactly, Sister Mercy. I take such opportunities again to be alone in prayer for the town as we leave it, to pray for those souls who found healing and the grace of salvation under our tent of revival, and to commit them to the care of God. As did our Lord, I find that when I rise early and seek the heavenly Father in solitude, I am able to pray with great fervency of spirit."

The first evening's service at Sweetriver went much according to the usual pattern. The majority of those present were women, who, keeping their questions and what winks and comments they had seen and heard among the men of the town regarding the "pretty young preacher lady" to themselves, were yet hopeful about what the traveling evangelist might be able to accomplish to improve the morality and general religious sentiment in the community.

By evening's end, after the hymn singing and the prayers for healing and revival—not to mention Bart Wood, the town's most notorious drunk, coming forward to repent and dedicate his life to righteous living—all the town's wives were abuzz with enthusiasm for the next two services, pledging to join Sister Mercy in canvassing the town with flyers and invitations.

None of the religious wives were disappointed. The healing service on the second night brought twice the number to Brother Mertree's tent.

From her vantage point at the organ, Sister Mercy was gratified to see the two young men they had encountered on the trail, Jess Forbes and the other fellow with the odd name. Maybe they had lost their money in that poker game they had spoken of and had come to the revival to repent.

She glanced at them from her place at the organ as they took their seats and gave a slight nod of greeting. The fellow named Jess was looking the other direction just then. But the one called Jeremiah saw her glance and returned it with a smile of his own.

The two men's appearance put an added sense of purpose and zeal into her fingers as they made their way along the instrument's keys, and she sang "What a Friend We Have in Jesus," her voice containing even more enthusiasm.

The evening was one to remember for more reasons than that. There were three healings, and six more men and one of the saloon women came up for prayer, including Bart Wood again, who laid one hand on his partner, Slim "One Eye" Jackson, while he held the other in the air, praying so loud everyone could hear—though the God-fearing members of the assembly couldn't believe their ears—for Slim to know the same peace he himself had found the night before. Judging from the tears of remorse for his life of sin that fell and the loud cries for forgiveness, Slim's one good eye was indeed going to be single for the Lord from that night on. He and Bart stood up from their knees, vowing before the town to mend their ways and never touch another drop of liquor.

The whole town had heard about Shifty Snyder's accident, getting thrown from his horse two days earlier while out mending fences on his ranch. His horse had run off, and Shifty had crawled all the way back to his house, splinted the ankle up tight himself, and then ridden to Doc's place for a crutch so he could walk. He'd been hobbling around town on it ever since and had fallen flat on his face right in front of the sheriff's office once when he got the end of the crutch stuck between two boards of the sidewalk.

The *Praise the Lord, I'm healed . . . I'm healed!* that erupted from his lips after Reverend Mertree's passionate prayer for healing was enough to stir the heart of even the most skeptical. But it was with wondering eyes and *Hallelujahs* and *Praise the Lords* of their own that the congregation witnessed Shifty dig from his pocket every dollar he said he'd won at the gambling table that day, which amounted to sixteen dollars and thirty-five cents, and place it in Sister Mercy's hand for her to put in the collection plate.

"Give it to the poor, Sister," he had implored earnestly. "And whatever's left over, I want you and the good reverend to have it to further your work."

"Thank you, . . . thank you, Brother Snyder!" she had replied, her eyes sparkling with joy and thankfulness.

Nothing can compare with seeing lives transformed right before your own eyes, Sister Mercy thought to herself as she handed the plate to the next row.

Following Shifty's generous example, and Bart's and Slim's after him, the good people of Sweetriver found their pockets overflowing with financial gratitude for Brother Joseph Mertree's Tent of Meeting and Healing. They were thankful that the Lord had led Brother Mertree and Sister Mercy to minister the Word of God to their community.

With still one more service to go, Sweetriver would likely never be the same again. Or so thought Sister Mercy with a smile on her face as she lay down in the hotel later that night before falling asleep.

Traveling between towns had its unpleasant moments. She wished Brother Joseph would treat Beula with more consideration. But she knew she didn't understand everything. And she could hardly argue with the fact that God was doing a mighty work through the evangelist.

She felt so fortunate to be part of it.

7

DIFFERENCES
OF OPINION

The following afternoon Sister Mercy walked along the

sidewalk of Sweetriver's main street. In her hand she car-

ried flyers. As she went she spoke to those she met, inviting

them to attend the third and final meeting that evening.

She hurried past the Silver Ox Saloon, doing her best to

pay no attention to the music and raucous sounds of talk

and laughter inside. A few doors farther down, she entered

the dry goods store, where she passed out several papers, invited the proprietor to come, and greeted three ladies she had seen at the previous two nights' services.

One of the women, as she was telling her friends before Mercy arrived, had been skeptical at first. But she now believed the good evangelist's intentions toward his young assistant were altogether honorable.

"I intend to come again this evening," she added, as much to Mercy as to her friends, "and bring my brother and husband with me! Both of them *need* a good dose of repentance. If he can do them any good, I'll make a generous donation to Brother Joseph's work."

"Thank you very much," the young assistant said, leaving the women with flyers and exiting the shop.

"Sister Mercy, good afternoon," said a voice behind her.

She turned on the boardwalk and saw a figure walking toward her from the direction of the saloon.

"Mr. . . . uh —," she stammered, caught off her guard.

"Eagleflight," he said for her, hastening his step until he reached her. "It's a peculiar name to remember," he added, falling into stride beside her, "and a mouthful to say even if you do remember it!"

"It's not that," she replied nervously.

"You mean you did remember it?" he laughed.

"Yes, yes I did, that is — after I thought about it for a minute."

"Thought about it — when?"

"You were at the meeting last night."

"And you remember the names of everyone who attends your revival services?"

"Well, no . . . not exactly. It's just —"

"Ah, I see," he interrupted with a good-natured smile, "you decided to make an exception in my case!"

"Perhaps that is it," she replied. "It is an unusual name, you must grant. And I was encountering it for the second time. When I saw you come in, my mind wouldn't let go until I remembered. It sounds like an Indian name."

"That's what everyone thinks."

"Are you of Indian blood?"

"Not that I know of, Sister. My old man's grandfather, so the story goes, took the notion into his head of being a preacher, just like your Rev. Mertree. That was back when the family line was still in Europe—Germany it was."

"I'm afraid I don't understand."

"An evangelist like you, Sister Mercy . . . surely you know all about the prophet Isaiah and what he says about eagles?"

Her face continued to wear a blank expression.

"The old German's name was Adlerberg, which actually meant 'Mount of the Eagles,' or 'Eagle Mountain.' They had lived for generations in the mountains of Bavaria. So when he immigrated to the States, he changed his name."

"I'm sorry—I still don't get the connection with *your* name."

"Well, I reckon he didn't figure Adlerberg sounded American enough. But then you don't go around with a last name like Eagle Mountain either. He could have just called himself Eagleberg, and I've met a few Eaglebergs or Eaglebergers in my time. But my great-grandfather, like I said, had it in his head to be a preacher."

"I still don't see what that has to do with your name."

"When he came to this country, he brought a little of old Isaiah into the translating of his name to give it what he figured was a biblical ring. At least that's kind of how I figure it. Maybe he was just fond of eagles flying around those Bavarian mountains. Anyway, whether it was Isaiah or the

Alps, my old man's father was born Thomas Eagleflight, and my father was Andrew Eagleflight, and here am I, the third Eagleflight in a row."

"With as biblical a name as all the rest."

"I reckon that's true, but I never give it much thought. An accident with no significance whatever. I'm German through and through, but everyone I meet takes me for a Sioux, Iroquois, or Cherokee."

"And are you inclined toward the ministry, Mr. Eagle-flight?" asked Sister Mercy seriously.

A great laugh, not of derision but from the sheer humor inherent in the question, erupted from the young man's mouth. "I've just come out of the saloon from five hours of poker, I've got a six-gun strapped to my side, and you wonder if I'm inclined toward the ministry!"

"Wasn't your great-grandfather a man of God?"

"He came to America, spiritualized his name, went to work in a shipyard, and never cracked the Good Book that I know of the rest of his life. And neither did my grandfather or my father after him. But my grandfather always talked about being a gentleman. That's the only thing I remember of him. He said to me over and over when I was a kid, 'Son, no matter where you go, no matter what you do, no matter what kind of man or woman you face, if you're a *gentleman,* then you can hold your head high alongside anybody, rich or poor, king or slave.'"

"Why were you at the revival last evening then," asked Sister Mercy, "if you're not interested in spiritual things?"

"Did I say I wasn't interested in spiritual things?"

"I only assumed—"

"I only said my grandfather taught me to be a gentleman more than he taught me anything out of the Good Book.

33

But to answer your question, curiosity, I suppose, brought me to your tent, like most of the others. Maybe to see your face again."

She turned away momentarily, feeling the heat rising along the back of her neck.

"It wasn't curiosity that led them there, Mr. Eagleflight, but the conviction and prompting of the Holy Ghost."

"Come on, Sister Mercy, even you can't believe that. It's a sideshow, an evening's entertainment—that's why people in a town like this turn out."

"And the healings and saving grace that fell upon the whole congregation—what do you make of that?"

"Probably not what you make of it."

"Whatever do you mean?"

"I think it best that I keep my opinions to myself."

"Didn't you see Brother Joseph heal the man with the broken ankle?"

"I saw the whole thing."

"The man threw away his crutch and walked away!" declared Sister Mercy, more in disbelief that the man would not recognize the incident for a miracle than in annoyance with what he had said. "Surely you cannot deny the Spirit's working?"

"I don't deny a thing. I just say I don't make of it all you do, that's all. I think we ought to just leave it at that. I'm not trying to say a thing to upset you."

They walked along a while longer in silence. A few people passed them on the sidewalk, but Sister Mercy seemed not to notice. Still clutching the flyers in her hand, for the moment she passed none out. She stared down at the thick boards under her feet as they went, seeming nervous and distracted. At length she spoke again.

"You know, poker is an evil game, Mr. Eagleflight."

"Why do you say that?" he asked, no irritation but only question in his tone.

"It's gambling."

"Uh—yeah, that's true," he said slowly, not seeing the connection.

"Gambling is wrong."

"A wile of the devil, is that it? Like your Reverend Joseph told me out on the trail when Jess and I happened upon you?"

"That's right."

"What makes gambling wrong, Sister Mercy?"

"Everybody knows it's wrong. Why else would you use a saloon to gamble?"

"If you're going to gamble, you've got to do it someplace," he laughed.

"A saloon is a sinful place."

"Why?"

"What is a saloon for but to drink alcoholic spirits?"

"People drank wine in the Bible. Jesus drank wine. He wasn't too good to go into saloons."

"You can't use *him* as an example."

"Who *else* are you going to use?"

"He was the Son of God. He could go into an evil place without being stained like we will be when we do."

"All right, let's say I agree with you that a saloon is a sinful place. I still don't see how that makes poker sinful. What if you were to see Jess and me playing poker, say, on that bench over there outside the general store? Would you walk up to us and say we ought to repent of our sinful ways because we had cards in our hands and were sitting on that bench?"

Sister Mercy did not answer immediately. When she finally did, it was not in direct answer to the question the young man of the West had posed.

"Gambling is wrong, Mr. Eagleflight," she said again.

"If I knew it was wrong, I wouldn't do it."

"Why not?"

"Because it'd be wrong to do something wrong. I don't believe in doing things that are wrong."

"Gambling *is* wrong," Sister Mercy repeated.

"OK, then let me say it this way—it would be wrong to do something that you *knew* was wrong. If I knew it was wrong, I wouldn't do it."

"People do things all the time that they know are wrong."

"Do they? Don't you think mostly people go by their own code, that some things they do may look wrong to someone else but not to themselves?"

"Wrong is wrong, Mr. Eagleflight. Even if what you say is true, it doesn't change the fact that people do wrong things all the time."

"Maybe *people* do, but not me. I happen to be someone who tries to do what's right. If I see something's wrong, I don't do it. Ain't no other way to live, as I see it."

"Then I don't see how you can gamble and play poker and go into saloons."

"I reckon because I don't see the wrong in it. If I did, like I say, I'd stop. So now we're back at my question about what you'd think if you saw Jess and me playing poker on the bench there. Would it still be what you call *wrong* if there was no saloon or liquor involved?"

"You can try to confuse me with your trick questions all you want, but that doesn't change a thing."

"I honestly wasn't trying to confuse or trick you, Sister

36

Mercy," he replied with a sincere expression. "I just don't see the sense in what you said."

"That's the devil's way, using the clever reasoning of man to thwart the truths of God."

"Don't you think if you're going to preach the gospel, it ought to make sense?"

"The things of God are foolishness to the sinful mind of man."

"Where did you come up with a silly notion like that?" exclaimed Eagleflight.

"Silly! Do you dare call the Word of God silly? Those words are straight from the mouth of the apostle Paul!"

"Are you sure the apostle meant that the gospel's not supposed to make sense?"

"There you go, trying to confuse the issue with your clever reasoning again. Nothing you say can change my mind, Mr. Eagleflight. Gambling is wrong, and the Word of God is true, whether you think it makes sense or not."

Again there was silence for several seconds.

"If you will excuse me," Sister Mercy said after a moment, "I must leave you to pass out my leaflets." She turned to cross the street.

"May I ask you one more question?" said the young man.

Sister Mercy hesitated. "If you promise not to mock the Word of God," she replied.

"I have not been trying to do so."

"Go ahead then," she said, standing in the dirt at the edge of the street.

"What do you think of games of dice? What about if you walked into the Silver Ox and saw—"

"I would *never* enter a saloon!" she exclaimed.

"I'm sorry. Then what if I told you that Jess and I had been playing a game of dice—what would you say then?"

"The same thing, that gambling is wrong."

"A wile of the devil?"

"That's right."

"Do you know what *casting lots* is?"

Sister Mercy felt a sudden discomfort and was unable to keep her face from showing it.

"I see you do," he said. "It's the biblical expression for using something like dice to make decisions, little colored stones, or stones with various markings on them. Dice came from the Bible, Sister. God invented the use of dice and even told his people to use them."

"That's *not* the same as gambling," huffed Sister Mercy.

"What do you think they did for Jesus' robe but gamble for it?"

"Those were wicked men who killed the Savior!"

"Perhaps. But the disciples threw dice to decide who should replace Judas. Were *they* wicked for casting lots?"

"There you go again, twisting the words of the Bible all around! It would seem you know more about the Holy Scriptures than you like to let on, Mr. Eagleflight."

"Everybody knows a little of the Bible, Sister Mercy."

"But not everyone uses what they know to attempt to deceive the innocent."

"Which I have not been trying to do with you. Besides, I might make just the same comment about your so-called Brother Joseph."

"I will not listen to another word of your blasphemy! Good day, Mr. Eagleflight!"

With those words, Sister Mercy turned and strode angrily across the street.

8

FINAL
CLIMAX

Sister Mercy did not know whether to be relieved, upset,

or concerned for Jeremiah Eagleflight's soul when neither

he nor his nephew made an appearance for the third and

final revival service in Sweetriver.

She had unconsciously looked for him as she sat at the

organ playing hymn after hymn while the tent filled for the

service. Of course, had he walked in, she would not have

glanced in his direction nor cast him a look of welcome. He had offended her religious sensitivities, and it seemed only appropriate that he realize it.

Their conversation earlier that day had unnerved her. She had been unable to get it out of her mind. The fellow was an obvious heathen, just the sort of man the western frontier was full of—gun strapped to his side, playing poker all the time. . . . He probably drank a quart of whisky every night too, she thought.

It was for the salvation of such men that she had wanted to become a minister of the gospel, or at least an evangelist's assistant for now. This was "the great mission field of the West," Brother Mertree had said the night she had first heard his heartfelt plea for those of like missionary zeal and evangelistic vision to join his campaign to take the Word of God west.

"Join with me," he had challenged the young women at the meeting, "join the eternal crusade against the evil lawlessness that grips the prairies and western territories of our fair nation."

She had answered that call. And yesterday she had come face-to-face not with the vague, nebulous, impersonal "mission field" the evangelist had spoken of but with the eyes and mouth and voice of one particular heathen westerner who poked and jabbed so uncomfortably with his questions that she hadn't enjoyed the encounter at all. The fact that she hadn't been able to answer him satisfactorily bothered her not nearly so much as that she found herself thinking more about his face than praying for his soul.

It was therefore with a mixture of unfamiliar and confusing feelings that she rose from the organ promptly at seven o'clock to speak her own words of welcome, encouragement, and religious exhortation to those present and then, after a few more hymns, to introduce Brother Joseph for his final eloquent and rousingly emotional address.

The crowd was about the same size as the night before, perhaps slightly larger. The manifestations of the miraculous were not quite so dramatic, though another healing or two gave rise to a passionate outpouring in prayer for the town and region in general on the part of Brother Joseph, punctuated by numerous *Amens!* from the assembly. His challenge to the "righteous" element of the community to continue to spread the "revival begun here under the Tent of Meeting," combined with further testimonials from Bart Wood and Shifty Snyder, succeeded in raising the emotional current under the healing canvas to a highly excitable pitch. The organ accompaniment to the final choruses of "Bringing in the Sheaves" could scarcely be heard above the words of the hymn, along with numerous *Amens* and *Hallelujahs*.

As a result, the final evening's "love offering for the work of God" was nearly a hundred and twenty-five dollars, half of which, Brother Joseph promised, would be on its way the next day to the Foundation for Evangelism in the Western States and Territories, located in St. Louis, whose sole purpose was helping to fund the building of new churches in the West.

"A personal letter from me will accompany the donation to this most worthy cause," Reverend Mertree added, declaring his conviction that the fair community of Sweetriver, Kansas, should be put at or near the top of their list of sites for immediate consideration.

"I am all but certain," he went on, "that once the committee for the designation of funds hears of the great revival under way in this community, they will wholeheartedly approve my recommendation."

This news could not have fallen on more receptive ears and resulted in an additional fifty-three dollars being added to the collection plate at the conclusion of the service. A church was exactly what many of the women — coming to him afterward to thank the evangelist and contribute further to the cause of spreading the gospel in the West — told Brother Joseph they had been praying for ever since their arrival in the region.

The revival services could not have been a greater answer to prayer, the women all affirmed as they left for their homes. It was only too bad the meetings were so brief, though they understood that there were many fields equally white unto harvest as their own, and they knew that Brother Joseph must do as had the apostle Paul and move still farther abroad into regions where the unsaved needed him.

Listening from her seat at the organ, Sister Mercy softly played the final strains from the final hymn over and over, watching as the citizens of Sweetriver paid their last best wishes and respects to Brother Joseph and then filed out of the tent to their homes.

She had heard such conversations with admiring and grateful women many, many times at the end of their revival services. It seemed they always wanted to give every penny they could in the hope of bringing a permanent church to their town. Sister Mercy was well aware of Brother Joseph's affiliation with the church-building foundation in St. Louis, for he spoke of it on the third evening at nearly all their revivals.

On this particular evening, however, the words of the scattered conversations throughout the tent only vaguely echoed through the back of Sister Mercy's subconscious.

She had been distracted all evening. As she watched the tent slowly empty, she was reminded again of the young man who wasn't present, whom she kept telling herself she did *not* want to see again. She could not help glancing around, even as the crowd thinned, to see if maybe he had come at the last minute after all.

She would be glad to see the tent folded up and to get on the road for their next stop and away from Sweetriver for good!

Thirty minutes later, after saying good night to Beula, Sister Mercy made her way from the site of meeting through the quieting streets of Sweetriver. The sun was gone for another eight or nine hours, the breezes of the day had nearly settled themselves down for the night, and dusk had fallen on the prairie. The darkness of the May evening would be complete in another half hour. Most of those who had been at the services were by now back in their homes. The sounds she heard were animal rather than human in origin—the barking of two or three distant dogs, the occasional low of a cow from one of the surrounding ranches, or the stamp and snort of a horse in the livery stable behind her. The roosters' chief business lay at the other end of the day, and most of them had gone to bed so as to be ready for the sun's return.

As she walked toward the hotel, she had to pass the Silver Ox Saloon.

The sounds of music and laughter and boisterous talk from inside its doors reached her ears and grew louder as she approached. She wished Brother Joseph was at her side, but he had gone out to walk and pray before retiring.

She quickened her pace but was anxiously conscious of

the echo of her booted feet along the boardwalk of the quiet street. She drew alongside the bright window of the saloon, hastened her step even more, and sought to keep her gaze toward the street so as to see nothing inside.

Suddenly a burst of laughter erupted, and she heard a voice she knew cry out, "You see, gentlemen, sometimes there *are* circumstances justifying a draw to an inside straight!"

"I'm beginning to doubt that that run of yours is all luck, Forbes," grumbled another man in an unfriendly tone.

She was past the doors now. She heard the sound of a chair scraping against the wood floor and what sounded like men standing up. She hurried by the second window, relieved that the sounds from inside the Silver Ox were already beginning to fade behind her.

Just then another voice sounded above the rest, more familiar even than the other. She could not help arresting her step and turning her head slightly to listen.

"Jess is the luckiest man with cards alive," she heard Jeremiah say. "I've never seen him cheat, and I've seen him win more big pots than any cardsharp I ever heard of."

"So *you* say, Eagleflight!" rejoined the second man angrily. "But then you and he ride together, so why should I take your word for it?"

"Because I'm telling you the truth."

"Bah, the truth! I wouldn't trust either of you to tell the truth any further'n I could throw you!"

"You better trust me, Jackson, or *I'll* throw *you* out of here before you cause anybody else, or the owner of this place, any trouble. You've had too much to drink since you came in an hour ago, you're not such a good poker player as you think, and you're a lousy loser."

"How dare you, Eagleflight!"

"Look, Jess won that pot fair and square. I saw the whole thing, so did everybody else here."

"Yeah, well maybe you didn't see him pull a card outta his sleeve!"

"Don't be ridiculous. You saw him only take one card. And you trying to win a pot that size with nothing more than a pair of kings . . . that's bad poker playing, Jackson. Now either sit down and enjoy the game with the rest of us, or go home and sleep it off. The rest of you fellas agree with me?"

Acknowledgments and more words spread around the table, urging the man called Jackson to sit down and quit causing trouble.

Sister Mercy heard the man curse. A chair crashed to the floor, and she heard a heavy boot stomping toward her.

The sound terrified her. She realized she'd been standing still next to the window the whole time, listening to the conversation.

Again she continued her flight along the sidewalk toward the hotel, now breaking into a run.

The doors flew open behind her.

Sister Mercy did not look back nor even hesitate but picked up her terrified feet all the faster. She could not help hearing as the man shouted back into the saloon.

"I'll get even with you for this, Eagleflight!" he cried. "I'll get even with you both. I'll get what's coming to me, and you'll get what's coming to you! You hear me—and I always pay my debts!"

She flew into the hotel and straight up the stairs to her room. Her heart pounded more from guilt at having stopped outside the saloon than from fear of what she had heard, or even from exertion caused by the run.

Twenty minutes later, calmed and lying in bed, Sister Mercy's heart was no longer pounding, but she was no nearer repose or sleep than she had been on the sidewalk outside the Silver Ox.

Indeed, sleep would be difficult to come by tonight. Too many unsettling things raced through her mind to allow for the contented feeling of satisfaction that usually followed the final night of a revival.

Not the least of these was the man who was the object of the poker player Jackson's violent threats.

OVERHEARD
UNMASKING

Sister Mercy awoke to the gray light of predawn.

She had slept but fitfully. Neither body nor brain felt

rested. She had dreamed hazily unpleasant dreams but

could remember nothing of them. Only vague sensations

remained of danger and uncertainty, as if she had been cast

adrift in a strange land with nowhere to go, no friends, no

relatives, and even where she did not know the native language of the region.

She lifted her sleepy head from her pillow and glanced around the drab gray room.

The previous night returned vividly to her—the wonderful service and then the experience outside the saloon on her way here to the hotel. Now she began to remember the cloud of distraction and agitation that had gnawed at her all day and into the evening. That must have been what had caused her to sleep so poorly and led to the dreams, as well as the headache she now realized she had.

But this is a new day, she told herself.

It was time to shake off the cobwebs of the past. The sun would come up—she could already hear a few well-rested roosters getting ready—and would lift her spirits. By afternoon they would be on their way toward the next town. She reminded herself how fortunate she was to be about the Lord's business in the world.

She drew in a deep breath. More sleep was out of the question now. She had a headache and was wide awake, however poor had been her sleep. She might as well get up. Perhaps she should go out early, as Brother Joseph spoke of so often, and pray for the town before they left. It might be just the tonic she needed to lift her spirits.

She climbed out of bed, dressed, quietly stole from the room, went downstairs, and walked from the hotel into the gray deserted street.

No sounds came from the direction of the Silver Ox now. That was a relief. She nevertheless unconsciously shuddered at the memory of the previous night, then turned and walked along the boardwalk in the other direction.

The town of Sweetriver was not a large one. Within five

or six minutes she reached the last houses of the main street. Turning to her right, Sister Mercy walked the long dirt block toward the next street running parallel to the one she had just left, also extending the length of the town and emerging near the location of Brother Mertree's now-silent Tent of Meeting and Healing. Here no boardwalk had been built, and Sister Mercy walked slowly along the edge of the hard-packed dirt street, thinking quietly about the occupants of the houses she passed and praying in the general and undefined fashion of which she was capable.

By the layout of the town, she was making her way in a generally eastern direction. As she drew near the end of the street, having been walking at a leisurely pace, the horizon brightened in the distance in front of her. Noticing the approach of the sun, her thoughts drifted away from the town, the houses she was passing, and even where her feet were taking her.

How much time thus passed as Sister Mercy sauntered slowly along, she couldn't have told.

Voices brought her out of her reverie. At almost the same instant, the sun broke over the horizon with its upper edge. The livery stable sat close in front of her, but the bright rays momentarily blinded her eyes, and she could not see the speakers.

The first voice to intrude upon the peaceful morning contained an unfamiliar tone. Yet she did not have to see the speaker's form to recognize the voice as Brother Joseph's! It came from behind the closed front door of the building.

Instinctively, something told her she shouldn't be seen. Yet some unknown impulse drove her to listen—she wanted to hear more of the exchange.

Without pausing to think, the young evangelist hurried to

the side of the livery, ducked between two beams of an empty horse stall, then crouched down in its corner on some straw. Leaning against the outside wall of the building, she could just make out the voices on the other side of the thick, rough-cut slabs of board, though she had difficulty hearing over the beating of her heart.

"—exactly what I agreed to. You put back in the sixteen-thirty-five I gave you the other night, so we're square there, and this is the twenty I promised for your fine piece of acting."

"I put in another five last night!"

"I thought that was from the goodness of your heart, Snyder," remarked Brother Joseph sarcastically.

"If you don't give me the five back, plus an extra five for the second night's testifyin', Reverend," retorted the other angrily, "then this whole town's gonna swarm down on you afore you can git that tent packed and yourself an' that filly an' black slave outta here."

"Keep your voice down, you fool!"

"All I want's what's comin' to me, Reverend."

"All right, all right! Here's the twenty plus the five you added—twenty-five dollars."

"And the other five."

"Yeah, another five! By the time you thieves get through with me, I won't even clear two lousy hundred on the whole crusade!"

"Preachin's a tough life, Reverend," said the other, with derisive humor in his tone.

"So, . . . what about you, Wood? I gave you, what, eight bucks to put in . . . you gave me that back in the collection and now got the twenty coming. You going to try to tell me you added something of your own to the plate last night too?"

"A reformed hypocrite and drunk like me, Reverend!" he

laughed, with a voice that indicated all too clearly that he had been drinking heavily. "I ain't gonna tell you nuthin' but God's truth!"

"I wouldn't believe a word either of you told me!"

"Believe this, Brother Joe," said Wood, slurring his words. "I want twenty-five, jus' like Shifty here."

"I figured as much. I should have known better than to trust the likes of a couple of shysters like you!"

"I'll take Slim's cut too."

"You'll do nothing of the kind! Where is the fool, anyway?"

"I'm afraid he done lost his salvation, Reverend. Why he got hisself so drunk last night he passed out halfway up the stairs o' the boardin' house."

"Then he gets no twenty."

"He'll be riled something fierce, Reverend," put in the first man. "He's like to kill you if you try to double-cross him like that."

"I told all three of you that if you weren't here at quarter to six the morning after the last meeting, you'd get nothing. You heard me, and you all agreed—him included. If he's riled, then you remind him of that! I kept my word, but he didn't keep his. Now get out of here before someone sees you!"

The conversation ended abruptly.

Sister Mercy heard a door squeak open and the sound of two booted feet shuffling their way across the sawdust to the road. A minute or two later the door opened again, then shut. In disbelieving agony, she waited as long as she could stand, then crept on hands and knees to the edge of the stall to peer around the edge of the stable.

All she could see were the retreating forms of three men.

Walking back toward the main street, side by side, were the two men she recognized as Bart Wood and Shifty Snyder.

Going the other direction, along the side street she herself had taken only a short time earlier, continuing his final round of morning prayers for the community, strode the confident figure of Brother Joseph Mertree, healer of bodies, savior of souls, and self-styled evangelist to the western states and territories.

Sister Mercy's shocked and horrified eyes followed him till his form disappeared from sight among the houses of Sweetriver.

Slowly she slumped back and sat down against the wall of the livery stable.

It could not be possible! Her ears had played some cruel trick on her heart! Her countenance glazed over with incredulous denial, and she stared with empty mortification toward the ground.

How long she sat without moving she did not know. When she again became aware of existence, the sun was high enough above the horizon to indicate the passage of some extended duration of time.

Slowly reality began to dawn upon her stupefied brain. The wide eyes of innocence gradually reddened, then filled with hot tears of anguish.

She buried her face in her hands and wept bitterly.

Fifteen minutes later an old semi-invalid who lived on the south side of town and who had little to occupy his time besides feeding his chickens and hogs every morning observed a figure wearing a long black dress and matching bonnet running toward the hill a half mile from his place. His eyes followed her with mild curiosity until she disappeared among the dozen or so oaks scattered up its side. He then returned his attention to scattering breakfast out on the ground for his hungry hens.

He hadn't been to the meetings, barely even remembered what a revival was, and hadn't any idea who the strange young lady might be.

10

PARTING
OF WAYS

The morning was well advanced when finally Brother

Joseph had waited as long as he considered was safe.

Every minute more he delayed compounded the risk ten-

fold that Wood or Snyder would drop an untoward word

where the wrong ears might hear it or that the fool they

called One Eye Jackson would awaken from his drunken

stupor and come after him.

"Are you sure she said nothing to you?" he snapped at Beula for the eighth time as he checked the final harnesses and straps on the team.

"How many times I gotta tell ya, Joseph?" she snapped back crossly. "I ain't seen her since afore las' night's meetin' when I shut mysel' in da wagon!"

"We can't wait for her any longer. We've got to get out of town." He jumped up on the bench and grabbed hold of the reins.

"I done heard you play da organ," said Beula with a chuckle, "an' you can't hold a candle t' Miss Mercy!"

"You let me worry about the revival services, and you just do what you're told!" groused the evangelist rudely. "She knows where we're heading. When she gets out of whatever trouble she's in or comes to her senses, she'll catch up with us."

"Wif what? You neber gib her no money."

"She's well taken care of."

"An' if she don' come?"

"I managed fine before I hooked her."

"Hoodwinked her, don't ya mean!"

"Shut up, Beula! What you know about spiritual matters would fit on the head of a pin."

As he spoke, Brother Joseph cried to the horses and lashed the reins. The team jerked into motion, and the traveling evangelism show was off again, minus a third of its membership.

"I knows yor take be twice as high since Miss Mercy come along as afore. I ain't as dumb as you gib me credit fo'!"

"You're twice as dumb as anyone I've ever met! Now get in the back!"

"You'd neber dare talk t' me like dat if Miss Mercy was here."

"And she's not here, is she!"

"An' you's worried too, I can tell."

"You can keep your fool opinions to yourself!"

"You thinkin' 'bout dat floozy you hired back in Alabama t' talk all religious like dat den run off wif da deputy."

"Mercy Randolph is so innocent she'll cause us no trouble. That's why I replaced the floozy, as you call her, with a young woman running over with missionary zeal. I'm not worried about a thing . . . except how you're going to get the tent up all by yourself. You're not as spry as you once were, Beula." His voice contained not humor but ridicule.

"I could still whup ya like I did when ya was a pup an' yer mammy put me in charge o' the place!"

"Don't try it now, Beula, or you'll be out with Mercy. I don't need to tell you this is no friendly land for a black woman."

For the moment Beula kept her peace. She hated being dependent on Joseph. But he was her lifeline, and she knew it.

"Now shut your ugly black lips and get out of sight back there like I told you. Otherwise, when we stop tonight, it'll be *me* whipping *you!*"

Beula obeyed. She always did. Just so long as she had the chance to air her grievances once in a while, she could live with Joseph's ill-treatment. What right did she have to expect better anyway? The only difference freedom made was that she didn't have to keep it all to herself anymore. But it didn't mean that anything had actually *changed* as a result of the slaves being turned out on their own close to thirty years before.

Meanwhile, from her lonely vantage point behind several oaks on the gently sloping hillside overlooking Sweetriver, Sister Mercy watched the familiar wagon gradually shrink from sight as it rumbled away from the town and westward across the prairie.

She'd watched her two companions all morning. She felt sorry for Beula. The stout former slave had the tent dismantled and the wagon mostly packed to begin the day's journey before the good evangelist had returned from his "morning prayers" and leisurely breakfast at the hotel.

She'd seen him walk back into town several times. She knew well enough he was looking for her. By now the hotel clerk had probably been browbeaten four or five times by Brother Joseph.

Then they had moved the wagon away from the livery and had driven the horses half or three-quarters of a mile along the road, getting as far away from Sweetriver as possible while still remaining visible for what Brother Joseph hoped would be Sister Mercy's last-minute appearance.

She'd wondered why they always set up the tent on the side of town toward the direction they would travel next.

Suddenly it was all so stark and clear! *It is called making a getaway,* she thought with a laugh of irony.

She'd also been curious why they never remained behind a day or two to visit and encourage and pray with the new converts or give them Bibles or teach them anything about their new lives as Christians. It was one of the many aspects of her evangelistic work with Brother Joseph that she had never understood. She had never even seen any Bibles or teaching materials.

But he'd had an answer for everything. There was a great deal she couldn't understand, he'd told her many times. He would tell her everything as she grew in the ministry. For the time being, she could trust him and trust God to minister to the souls of the newly saved.

Brother Joseph, indeed! *Oh, how could I have been so naive!*

She lay down, face cradled against the bent elbow of her arm, and wept quietly for a few moments. She would weep again—many times. But the initial anguish following the shattering minutes outside the livery stable gradually gave way to the vague sense that a great change had come upon her and that from this moment on life would never be the same again.

What that change would be, it would yet be some time before she would pause to consider.

For now it was enough to know that the past had been severed. Her future, empty and colorless as it presently seemed, lay before her.

When Sister Mercy looked up again and peered into the distance, a slight cloud of dust was the last and final reminder of her months as assistant to Reverend Joseph Mertree.

She drew in a breath.

Then for the first time, with the finality of seeing the wagon disappear past the edge of the prairie horizon, she began vaguely to wonder what she ought to do next.

11

MINISTER
OF THE GOSPEL

This had not been one of his better mornings.

It didn't usually matter to Jeremiah Eagleflight if he lost at cards himself. Jess always made up the difference, and they came out far enough ahead at least to keep a roof over their heads and food in their stomachs.

After an incredible two-day run, however, suddenly his nephew's luck had gone south faster than the Rio Grande in spring. In less than an hour, they'd walked out of the Silver Ox with a grand total of two dollars and thirty-seven cents between them.

"I tried to signal you, Jess. I could tell ol' Zeke was sitting on something mighty hot. You should have suspected three of a kind from one look in his eyes."

"What did you expect me to do?" Forbes shot back. "Fold it in when I was holding a pair of aces and a pair of queens?"

"It just seemed like you wasn't usin' your head."

"After losing eleven pots in a row, I figured this was the one where I'd turn it around. What are you mad at me for, anyway? You wasn't bringing us in much that I could see."

"I'm not mad, Jess."

"You sure could have fooled me!"

"I just hated to see our hard-won money disappear into the pockets of that rancher Zeke Simmons and the drifter that wandered into town last night. You're a better poker player than both of them put together."

"Yeah, well maybe I used to be," rejoined Forbes sarcastically.

"I suppose we better figure out what to do now, either see if one of the ranches around is hiring on so we can get our stake back, or else shove on to Denver like we talked about."

"Simmons'd probably relish hiring us to punch his cattle and get our own money back at fifty cents a day!"

"We've done worse," said Jeremiah, "though it's sure harder work than cards. From what I hear, he's got the biggest spread in these parts."

"Before we do anything, I'm gonna walk it off." With those words Forbes turned and sauntered off down the boardwalk, still shaking his head in disbelief at how he could have lost so much money in such a short time.

Eagleflight watched his partner go, then glanced around, sucked in a deep draught of the warm midday air, exhaled, then slowly moved off in the opposite direction, toward the hotel.

It had been two days since his heated talk with the young Christian zealot. He'd heard that the evangelist's wagon had departed from the community yesterday. It was therefore with surprise that his ears heard the familiar voice even before he rounded the corner at the other side of the hotel.

". . . and call upon you to repent and give your lives to the Lord."

He strode around the side of the building to see the evangelist's assistant, standing on a crate a few feet away from the sidewalk, conducting a street-side service. Five or six men and a little girl holding her pet were gathered around, listening casually.

Eagleflight approached as Sister Mercy continued to preach from her makeshift pulpit.

"Please listen to me, brothers—the Bible says the wages of sin is death, but the gift of God is eternal life through Jesus Christ the Lord. Won't you take that free gift that he offers you by his grace? Take it and live, my friends, and turn from the sins and vices of the fallen nature."

She paused and glanced around at her handful of listeners, a look of imploring desperation on her face. By now the girl and her cat had wandered off, and most of the small party of men had likewise continued on their way, each tossing a coin into the upturned bonnet sitting on the crate at the would-be evangelist's feet. Only one of the tiny congregation, a gruff man who appeared uninterested but remained longer than the rest, still stood, waiting for what she would say next.

She saw Eagleflight moving toward her along the sidewalk. Rather than meet his gaze after their uncomfortable parting two days earlier, she turned her attention to the man standing on the sidewalk a few yards away.

"You, sir," she said, "do you not want to know the joy that comes with the salvation of—"

By now the man had had enough religious talk for one day and turned to go.

"Excuse me, mister," said Eagleflight as he reached the scene, "aren't you forgetting something?" He glanced toward the makeshift collection plate.

The man threw him an annoyed look, wondering what business it was of his. But thinking better of pushing the matter further, he dug into his trousers and tossed in a dime, then walked off without a word.

Eagleflight glanced up into the tired, disillusioned face.

"Sister Mercy," he said, "what are you doing here?" His voice was soft and full of concern.

"I was trying to preach the Word of God. It doesn't look like I was too successful at it," she said, pursing her lips and lifting her eyebrows. A more discouraged tone and countenance it would have been impossible to imagine.

"But why?"

"I'm a minister of the gospel."

"That's not what I mean, Sister Mercy. Why . . . are you *here?* I thought you and Brother Joseph were long gone."

"Brother Joseph *is* gone." She stooped to climb down from the crate. He stepped forward and reached up a hand. She took it, and he helped her down to the street.

"And . . . you?"

"I decided to leave his employ."

"And you've taken up holding street services on your own?"

"I have to pay my bill at the hotel."

"He didn't pay it?"

"Only through the revival. I already owe for two more days, and it's fifty cents a day."

"He gave you no money? What kind of man is he?"

"Not the kind I thought he was."

She reached for her bonnet. Eagleflight took it from her and emptied the contents into his hand.

"There's only sixty-five cents here. That's not going to get you too far. What are you going to do, Sister Mercy?"

She sighed. "Hold services, I suppose, and try to raise enough money to buy a train ticket back to either Indiana or Kentucky."

"Sounds to me like you're stuck between some pretty far-away options."

"I suppose I am," she said with a crestfallen expression. "My home is in Kentucky, but I was away at college for three years in Indiana. That's where I joined Brother Joseph."

Eagleflight put his hand into his pocket, took out what was in it, and added it to the rest.

"Here's a dollar and fifteen cents, Sister Mercy. That'll get you square with the hotel manager. Now you take the rest and whatever else you got and get a stagecoach or a train back home or back to your college or wherever you want to go. This is no place for a pretty girl like you to be all alone."

"I'm afraid I've got nothing else. That sixty-five cents you're holding in your hand is all I've got to my name."

"That's all! What have you been eating on for two days?"

"I haven't had anything to eat since Reverend Mertree and Beula left."

"I thought you looked faint! You come with me, Sister Mercy," said Eagleflight, taking her arm and leading her to the shade of the sidewalk. "The hotel bill can wait. We're going to get you something to eat!"

"I'll be all right, Mr. Eagleflight. I simply cannot take your money."

"Why not?"

"After the way I treated you the other day, I would be mortified to accept it."

"Don't worry about the other day."

"Now it turns out I was as wrong about some things as I thought you were about some others."

"I always did ask too many questions."

"You had every right to question me like you did. I had no right to get so angry. I'm very sorry."

"Apology accepted. But I'm still going to get some food inside that belly of yours before you keel right over in this hot sun!"

"I still feel awkward about taking your money. I'm afraid it wouldn't be proper."

"Are you saying I don't have as much right to contribute to the Lord's work as those other men who were listening to you?"

"Realizing how you feel about the Lord's work, Mr. Eagleflight, I know you would be giving the money to me, not to the Lord."

"With all respect, Sister Mercy," he replied patiently but with a hint of growing exasperation in his tone, "I don't think you have the slightest inkling how I feel about the Lord's work. You jumped to conclusions that I don't think are altogether accurate."

"I don't know how I could have misunderstood you."

"Nevertheless, you may not be as right about what you think I think as you think you are."

Sister Mercy smiled. "Whether you're right about that or not, it is an interesting way to say it."

Eagleflight laughed. "Besides," he said, "what's the difference if I give it to you or to a collection plate in some church? Isn't helping your fellow man a part of the Lord's work?"

He paused briefly, as if waiting for an answer. But before she had the chance to reply, he spoke again. "In any case," he went on, "whether you like it or not, and even if you don't know if it's right for you to accept it or not, you *are* going to eat something, even if it's my money that buys it. Now, come with me—we've been talking long enough when you should be eating!"

Realizing that further expostulation would be pointless, she smiled her thankful acquiescence and allowed him to lead her back along the boardwalk, around the corner, and into the hotel.

A DISCOMFORTING QUESTION

An hour later, after a modest-sized lunch had nearly disappeared from the table, Sister Mercy smiled at Jeremiah Eagleflight.

"I don't like to see you spend your money on me, Mr. Eagleflight," she said. "But I have to confess that I did very much enjoy that."

"I'm happy to hear it—best thirty-five cents I've ever spent."

"I wish you'd eaten more."

"I haven't been two days without food! Besides, we have to save some of your dollar eighty for your dinner tonight. And when you give the hotel its dollar, that'll only leave you forty-five cents. Let's see, the way I figure it, you're going to run out of money for any more meals just about two-thirty tomorrow afternoon!"

She laughed. "What about you," she said, "you *do* have more than what you gave me?"

"Not a plug nickel."

Her face showed alarm. "Then you must take your dollar and fifteen cents back!" she exclaimed.

"And leave you penniless?"

"I'll hold more services. Today's Wednesday—I'll spread word around town that I'll conduct a church service on Sunday. People will come, and I'll take a collection."

"Don't you think folks in these parts are about religioned-out for a spell?"

"You can't ever have too much of God, Mr. Eagleflight."

"You'll have starved before Sunday!"

"No I won't. The Lord will take care of me."

"The Lord takes care of those who take care of themselves, Sister."

"That's not in the Bible, Mr. Eagleflight."

"I didn't say it was. That doesn't mean it's not true."

"Only the Word of God is true."

"Do you really believe that?"

"Of course I believe it."

"Well, I don't want to argue with you again. I'm starting to like you, Sister Mercy. I don't want to spoil a good friendship just when it's getting going. Anyway, it's four days till

Sunday, and by then you'll owe the hotel two or three dollars, not to mention what it'll cost to eat between now and then. And if you're lucky and anyone comes to your service, you might collect a couple dollars."

"I tell you again, Mr. Eagleflight, the Lord will provide."

"Maybe so, but he just might do it by helping me find some hard honest work instead of waiting for you to pass the collection plate. So you pray all you want. I'm going to start asking around to see if I can make a few dollars breaking a horse or mending some fences or shoveling out some stables."

"What does that have to do with me?" asked Sister Mercy.

"What it has to do with is that I figure I'm just about the only friend you got around here, and so I'm going to try to scrape together enough money to get you on a train or stage so you can go home."

"But . . . why would you do that—for me, Mr. Eagleflight?"

He looked at her for a moment, then answered. "Because I like you, Sister," he said. "You seem like a nice and an innocent girl. I don't know what happened with you and the reverend. All I know is I don't want to see you get hurt. If I can help you, well, maybe that's *my* way of doing what you call the Lord's work. You may wait for the Lord to provide, like you say. But my way has always been, if I see something that needs doing, I go and do it. If I see somebody that needs something, if I can help them get it, then I'll do what I can for them. No big mystery in it. That's just sort of how I look at life, I reckon."

Sister Mercy was quiet for a long time, a thoughtful, half-puzzled expression on her face. "You're not like any heathen I ever met before, Mr. Eagleflight," she said at length.

"I haven't been in the habit of thinking of myself as a

heathen, Sister Mercy," he smiled, seeing humor rather than offense in her comment.

"You aren't a believer."

"How do you know?"

"Because you didn't come to the last revival meeting, and—well, you're a gambler, and you go into saloons."

"And all that tells you what I believe in my head, does it?"

"You mock the things of God," added Sister Mercy.

"What! How did you draw that conclusion?"

"From everything you say."

Now it was Eagleflight's turn to be pensive. When at last he spoke, his tone was so soft and earnest that Sister Mercy could not possibly take offense from his words. It was clear that he was trying to get at the truth and was not splitting hairs for the sake of argument.

"I am sincerely sorry it has seemed to you that I feel mockery in my heart toward the things of God. I mean that deeply, Sister Mercy. I love the truth, and I would never ridicule something I felt was true. Whether everything you say about God *is* true, I have to tell you, I honestly don't know. I'm not criticizing what you believe or mocking God or the Bible or anything. I just say I don't know everything there is to know about God. Ain't that a fair enough thing for a person to say?"

"I suppose so," replied Sister Mercy tentatively.

"I believe in the truth," Eagleflight went on. "And I believe in living by what a person knows is true. Maybe that doesn't qualify me as a saint, but then . . . well, that's the code I live by anyhow. That's about as honest as a man can get about what's inside him. Not too many men I've run into know *what* they believe. So I'm just playing it as straight as I know to play it with you, Sister. Fair enough?"

Sister Mercy nodded. She wasn't quite sure what to make of everything he said, but she sensed a difference in his mode of expression from any man she had ever met, especially Brother Joseph.

"Now, Sister, if you'll let me, I've got one request to make of you and one question to ask."

He paused and gazed seriously across the table at her.

"I don't want to rile you or argue with you," he went on, "or make you think I'm mocking spiritual things. I'm just wanting to understand, that's all. Honestly. So I won't say anything more unless you tell me to."

"Go ahead, Mr. Eagleflight. You did buy me lunch, and I suppose that entitles you to one request and one question," she said with a smile.

"All right. The request is this: If we're going to be friends, no more of this *Mister* Eagleflight business. I know Jeremiah isn't much better, but it's the only first name I've got, so I'm stuck with it."

"I think I can grant you that request, Mr. Eagle — I'm sorry — *Jeremiah*. Maybe it won't be as easy as it seems!"

"I appreciate that you tried anyhow," Eagleflight said with a smile. "It sounds nice to hear you say my name."

He turned serious again, then continued. "My question may not be easy either, Sister Mercy," he said. "Are you sure you want me to ask it?"

"I don't know — I don't suppose I have any choice now."

"Still, I won't unless you say to."

"Then do, Jeremiah."

He sighed deeply, then looked her full in the eyes. "All right then, this is the question: Do you really, all the way down in your heart — do you *really* believe all those spiritual-sounding words you say about everything?"

The question jolted her. She stared back at him across the table with wide eyes and a blank expression.

"How can you even say such a thing?" she replied after a moment, slowly and still confused. "Are—are you asking if I'm really a Christian?"

"No. I figure that's a mite more theology than I'm game for at the moment. I don't know about what makes a person a Christian or not. I'm only asking if you really believe everything you're talking about."

"But . . . of course I believe it. I studied, and I went to the Young Women's Missionary College in Evansville, and I dedicated my life to being a minister of the gospel."

"I don't doubt any of that. But do you really *believe* it all?"

"How could I not?"

Eagleflight did not answer immediately. He allowed the implications of his question to settle before speaking again.

"I have no doubt," he said at length, "that you believe it, in a manner of speaking, in your brain. But I want to know if it means something down deeper in your heart."

She was looking at him intently, not sure whether to trust the words her ears were hearing. He went on. "You see, Sister Mercy, you have a ready answer for everything. You're full of religious *professions,* but they all sound so rote and pat, like you memorized them out of some book you got at that school. Every time I ask you something—whether it's about poker or your revival services or saloons or Jesus drinking wine in the Bible—you've got a quick reply. But it's all out there kind of distant-like, Sister. It's just religious words— leastwise that's what it sounds like to me.

"Your preaching's the same—words with no *life* in them. If you're wanting to be a minister of the gospel, it seems to me you might oughta have some good news to give folks.

Looking at your dour face standing on that crate today wouldn't make me feel like doing much in the way of repenting for what you might call my sins.

"If being a Christian's all you say it is and all it's cracked up to be, it strikes me that it's gotta be about more than words. You talk about the life, but where is the life? All you're doing is saying words *about* it. Seems like more important might be how folks live and behave and think.

"Why do you think those men you were preaching at an hour ago finally walked away? I'd say it was 'cause you were just saying words that probably didn't mean a thing to them. You and I've spent enough time together these last couple of days that I feel I can be honest with you. And to tell you the truth, Sister, I don't think I really know anything about the deep down *you*. All you let anyone see is a religious shell that's built with a bunch of pious phrases out of the Bible."

He paused and glanced away. The look of pain in her eyes stung him. He realized his words had been like a slap across her face.

He looked back and again sought her eyes.

"I'm sorry, Sister," he said compassionately. "I didn't mean to hurt you. But I'd like to uncover the real live person who's down there inside your skin. I think it might be somebody I'd like to know. But I've got to find out who it is first. And right now all your religious words are getting in the way. You sound like a religious book, not a flesh-and-blood real person. I think your religion might be keeping you from even knowing who you are yourself."

TEARFUL
SOUL-SEARCHING

Mercy Randolph had never cried so much in two days in
all her life.

Nobody had ever said the kinds of things to her that
Jeremiah Eagleflight had. She hadn't known whether to be
angry, hurt, ashamed, defensive, or what. She had been all
four, several times each, since Wednesday and had felt a
hundred other emotions as well.

She had gone back and forth a dozen times between the two extremes of response available to her.

On the one hand, there was the standard retreat she had been taught to protect herself with in such situations. The man was an obvious unbeliever, a heathen, totally unable to understand the ways of God, which were higher than man's ways. His attack was exactly the kind of persecution for the gospel's sake she had been told to expect, and she must give thanks for her ill-treatment and then do as the Savior had commanded and pray for the man's soul. It was one of the first principles of ministering for the Lord they had been taught at Evansville.

Of course she could have nothing more to do with him, she said to herself, for Paul's words in the third chapter of Second Timothy, verse 5, were unmistakable. And did not, just a few verses farther, the great apostle say very clearly, "All that will live godly in Christ Jesus shall suffer persecution. But evil men and seducers shall wax worse and worse, deceiving, and being deceived"?

There was a certain comfortable, self-assuaging place into which she was able to withdraw with such Scriptures.

But the minute she did, suddenly a completely opposite slant on the whole thing would assault her.

Obviously Jeremiah Eagleflight was no evil seducer bent on deceiving her. She couldn't really call him such.

One look at his tanned, rugged, handsome face, one glance into his honest, searching eyes—as light a blue as the sky itself!—and one word from the tender, soft-spoken tone of his voice could tell anyone that in a second.

She was alone, penniless, vulnerable, and he had even called her pretty. Yet far from taking advantage of her in any way, he had treated her with the utmost courtesy and honorability, to the point of giving her all the money he had to his name.

Even Brother Joseph had never been so kind.

Just as soon as she grew sympathetic to the cowboy, however, the inner voices of her religious training would once more assert themselves, telling her that his being a good man meant nothing in God's sight. The passage about righteousness being "as filthy rags" flitted vaguely through her brain, and along with it something Paul had said about the disobedient and ungodly and their "foolish hearts being darkened."

Then she found herself back on the other side of the fence again!

Even if he was a good man, how could she listen to what he might say about the things of God? How could he think clearly with the "darkened" mind of a heathen unbeliever?

Then there was everything he said about the truth. He claimed he wanted to know what truth was. As uncomfortable as everything he'd asked and said was, she could not escape the feeling that he meant it, and that maybe he really *did* want to know the truth. He was as straightforward as any man she'd ever met. He was even honest about telling her that he *didn't* know much about God.

A *deceiver*. . . an *evil* man . . . those were the *last* words anyone who knew him would use to describe Jeremiah Eagleflight.

Then how could he have said those awful things?

And there she was once more—for the fiftieth time—stuck on the thorny point of her dilemma. Believer or not, if Eagleflight actually was an honest and truthful man—at least as far as he was capable of being—how could she not look squarely into the face of the startling and unpleasant questions he had asked?

Even if he *wasn't* an honest man, did that make his words any less valid? How could she not look at what he had said! It wasn't even a question of whether *he* was honest and truthful . . . but was *she?*

Round and round her mind twisted itself into knots.

She had left Sweetriver an hour ago, walking in no particular direction into the surrounding ranch land and rolling hill country. She paid no attention to where her steps led, her feet wandering as randomly as her thoughts.

She could *not* look straight into Jeremiah's question.

It was too painful. It undid everything she had always thought she believed. It undid all her training at the Missionary College. And it reminded her of home.

Yet . . . wherever she inwardly turned to try to escape it, there were his words still staring her in the face. *Do you—Mercy Randolph—do you really believe all those spiritual things you say—all the way down in your heart?*

The words stung deeply as she recalled them. Once more her eyes filled with the hot tears of silent, terrified uncertainty.

"Oh God, oh God," she cried softly, "I don't know what to think!"

As she said the words, she broke into a fit of sobbing, then fell to the ground and buried her face out of sight in the tall dry grass of the prairie.

14

LABOR AND
PROVISION

Jeremiah Eagleflight had been watching the hotel as

best he could from down at the end of the street at the liv-

ery stable. He had not seen Sister Mercy leave the building

all day Thursday. But then today, which was Friday, around

ten-thirty she had emerged onto the sidewalk and walked

off in the opposite direction and out of town.

He excused himself, told the proprietor he'd be back in

ten minutes, wiped his hands halfway clean on a bale of
fresh straw, then his boots on the stiff edge of the same bale,
and headed up the street.

He'd told the man two days ago on Wednesday afternoon
that he'd give him a hard, honest ten-hours' labor for a dollar fifty a day.

"I'm not looking for no help, mister," the livery man had
replied.

"And I'm not looking for long-term work," Jeremiah had
replied. "Just a few days, and I'll be the best hired hand you
ever had. Believe me, after a week, you'll beg me to stay
longer."

"So *you* say."

"A dollar and a half, and let my partner and me throw
down our bedrolls on a pile of straw over there."

"I don't know. . . ."

"Look, anytime you're dissatisfied with anything I do, you
tell me to take a walk, and I'm gone. But from the looks of
it—" as he spoke Jeremiah glanced around at the stables
and inside the barn— "you got some stall boards starting to
get loose, you got more manure piled up out back than you
know what to do with, looks to me like you're running low
on straw and hay, and the whole inside of your place is a
mess."

The man followed Jeremiah's gaze all around, knowing
full well he was right, but reluctant to admit it.

"You pay me a dollar and a half, and I'll straighten up the
barn, repair your fencing, get rid of that manure for you,
and if you tell me which of the ranchers you get your grass
from, I'll take that wagon there out and bring in another
load or two."

"All right, all right, you got a deal," the man had

consented. "But like I say, I ain't been looking for no one, so you better give me a hard day's sweat. I ain't made of money, you know."

"None of us are, mister," Jeremiah said with a smile. "Oh, and one more thing. I'll work for you the rest of today to show you what I can do. I figure seventy-five cents is fair. That sound about right to you?"

The man nodded.

"I got to be paid every day."

"Why's that?"

"My own business," answered Eagleflight.

"Sounds crazy to me. I usually pay by the week," said the man, eyeing Jeremiah with a questioning gaze.

"I thought you said you didn't use hired help?"

"I don't. I'm just saying that *if* I did, I'd pay once a week."

"Well if you want me, it's gotta be by the day."

"All right," finally agreed the man. "I reckon it's fair for an honest day's work."

"And after today, once you see if I can work or not, I've got to have my day's wage in advance, starting tomorrow morning."

The man broke into a laugh. "What kind of numbskull do you take me for?"

"One who's a good judge of character," replied Jeremiah seriously.

"Yeah, well maybe I am at that! And you're starting to look to me like a con man trying to stiff me outta a day's wage!"

"Then you're not the judge of character you think you are. I'm an honest man. I'll give you a full return of work for your money, and you can trust me. I'll work the rest of today. You can decide for yourself what you think. If you want me to stay on, starting tomorrow morning, it's the full day's wage in advance. Those are my terms."

The man had groused a little more. But when Thursday morning had come, he had given Jeremiah the full day's wage. By evening he was congratulating himself for finding such a hard worker at the bargain price of only a dollar and a half a day.

Jess, meanwhile, had talked his way into two or three more poker games and was confident about winning back what he'd lost. But Jeremiah would rather trust his back and arms than fleeting illusions of an ace-high full house.

On Friday, therefore, Jeremiah made his way up the street with three dollars in his pocket—two-and-a-half-days' wages, less the seventy-five cents he had used to buy himself and his nephew enough food to keep them alive.

Glancing around to make sure Sister Mercy was not returning, he walked into the hotel, across the lobby, and to the counter. The proprietor glanced up from his desk, rose, then nodded, sniffing once or twice at the unmistakable stable odor that had accompanied Jeremiah into the room.

"You, uh . . . wanting a room?" he said, not sure whether or not the business would be beneficial to the rest of the hotel's guests.

"No," replied Jeremiah. "I just wanted to ask about the young lady you got staying here—Mercy Randolph."

"*Sister* Mercy?"

"That's it."

"What about her?"

"She owes you for a couple nights, I believe."

"She does, plus half for Wednesday."

"Why's that?"

"When she started to pay me she said it was nearly all she

had, so I made her keep half of it for food. I don't know why I'm such a sap for strays."

"Did she say how she plans to pay you?"

The man laughed. "She says she's a gospel minister. That's a good one, ain't it!"

The man laughed, but Jeremiah continued to stand waiting without joining in.

"She says she's gonna hold a service on Sunday and take a collection. Ha! After everyone in town gave when she passed the plate around for that evangelist, I don't look for her to raise twenty-five cents!"

"Why do you let her stay then?"

"Like I say, I'm a sucker for strays."

"She say where she's going to hold her service?"

"Aw, I told her she could do it here in the lobby, long as she don't raise no ruckus."

"Where—right here?" asked Jeremiah, glancing around the empty room.

"I'll bring in a few chairs from the dining room if she needs them."

"How's she going to get people to come?"

"She'll probably go out and tell them."

The man let out a sigh. "I don't know how I keep this hotel afloat," he added, mostly to himself. "What'll it be next after a church service! If ever there was a lost lamb, she's it, whatever she may think she is."

"She *is* a minister of the gospel, mister," said Jeremiah.

"Yeah, well, maybe so. And maybe I'm Abraham Lincoln come back from the grave! I never heard of no woman minister as long as I lived. Anyway, what's it all to you?"

"Just this—" Jeremiah pulled the two dollars and two fifty-cent silver coins from his pocket and plunked them

81

onto the counter with a metallic ring. "—Here's three dollars. That gets her square with you and pays her up through sometime around next Monday or Tuesday by the way I figure it. You let her stay as long as she likes, and you make sure she gets enough food to eat too. If you need more, I'll be back."

"Uh—thanks, young fella!" said the proprietor, losing no time to deftly scoop the four coins off his counter and deposit them in his cash box with a clank. "What's your name?"

"Never mind my name."

"But who should I tell her—"

"Don't you tell her a thing. You just say her bill's been taken care of, that's all. You say a word about me being here, and it's the last of the inside of my pockets you'll see!"

"I understand. You've got your reasons, right?" said the man with a sly wink.

"Yeah right, I got my reasons," replied Jeremiah, "though not what you think. You just make sure she's well provided for and that she knows nothing. I reckon I'm a sucker for strays too."

"I understand."

Jeremiah turned and strode briskly across the wood floor and outside. Glancing quickly to the right and left and seeing no sign of Sister Mercy, he turned and walked back in the direction of the livery stable.

15

LETTER
FROM HOME

Sister Mercy sat at the tiny desk in her hotel room,

staring down at three yellow sheets of paper in her hand. She

could not keep tears from overflowing her eyes, nor did she try.

What had prompted her on this day to take the letter

from the bottom of her carpetbag she didn't know. It had

lain there undisturbed for months. Suddenly she had pulled

it out and begun unfolding the sheets and reading the plea
she had tried so hard to forget.

Painful as it now was, however, she again read the words
in her mother's familiar hand.

My dear, dear Mercy,

It was wonderful to hear from you. Thank you for such
a nice long letter. We are glad for the enthusiasm you
obviously feel. We miss you here at home and remember you in all our prayers and have been eagerly looking forward to your coming home for the summer.

Your father and I read your letter, however, with a mixture of many feelings it would be impossible for me to
describe in a response such as this. But I shall try my
utmost to set aside those emotions of my mother's heart
and speak to you woman-to-woman.

As you know, we were altogether in favor of your
going to Evansville to attend the Young Women's
Missionary College. We knew you were yet young to
move so far, not having been away from home before.
I know nineteen seemed different in your estimation
than in ours. In your eyes, adulthood had arrived. In
ours, you were still our little girl whom we were not
ready to have leave the nest of our home. Yet we knew
the time was right for such a change.

There is a certain self-reliance and confidence that is a
necessary part of growing up, an independence by
which young men and women gain the strength to face
life and to make decisions, the capacity to think things
through for themselves and to handle adversity. When-

ever such a time comes, whether at fourteen or twenty-one, I don't suppose it is ever easy for a loving parent. Yet adulthood must come, and independence from one's parents is an important aspect of it.

We had tried prayerfully to bring you and your younger brother and sister up, as the Scriptures say, "in the nurture and admonition of the Lord." You were always an obedient daughter, one we could not have been more proud of—

As she read the words, the tears flowed freely down Mercy's cheeks.

—and as you grew we could see so many evidences within you of virtue and character that indicated to us that you were beginning, as must all Christian young people at some point in their lives, to personalize your faith rather than merely slide halfheartedly into it because we had taught you the ways of God. We hoped and prayed that such an experience would lead to a greater level of maturity as you grew to stand on your own feet spiritually.

The independence of adulthood is important in a different way for young people like you, Mercy, who have grown up in a Christian environment. There is far more to living as a Christian than being from a Christian family. Christianity is a *way of life* that has to be learned, each man and woman for himself and herself. I had to learn it. Your father had to learn it. And you have to learn it too, Mercy—independent from us. You have to learn what being a Christian really means—for *you*.

That was another reason we were in favor of your attending the Missionary College—we knew it was time for you to find out how strong were your *own* spiritual convictions, without relying solely on the convictions we had taught you. This is another thing that is not always easy for parents, yet it is sometimes necessary if young people are to develop spiritual muscle of their own. Some young people can develop this fiber without having to go away—we think your brother Thomas may be one of these. But we knew that perhaps you needed to test your spiritual stamina in another setting than here with us.

Now you are twenty-two. You have been at the Missionary College almost three years and have learned many things. I hope and pray the instruction you have received will prove to be vital in your life and more than mere words and doctrines of rote learning.

And now you are thinking about embarking on a path that does not seem wise to us. You have written telling us of this opportunity to go west with Rev. Mertree. It is obvious from your letter that you are excited and want very much to "answer the call," as you said was his challenge on the evening of his talk to the girls of your college. We only want what is best for you. But this does not seem best.

Oh, dear Mercy, let me speak words of caution. As much as you find yourself desirous of leaping at what you consider a wonderful opportunity, it may not be the right thing for you. You are still young. I know age does not seem a great factor to you. But the fact that you are young means that you also lack experience. A few more years will enable you to know people and situations better. You have gained some of that valuable experience at the school, in a safe and supervised setting. But what you are now considering represents sailing out into unknown water, and we question whether it is a wise decision.

Dear Mercy, I say that not critically, but with the deepest love it is possible for a mother to cherish in her heart for a daughter. Another year or two spent solidifying your walk with God and maturing as a person can only help strengthen you and make your experience at the Missionary College all the more beneficial in your life.

You are feeling further independence rising up within you. As I said, some kinds of independence are good and necessary as one grows. But there is also a spirit of self-rule that can lead one away from what God wants if he or she seeks his or her own will instead. There are dangers to independence as well as strengthening benefits. The wrong kind of independence clouds sound judgment and leads to poor decisions.

Will you say in reply that we do not understand how you feel? Perhaps we do not. Yet parents usually understand more of how their sons and daughters feel than they think. Remember, we were once young ourselves.

Not everything good is necessarily the Lord's will. Some of the things you want to do may be good things, but if they are truly what the Lord wants, there is no urgency about them. It has been our experience that the Lord is seldom in a hurry in what he does. If you place your life in God's hands, he will make your desires happen even if you wait.

Sometimes one must choose between something that is good and something that is better. In this present case, I believe that prudence dictates that you do not make a decision without allowing time to settle your emotions. Find out more about Rev. Mertree's ministry. Think about the propriety of traveling with a man at your young age. Do not let your youthful enthusiasm place you in a compromising situation where you may be vulnerable to dangers you cannot anticipate.

You have said that the opportunity exists now, that he needs an organ player to accompany him this spring and summer and that such a chance may not come again. Those are not the words, if you will forgive my honesty, of a man trusting the Lord for the directions by which he orders the steps of his life. When someone attempts to pressure you into a decision, one learns in time to detect selfish motive. Persuasion and coercion are not methods by which the Lord usually leads. He makes his will known by the still small voice that speaks into men's hearts.

Be wary, Mercy. If the Lord has indeed chosen for people to hear his word, it will not be dependent upon you, as you indicate that the evangelist says. The Lord will do his work. You must not be influenced by a man's charismatic, outgoing, persuasive personality. Wisdom does not often come with charming words and potent personality, but more often in the calm, quiet, sedate voice of experience and reason.

Listen to wisdom, Mercy. Listen to *wisdom,* not persuasion.

Let me remind you of the words your father has read aloud many times in our home: *Incline thine ear unto wisdom, and apply thine heart to understanding. Happy is the man that findeth wisdom. Get wisdom, get understanding. Wisdom is the principal thing, therefore get wisdom!*

There are so many other things to seek, dear Mercy. But even saving souls in God's work is not so high a goal as wisdom. The Bible says so, and your father is constantly reminding us of it.

Choose the people you learn from and listen to with care. Look for wisdom in the faces and attitudes and words of those around you. Learn to detect it. Seek wisdom, Mercy—seek wisdom in the people you associate with. Remember your father's favorite proverbs, and find people from whom you can glean that priceless gift.

I am not saying you should never do something such as this. Please—just wait. Let time season the Lord's leading. Sons and daughters rarely like to be reminded of their youthfulness. But it is a reminder no less true that it may be unpleasant. Neither your father nor I feel this is the Lord's will for you right now. We strongly and lovingly counsel you against accepting Rev. Mertree's offer.

We will always encourage you to follow the paths that seem best to us. But if you choose another path, we will always uplift you in our love and prayers. Know, dear daughter, that once your decision is made, if you do go ahead, we will always be here for you. We only want what is best for you, and that is the only reason I speak as I do.

You are a good and virtuous young lady, Mercy. We think the world of you. Just do not be anxious to grow up too fast.

We care for you with all our hearts, and nothing will ever, nothing could ever, change that fact above all else.

I love you.

Mother

P.S. Your brother has taken over half of the loft and made himself a place to work on his science experiments. He spends all his pennies and nickels on chemicals he gets from Dr. Brown. Someday his curiosity may blow a hole in the roof. You and Thomas have certainly kept life interesting for us. What will your sister Rachel do now, I wonder!

When Mercy had first read the letter months ago in Evansville, the words rang in her ears as rejection. She had felt that her parents didn't really accept her, didn't recognize that she was an adult capable of thought and of making wise decisions.

How different her mother's words sounded as she read them now!

At last she could clearly see how much her mother loved her and that both her mother and her father had supported her and believed in her though they felt her decision a poor one.

She was not nearly so grown-up and mature and capable as she had thought. Much of what she had considered her faith had indeed been mere words she had learned. Her judgment had been clouded by independence of the wrong kind and, yes, by a little stubbornness as well. She hadn't listened to her parents' counsel, and now here she was, penniless and in the middle of nowhere.

What was she going to do? How she missed home! If she had the money for fare, she would be on a stage for Louisville today! She had felt so grown-up and ready to be on her own at nineteen. Now she felt like a silly little girl again!

She sat another ten minutes or so, still holding the letter. Gradually her tears dried. She refolded the letter, placed it between the pages of her Bible, then removed two fresh sheets of stationery from her writing case and laid them on the desk.

It was time to write another letter home.

She removed the lid from the small jar of ink, picked up her pen, dipped its tip into the jar, and set it to the page.

"Dear Mother and Father," she wrote, then paused a moment to think.

16

A MEMORABLE
SUNDAY SERVICE

"Come on, Jess, why don't you come with me?

asked Jeremiah, sitting up from where he had lain in the

livery stable and pulling on his boots.

"I went to that revival meeting with you," replied Forbes.

"I figure that takes care of my religious needs for about

six months. Too much of that stuff'll do strange things

to a man!"

"It'll make her feel good to see us there, Jess. What do you say—do it for her."

"Not even for you!" laughed Jess. "What's with you, Jeremiah? You getting sweet on the preacher lady?"

"She's alone, Jess—alone and I think a little confused right about now. I just want to help her, that's all. Everybody needs a friend sometime, and this is her time."

"Well then, you be her friend. Me, I'm gonna win some of our money back today. I can feel lady luck getting ready to shine her eyes down on me again!"

"You got any money?"

"Four or five bucks—enough to get me into a game."

Jeremiah stood, reached into his pocket, and flipped his partner a coin. "Here's a quarter. I worked two hours for that yesterday, busting my back loading up hay for the livery out at our friend Zeke Simmons's place."

"From the Silver Ox?"

"Yep," answered Jeremiah. "So don't you go gamble it away—them bales were heavy. You get yourself some breakfast with it."

"What about you?"

"I got enough to buy a little breakfast for myself, and a dollar for the collection plate. I'll get more tomorrow."

"I don't know what's got into you, Jeremiah! But I'll have breakfast on you, and if I hit it at the Silver Ox today, I'll treat you to the biggest steak dinner they got in this town tonight!"

"Whatever you say, Jess." Jeremiah walked toward the livery door.

"What do you think?" Jess called out behind him. "You figure it's about time we were pulling up and heading on? I've about wore out my welcome at the Silver Ox, especially if I get another run of luck."

"I can't leave till I know she's going to be OK, Jess. I've got to at least see her on a stage back to Kansas City or Louisville or somewhere."

He strode on out of the barn, leaving Jess shaking his head in disbelief at what had come over his formerly sane uncle.

Keeping his ears open, Jeremiah had learned that the service in the hotel was scheduled for eleven o'clock. After a late breakfast in the dining room, he wandered through and into the lobby at about five minutes before the hour. Eight or ten chairs had been arranged in two rows. None were occupied.

The proprietor gave him a glance from behind his desk as he entered. Sister Mercy was nowhere to be seen.

He took a seat in the second of the two rows, and waited.

At exactly eleven, he heard footsteps descending the stairs. A moment more and Sister Mercy appeared, Bible in hand, dressed in the same full black dress and bonnet she had worn every other time he had seen her.

She walked slowly to the front row without once allowing her eyes to rest on the lone figure in the room, sat down in front of Jeremiah, and likewise waited. She would give the latecomers a few minutes to assemble.

Four long minutes of agonizing silence went by.

Against all reason, and defying the clear evidence of her ears, at length Sister Mercy stood, walked forward several steps and turned around, fully expecting a roomful of hungry worshipers eager for the preaching of the Word. Her face turned pale momentarily at the single set of eyes staring back at her.

She recovered herself, opened the black book in her hand, cast her eyes down upon it as she turned with trembling fingers through its leaves, located her passage, then looked up, drew in a deep breath, and bravely began.

"Our Scripture for this morning's service," she said, struggling mightily to keep her quavering voice steady, "is taken—" She hesitated, but only briefly. She hadn't anticipated this! But it was too late to change it now. "—taken from . . . the prophet Jeremiah, the fifth chapter," she continued. She glanced down at the page, doing her best to read the fine type in spite of the tricks her eyes were playing on her. "'Run ye to and fro through the streets . . . and see . . . if ye can find a man, if there be any that executeth judgment, that seeketh the truth. . . . O Lord, are not thine eyes upon the truth?' Therefore, says the Lord," she continued, pausing to turn several pages, "from the twenty-ninth chapter, 'And ye shall seek me, and find me, when ye shall search for me with all your heart. And I will be found of you, saith the Lord.'"

She looked up, still holding the open Bible aloft in her hand, as she had been taught, to add to the dramatic effectiveness of sermonizing. Glancing slowly about the empty room as if there were a dozen present, but scrupulously avoiding the pained look of compassion Jeremiah was resting on her, she began to preach.

"Brothers and sisters, the prophet is speaking of . . . of the need of each man and woman to seek—to seek God with all their heart . . . and to hunger—"

It was all too horrid! Why hadn't she chosen some *other* sermon from her notebook to read? She hadn't even thought about what the words *said!* Now there they were, staring up at her from the folded paper resting between the pages of her Bible.

"—the need to seek . . ." She tried to go on, blinking her

eyes rapidly as she read the words she had copied down from the Preaching to the Lost class she had taken at the Young Women's Missionary College. ". . . God with their whole heart and soul and mind and strength. The prophet is speaking of the searching spirit of God, who goes to and fro throughout the earth looking for honest men, whose hearts—"

She was stumbling over the words in earnest now, fighting to maintain her composure, not even realizing that she was no longer reading from the paper but was fumbling forward blindly on her own. "—men who seek the truth . . . searching for . . . women who seek God . . . women who have searched with their whole hearts . . . to find . . . who want to know the truth . . . who are seeking to find out if—"

She could not continue. Suddenly she ran toward the door, Bible and folded sermon paper falling with a thud to the floor.

Outside she flew, eyes blurring with tears, and up the street . . . running . . . running, as fast as her booted feet and full skirt of petticoats would take her.

The humiliation was unbearable!

Her heart pounded within her. Still she ran, past the last houses of town, along the road toward the ranches in the distance.

Her brain was in a fog, as though clomping heavily along in an unconscious dream.

Gradually her legs grew heavy. She stopped, emotionally and physically exhausted, then crumpled to the ground, chest heaving in great gasping sobs.

Oh, if only I could die! Just crawl into the ditch beside the road and die!

She cried for several minutes, then slowly began to

breathe deeply as she regained her breath. She wiped a long sleeve across her sniffling nose, then wept softly again.

Another minute or two passed.

"Sister Mercy," came a voice above her.

The sound startled her. She lay where she was, head down, and did not move.

"Sister Mercy," repeated the voice.

"Go away!" she cried in embarrassed frustration.

"Please, don't you want to talk about it?" asked Jeremiah in the gentlest of tones.

"No, I don't want to talk about it!" she snapped, then stopped to sniff again. "What's there to talk about," she added, "except that I made a big fool of myself in front of the whole town!"

"It wasn't in front of anyone but me, Sister Mercy," he said, "and I do not in any way consider you a fool, but a very brave young lady."

"You're just saying that!"

"I brought you your Bible."

"It's all your fault anyway!" she went on, ignoring what he'd said. "If it hadn't been for you putting all those doubts in my head, I wouldn't have gotten so confused about everything. I was doing just fine until you came along."

"I'm very sorry. I didn't mean to—"

"Just go away and leave me alone!"

This time no answer came.

A moment more Sister Mercy lay where she was, then raised her head and glanced toward where Jeremiah had been standing. All she saw was his retreating form about twenty yards away, walking slowly back toward Sweetriver.

Her Bible lay beside her on the ground.

17

LOOKING
AHEAD

For two days Sister Mercy scarcely left her room.
Despondency engulfed her so deeply that it took away her
power to think, read, or pray. She barely ate.

Tuesday morning she rose from an adequate slumber, feeling once more the sensation of thought in her brain. She had
grieved long enough for the cleansing to do its work. Her

98

eyes opened and beheld the sun's morning rays through the window.

Then first began to awaken a glimmer of the question *What to do now?*

That she could not preach was clear enough! Whom had she been trying to convince?

But she was eight hundred miles from home—alone, penniless, without even money for a night's lodging, much less fare to get back home!

She sat on the edge of her bed and thought.

A hundred revelations crowded for her attention. With all the inward commotion concerning Jeremiah and his questions and her being cast adrift in a strange town, Brother Joseph and her recent past as an evangelist's assistant had not occupied as much of her thoughts as might otherwise have been the case. Perhaps she had subconsciously forced herself not to look at the unpleasant truth.

Now it was suddenly all so clear!

He had been using her, nothing more. An evangelistic con game—she had heard of such, even been warned of such. And now—awful revelation to admit!—she had herself been party to one! While she had been pouring her heart out in word and in song, he had been deceiving townspeople in community after community with phony conversions and fake healings!

And she had helped him do it! How could she have been so blind, such a completely naive and ignorant fool!

Her mother's letter had urged caution and had hinted at motives of the good reverend's that might not be the best. Her mother and father had suspected his duplicity without even laying eyes on the man, while she hadn't been able to see what was right before her eyes! Her mother had been right—she wasn't as experienced as she had thought.

All this time she'd had the illusion of doing the Lord's work when all she'd been doing was lining the pockets of Reverend Joseph Mertree! He probably wasn't an actual clergyman at all!

She wondered if Beula knew. How could she not, especially if the story they told was true, about her being a slave to his parents before the war whom he felt duty bound to care for now.

Suddenly another thought struck her. Did Brother Joseph's charade lend credence to all the dreadful things Jeremiah Eagleflight had asked? Maybe everything Jeremiah had said *was* true after all! Her being so easily and foolishly duped by Brother Joseph proved it!

No. She couldn't think about that yet.

She shook her head and stood up. If her faith was a sham and was nothing but memorized words she'd learned from others—no, she would *not* look at all that now! Maybe later, but she had had enough grief these last two days for a lifetime.

She wasn't going to let herself remember any of his words. They were too painful. After her mortifying scene in the hotel lobby on Sunday, she didn't deserve any more pain!

As if by sheer resolve and determination to steel her mind against any thoughts whose entry into her brain she did not control, she clenched her teeth and lips, walked across the room to the door, opened it, and descended the stairs to the lobby.

"Mr. Millen," she said timidly, but determined to face her problem as squarely as she could, "I'm afraid I'm in a predicament and don't know what to do about it."

"If you mean your bill—"

"Yes, that is what I mean. I don't have any money, as you know, and after last Sunday, I don't have any prospects of getting any."

"Don't you worry about a thing, Sister Mercy," said Millen kindly.

"I can hardly do that," she said with a nervous smile. "I have to pay you eventually. Every day I remain here I owe you another fifty cents. You've been very kind, but I cannot presume—"

"I said not to worry," he interrupted. "As I told you a few days ago, your bill has been taken care of."

"But I don't have the slightest idea what you mean, Mr. Millen."

"Aren't you the one who told me when you first came that the Lord would provide?"

"Well, yes, but—"

"Just take it on faith then, Sister, that he has done so."

"I can't just stay here like this forever. I have to eat too, and I also need to find some way to buy a ticket home, whatever you say about my bill to you."

"Ah yes, I see what you mean," said the man slowly.

"Do you have any work around here I could do, Mr. Millen?"

"I'm afraid not that I can—"

"I'll do anything—clean up, sweep, change the beds, maybe help in the dining room."

"I'm afraid, Sister Mercy, we already have people taking care of all that."

"Can you think of *anything?*" implored Sister Mercy.

The proprietor was silent a moment, thinking. "Hmm . . . there *is* Mrs. Simmons," he said.

"Who's that?"

"Wife of a big rancher south of town. Zeke's got the biggest spread in this whole Pawnee Valley. The Sweet River runs right across his land."

"What about his wife?"

"Well, she does a lot of things for the men and women around here—makes things, I mean. Blankets, dresses, clothes, hats, coats, trousers. . . . Why she even does a bit of cobbling with leather. She's as handy with her hands using cloth goods and leather and whatever else she's got as ol' Zeke is with cattle and horses."

"But why did you mention her?" asked Sister Mercy.

"'Cause sometimes she gets so loaded down with work she's got to turn it away if she's got nobody to help her. Everybody gets her to make their duds 'cause they're cheaper and better than store-bought—and last twice as long."

"I still don't understand."

"Sometimes some of the women in Sweetriver help her. But most of them are too busy with their own chores. Besides that, she and Zeke's got no kids of their own, so there's nobody to help out around the place. She does all the cooking for Zeke's hands too. So I was thinking maybe she could use a hired-on young lady like yourself."

Sister Mercy's eyes lit up. "Oh, yes—I see," she said. "Thank you—thank you very much, Mr. Millen! Can you tell me how to find their ranch?"

"It's about two or three miles due south. There's only one road heading that direction, and the Simmons place is the first house you'll come to after you cross the river, just past a little rise where you can't see what's coming along the road from the other side."

"Thank you. I'll take a walk out there this morning!"

18

CHANGING
OPPORTUNITIES

It was not much past midmorning when Sister Mercy made her way over the ridge the hotel man had described to her.

In her heart beat fear and uncertainty. Little did she know that her future was about to take a turn almost as great as it had that fateful day exactly a week before when she had watched Brother Joseph's wagon disappear across the Kansas prairie.

She crested the incline. There sat the ranch house exactly as Mr. Millen had described, nestled among oak, a few birch, and other variety of trees. A stream flowed nearby, emptying into the Sweet River off in the distance.

The house was large and flanked by several barns and stables. Cattle grazed in the distance. Several fenced corrals enclosed a variety of horses. Around the perimeter of one, several men were gathered sitting atop the rails of the fence, shouting encouragement to a young broncobuster who was doing his best to stay in the saddle of a wildly kicking horse he was attempting to tame.

They were so absorbed, they did not even see Sister Mercy as she approached along the road. She walked straight to the house.

A woman answered her knock.

"I'm—I'm here to see Mrs. Simmons," she said, her voice betraying her nervousness.

"I am Jody Simmons," the lady replied.

She was older than Sister Mercy had anticipated, in her mid to late forties, with ample gray mixed in with an otherwise full head of brownish hair and the lines of years showing around her eyes and mouth. She was slightly taller than average and of slender though solid build. Wearing a man's red flannel shirt, blue dungarees, and high leather boots, she looked as though she would be more at home in a saddle than in a dressmaking shop as Sister Mercy had somehow expected. Her face was ruddy and tanned, showing clear evidence of life under the hot prairie sun.

"I, uh . . . that is, the man from the hotel in town told me that you . . . he said you might possibly—"

"Why, you're the young lady from the revival services!" said Mrs. Simmons all at once, face brightening in recognition.

"Yes, yes I am," replied Sister Mercy. "How do you—I mean, were you at the meetings?"

"Of course, all three. I very much enjoyed your singing and playing on the organ. But, my dear, what *are* you still doing here?"

"That's what I was trying to say," said Sister Mercy sheepishly. "I am looking for a job, and the man at the hotel told me I ought to talk to you."

The look of confusion on the face of the rancher's wife did not diminish her smile of welcome.

"Well, come in. Please, won't you join me—I'm just rustling up some lunch for the men. Perhaps you could help me with the soup and then tell me all about it."

She opened the door wide, and Sister Mercy entered the spacious ranch house, already feeling more welcome and at home than any place she had been for months.

19

A NEW FRIEND

Three days later, as Sister Mercy walked up the incline

of the last half-mile before reaching the Simmons ranch,

her heart was light and her spirits gay.

She skipped along, hardly even conscious that, for the

first time since the Tent of Meeting had been dismantled,

she was humming the bars of "What a Friend We Have

in Jesus." As she reached the final refrain, her lips began

mouthing the words, the tune at last escaping into full song, "What a privilege to carry everything to God in prayer."

"'Morning, Sister Mercy," Mr. Simmons called out to her as he strode toward the barn, saddle over his shoulder.

She returned his greeting with a wave as she bounded to the door of the house and inside.

"Good morning, Mercy. You look happy today."

"Good morning, Mrs. Simmons. I am happy, for the first time in a long while."

"I am so glad."

She turned and led Sister Mercy into their workroom, which appeared to be a cross between a dressmaker's, a cobbler's, and a leathersmith's shop. Bolts of cloth and woven goods, hides of leather, a large table, two workbenches, tools, and all manner of assorted equipment were scattered in loose but orderly fashion about the large room.

"We need to try to finish the repair on Barton's saddle today. I'll do that myself, but I want to show you how to stitch pieces of leather together. I worked on Mrs. Dunakin's lavender dress last evening too. I don't know why that lady comes to me instead of ordering what she wants from the catalog at the general store. She's got to have every latest fashion from the East, but insists I design them for her!"

Mercy laughed.

"She brings me pictures of the newest hats and wants me to make them for her too!"

"And do you?"

"Not if I can help it. I don't mind making hats, and I want to teach you the craft. But most of the fancy and flowery things Mrs. Dunakin shows me are so ornate and ridiculous I wouldn't even know where to start! I keep trying to tell her that this is the West and that people live simpler here. But she has to keep up with what all her friends back in New York are wearing."

She led Sister Mercy to the far end of the room, where sat a large wood and cast-iron, foot-pump sewing machine.

"Do you remember how to operate it?"

"I think so," replied Mercy. "It's sure nothing like the sewing we do back home. If you could just help me get it started, I'm sure it will come back to me."

Mrs. Simmons took the dress from where it hung on a rack nearby and inserted the basted ruffle on the skirt into the machine. In another two minutes Mercy was feeding it through herself, keeping a steady rhythm with her feet as the needle flew up and down through the cloth.

"I'll be back in a few minutes," said Mrs. Simmons. "If you have any problems, just stop the machine."

When she returned, the seam was nearly completed.

"You're doing just fine, Mercy," she said. "I knew you were going to be a fast learner!"

Suddenly a look of revelation came over her face. She stood still a moment, finger to her lips, clearly in thought. "Yes . . . yes," she said to herself. "We've got that storage room on the east side full of Zeke's tools. I've been after him to move them for years. It's absolutely perfect!"

She turned to Sister Mercy. "I've just had a wonderful idea," she said, "though I don't know what you'll think. Are you happy staying at the hotel?"

"I don't know—I suppose it's as good as a place like that can be."

"You told me when you first came that you had no money. How are you paying Mr. Millen?"

"Well, actually," replied Sister Mercy with an embar-

rassed look, "I owe him for several days. I thought after I'd
worked for you a while that then I'd be able to—"

"Then it's settled!" interrupted Mrs. Simmons excitedly.
"We can't have you paying out every cent you make for a
tiny lonely little room at the hotel and the dreadful food in
that dining room! Not to mention having to walk the two
miles out here every day. No, that arrangement's no good at
all."

"But I don't see what else—"

"You're going to stay here, Mercy—that is, if you want
to! Having you here with me will be well worth your room
and board. I'll pay you for your work in the shop, and you
can help me with meals and other things around the place in
exchange for your food and lodging. What do you say?"

The lady's eyes were aglow with enthusiasm.

"Are you sure you really want me to?"

"Want you to?" repeated Mrs. Simmons. "The only question in my mind is how it took me so long to think of it! Do
you know how nice it's been these last three days having
another woman around? It's absolutely perfect!"

She paused, examining Mercy from head to foot. "If
you're going to live and work on a ranch, however," she
said, thoughtful again, "we simply must get you some new
clothes. Is that black dress all you have?"

"I have another just like it back at the hotel. I didn't have
very many clothes in the first place, and most of what I
owned left Sweetriver in Brother Joseph's wagon."

"We'll have to do something about that! We'll make you a
shirt and some dungarees. We'll start today—Mrs. Dunakin
will just have to wait!"

"Dungarees? Is it . . . proper for a young lady to wear
pants?" asked Sister Mercy anxiously.

"Do you think *I'm* immodest?"

"Oh, no, I didn't mean—"

Mrs. Simmons laughed. "I know you meant nothing, Mercy. I was only teasing you. To answer your question, I don't know if it's *proper* or not. Who's to decide that but you? For me, I'm more comfortable in dungarees than a long dress, so that makes it proper for me. I've got too much to do every day not to be comfortable. We'll have to get you some new boots too," she added, looking down at Sister Mercy's feet.

"These have years left in them," objected Mercy.

"Then you can put them on when you dress up for a fancy occasion. But for everyday, you need some tough leather ranch boots. It can get messy around a place like this, Mercy! We might be making Mrs. Dunakin a new dress in the morning and birthing a calf in the afternoon! Are you *sure* you want to accept my offer?"

Sister Mercy smiled. "I'm sure," she said.

"Then you and I are going to go hitch up the team right now. We're going back into town. We'll settle your account with Mr. Millen and get your things from the hotel. Then we'll get you fitted for a new pair of boots with Hardy McFee, who's the best bootmaker in the whole territory."

"I don't have any money."

"I thought we had all that settled by now, Mercy. You're working for me now, and you've already earned a small advance on your wages."

"I don't know how to thank you, Mrs. Simmons."

"Then don't even try. Besides, you'll earn every cent! One thing folks around here know about my husband and me— everyone on the Simmons ranch works hard."

110

A DANGEROUS
GAME

Jess Forbes prided himself on being good with a deck

of cards.

Which was his biggest problem around a gaming table —

his pride. Actually, he *was* good. He possessed instincts from

years of experience that, if he had just played the game with

a level head, would ensure his coming out in the black three

times out of four. Unfortunately for both himself and his

partner, a level head was not something he was able to maintain with much consistency.

When the luck was running in Jess's direction, a subtle feeling of invincibility began to take him over. If the cards kept falling favorably, his recklessness usually made quick work of whoever might be left in the game. Many a man had declared they had never seen the stakes of a poker table accumulate so rapidly in a great pile in front of one man as when Jess Forbes was having things his way.

But if his luck turned while the feeling of invincibility still possessed him, Jess could also lose money faster than any three men who kept their wits about them.

In the last two days, as he had predicted, his luck had turned, and he had parlayed what a week before had been a dollar and twenty cents into well over fifty dollars—big winnings during the middle of the week for a town like Sweetriver.

The tide was shifting again, however, though Jess himself was the only one in the Silver Ox not to recognize it. He would have been a rich man and could have put up in the finest hotel rooms if he only knew how to fold his cards at the right time.

The pot on the table in front of him had already grown to seventeen dollars, the largest single pot in three days, strengthened by an early pair of kings showing in the game of five-card stud now in progress. Jess had an ace underneath, and when a second ace had been laid on top of his initial three, he had settled down to betting in earnest. He knew he had the two kings beat, though he tried not to raise too suddenly or they would suspect the ace he had in the hole. Next to him a pair of fours was also up, making it a three-way race, though a man called Smythe was still in the game as well.

The dealer slowly flipped out a fourth card to each of the four remaining players. The two who had folded watched in silent amusement.

McGraw, holding two kings, was dealt a seven. A six landed on Smythe's pile, and he quietly gathered in his cards, folded, and sat back to watch the other three finish out the round. Hanks saw a third four land on top of his pile, to the sound of a couple of whistles and exclamations from the onlookers. A jack landed on Jess's own pile, leaving him low man of the three.

Hanks was high and tossed ten dollars into the pot. More whistles followed.

When Jess stayed in, a few eyebrows raised. He clearly had either a jack, an ace, or a three in the hole. McGraw, with his two kings and a seven showing, also stayed.

There were no raises. The pot now stood at forty-seven dollars.

The dealer glanced around at the three, then deliberately dealt each his last card.

The saloon erupted with exclamatory comments and whistles when a third king completed McGraw's set. It was followed by a queen added to the top of Hanks's three fours. Thinking better of a bluff, Hanks sat back and sighed. He didn't have enough of a poker face to try to convince anyone he was holding the fourth four. He folded his hand.

Finally the dealer tossed Jess's last card face up onto his pile. It was an ace!

Jess watched it fall with a stone-faced expression, snuck one more glance at the corner of his underneath card, then glanced up at the only other player left in the game.

McGraw looked across the table and smiled, then tossed in another ten dollars.

Jess eyed him steadily. "I'll see your ten," he said slowly, "and raise you another five." He shoved fifteen dollars into the middle of the table.

"That's bold poker playing, Forbes," said McGraw, "two aces raising three kings. You must be trying to convince me you've got that third ace in the hole. It's the only way you can win, and you figure me to think you wouldn't bet all that unless you had it. But I think you're bluffing, Forbes, 'cause you think you know how I think. But you don't. So I'm going to call your five, and up it another ten, just to find out what kind of man you really are!"

McGraw now shoved fifteen more dollars onto the table.

Jess watched with inward amusement, his feeling of invincibility unshaken. He knew his three aces had McGraw's three kings dead to rights!

When Hanks had folded, he'd been a little careless with his underneath card. Jess had seen the flashing edge of a king. He hadn't looked on purpose, but since he *did* know that McGraw couldn't possibly be holding the fourth king, why shouldn't he use the information to his advantage?

"Well, McGraw," he said at length. "You think I'm bluffing about this third ace I got here. If you're right, then your three kings wins. But if you're wrong, then it's going to take *four* kings for you to keep me from winning that pot. And I just don't happen to think you got that fourth king in the hole."

"Gonna cost you ten bucks to find out, Forbes," said McGraw. "My last raise is still sitting there."

"Yeah, well don't you worry about your raise. I'll see your ten, and I'm going to up it another—" He paused to look over what he had in front of him. "—another twelve. It's all I got, and I'm betting it against that fourth king." He put all that remained of the fifty dollars he had had into the middle of the table, which now contained a hundred and nine dollars.

McGraw watched, a slow smile spreading over his face.

"I don't know what gets into you sometimes, Forbes," he said. "I've been watching you play cards for a week now. Sometimes you're pretty good. But at other times you're so downright stupid, why my mule could play better poker than you! You get on a run and figure you can't be beat, and you quit thinking straight. Well, here's the twelve—I call you."

Jess turned over his ace with a triumphant look of satisfaction.

"You see, McGraw," he said, "I wasn't bluffing. I had the three aces."

He reached out toward the pot.

"Not so fast, Forbes," rejoined McGraw.

"You don't have the fourth king, McGraw."

"You're right there—" as he spoke, he slowly turned up his hidden card—"but where I come from, a full house beats three aces every time."

He slapped down a seven.

Jess stared at the cards, dumbfounded.

"Did it never occur to you, Forbes, that I just might be holding the second seven?" laughed McGraw, pulling the huge pile of money toward him. He was joined in laughter by everyone around the saloon who had been watching.

Jess leaned back in his chair, eyes wide in disbelief, suddenly realizing his inane folly.

Sweetriver's hospitality had suddenly dried up.

He was getting out of there today and never coming back! Maybe they'd ride on into Denver. He'd always had good luck in Colorado.

Jess had no more time to contemplate his future, however.

Suddenly the doors of the Silver Ox swung open and banged against the walls.

"I'm here to collect what you stole from me the other night, Forbes!" said an angry voice.

Everyone looked up. There stood the onetime convert known as One Eye.

"Look, Jackson," said Jess half-humorously, not realizing the danger, "you see that pot in front of McGraw? Well, half of it's mine. Look for yourself—I don't have a cent left to my name!"

"Then I reckon I'll have to take it outta your hide!" growled Jackson.

21

HORSEFLESH
AND BLOOD

Jeremiah had scarcely been thinking of his partner all

day. He'd been in the saddle most of the morning trying to

tame a paricularly obstreperous two-year-old filly. The rest

of the time he'd been on the ground—like right now!

He had been thrown four times, his whole body hurt, and

he was about sick of the smell of horseflesh in his nostrils.

Like Jess, he had begun to consider practicalities—it was time to think of moving on.

If the truth were known, Eagleflight's thoughts were not on his partner *or* the filly. It had been a couple of days since he'd been in the hotel to give the man another dollar, only to have had his own words thrown back at him.

"Now it's my turn to tell *you* the young lady's bill's been taken care of," said Mr. Millen, handing him back his coin.

"You mean to tell me she paid you up?" he'd asked.

"That's not what I said. The bill was paid, but not by her. Mrs. Simmons came in with her, squared the whole tab with me—which was only one night's lodging and three meals' worth above what you'd already given me for her—and then checked her out."

"Was Sister Mercy leaving town?"

"Don't know. They went upstairs, got what little she had in her room, and left. That's the last I've seen of your young preacher friend."

Jeremiah left the hotel puzzled by the sudden turn of events, making no immediate connection with the name of her benefactor.

Of course he was glad for Sister Mercy's sake. Maybe the lady had bought her a stage ticket out of here and back to someplace where she would fit in better and find what she wanted her life to be about.

Yet he had been thinking about her for two days, regardless. He wondered if he had done right by instilling doubts in her mind. Maybe she was right and some of it was his fault, and he now regretted that he had not had the chance to see her again and wish her well.

"Hey, Eagleflight," the owner of the livery stable called out from the barn.

Jeremiah glanced up from where he sat, then slowly pulled his tired frame to its feet.

"I think it's time you gave that filly a rest."

"She's as frisky as she was three hours ago," replied Jeremiah. "It's me who needs the rest!"

Slowly he walked toward the barn, took off his hat, and dropped wearily onto a hard-packed bale of straw.

"Zeke say when we could get another load of straw?" asked his employer.

"'Bout a week," answered Jeremiah.

"It was a week ago you was out to his place, wasn't it?"

"Something like that."

"Then it's about time you hitch up the wagon and get yourself out there again."

"You want me to go today?"

"I don't know, tomorrow'd likely be—"

Both men glanced toward town when the gunshot rang out.

Jeremiah jumped to his feet, an unconscious feeling of dread sweeping through his frame. He ran out the door and toward the street, all hints of weariness suddenly gone, then stopped and glanced in both directions.

In the distance he heard shouts. People were running in the direction of the saloon. A horse was galloping off out of town.

He quickened his pace. *"Jess . . . Jess!"* he whispered, breaking into a run. A bad feeling suddenly stung his gut. When trouble was around, it usually managed to find Jess.

By the time he burst through the saloon doors thirty seconds later, a crowd was gathered around the table where a king-high full house had moments earlier beaten three aces. Jeremiah rushed forward. A premonition told him who lay in the midst of the circle of men.

He pushed his way through roughly and knelt down.

"*Oh, Jess* . . ." he breathed. An ugly hole in the right side of his belly had splattered blood all over Jess's shirt, and blood from the wound now dripped into a dark red pool on the hardwood floor beneath him.

He leaned forward and whispered something into Jess's ear. Jess opened his eyes into two thin slits. He tried to speak, coughed slightly, then winced in pain. "Jeremiah," he mumbled faintly, "we gotta—gotta get out of this town. . . ."

"Why's that, partner?"

"My dang luck turned on me again."

"I can see that," whispered Jeremiah. "But don't you worry—"

"No, no, not this—I mean the cards. . . . McGraw there . . . he suckered me into some blamed high stakes—"

He stopped, coughing again, and was unable to say any more.

"You quit talking," said Jeremiah. "Then as soon as you're back on your feet, we'll be moving on."

Jeremiah rose slowly to his feet, looked around, and sighed.

"Anybody go for the doc?" he asked.

Several men nodded.

"Look, Eagleflight," said McGraw, stepping forward, "we was just playing us an easy game, till your friend here took it into his head to raise too high with only three of a kind."

"Forget it, McGraw," said Jeremiah. "I know Jess better than any man alive. I know how he plays poker, and I have no doubt you beat him fair and square."

"You can have the whole pot back."

"Money's the last thing we need, McGraw—that is, unless the doctor can do something for him. You can help with that if you want. I've only got a couple dollars to my name."

"You can count on me, Eagleflight."

"Doc's here!" someone shouted.

The small crowd stood back. A thin man carrying a black leather medical bag made his way forward, stooped down, and proceeded to examine the wound.

"Don't look good," was all anyone heard him say.

22

An Offer

Jeremiah did not get out to the Bar S for the second load of straw that day or the next. His work at the livery, which amounted to only about half a day, alternated with anxious walks back and forth to Doc Haggerty's place. To make up for yesterday afternoon, he accepted no pay for the day. Once his partner had been carried to and made comfortable at Doc's, he said, the rest of his day's work hadn't been worth getting paid for.

Jess had fallen unconscious just as Doc had arrived at the Silver Ox. He hadn't woken up again. While the unconscious man lay on his table, and as his partner looked on, Doc Haggerty dug the slug from One Eye's .45 out of Jess's side, then bandaged him up.

"He's lost a heap of blood," Haggerty said, finally glancing up at Jeremiah with a sigh. "I don't give him much better'n a fifty-fifty chance."

The sheriff rode out to Jackson's shack in the hills within the hour with four or five men, but Slim was long gone.

The second day after the shooting, figuring there wasn't much good he could do hanging around the Doc's, Jeremiah hitched the team to the wagon around midmorning and headed out to the Simmons place.

As he rode up to the barn, the rancher strode out to meet him. "'Morning, Eagleflight."

"Simmons."

"Heard about your partner."

Jeremiah climbed down.

"I'm sorry," said the rancher somberly.

Jeremiah nodded in acknowledgment.

"Listen, Eagleflight, if there's anything I can do . . ."

"Thanks, Simmons," replied Jeremiah. "I appreciate that."

"Ol' One Eye always was a bad apple. . . . Well, I'll get a couple of the boys to help you load her up."

As Jeremiah watched the rancher open the double doors of the barn, he reflected on all the people he and Jess had met through the years. *Zeke Simmons is a real gentleman,* he thought. He reminded Jeremiah of his grandfather.

Forty minutes later, the wagon was nearly loaded. Zeke

reappeared, hoisted a couple of bales up to his foreman, standing on the back of the wagon, then signaled Jeremiah to one side.

"I want to talk to you for a minute, Eagleflight," he said.

Jeremiah followed him until they were alone.

"How much is ol' Lars paying you at the livery?"

"Dollar fifty a day."

"You like it?"

"It's work. Can't complain."

"You got any commitment with him?"

"Nope. I told him I didn't want nothing but day-to-day work."

Zeke thought for a moment, reflecting on what Jeremiah had said. "Summer's just about here and I need a few more men. If you're of a mind to take on something a little more permanent, and if we don't put Lars in any kind of bind, I'll give you two a day."

"How permanent? Jess and I don't like to get too tied down. We pretty much stay on the move."

"Your friend's not going anyplace for a while, Eagleflight, even if he does pull through."

Now it was Jeremiah's turn to stop and think. Zeke was right, he knew that. "So—how permanent?" he asked again.

"I don't expect nothing more than two weeks at a time. Out in the West here, you can't expect more. Most men are like you and your partner—they want to keep moving, no grass growing under their feet, you know. I pay every two weeks. If a fella leaves before that, he doesn't get paid. I don't suppose that's too permanent, but it keeps me with enough hands to run my spread."

"Two bucks, you say—a day?"

"Two dollars a day, plus room and board."

Jeremiah's face took in the new information with a nod of pleasure. "That's mighty good wages, Zeke," he said.

"Best in Pawnee Valley."

"How do you afford it?"

"My men work hard. It's a fair exchange. Everybody for a hundred miles knows that the hardest work, the longest hours, the best food, and the highest pay is at the Simmons ranch in Sweetriver. Believe me, I don't have much trouble with men leaving after two weeks."

"Men must be standing in line to work for you," remarked Jeremiah.

"Not exactly," Zeke went on. "Finding men who know how to work and who aren't looking to get paid more than for what they put out, that's not easy. But there's always some who'd like to get on here."

"Then why me?"

"I'm always looking for fellas who know the value of time. If a guy works for ten hours at half effort, he figures he ought to get paid for *full* effort. But I got a lot to do here. This is a big ranch. I'm not running an institution for broken-down cowpokes who want an easy time of it. I'm looking for men who don't mind taking orders and who know how to work hard."

"I figure if you take a job, taking orders and working hard goes with the territory."

"Not everyone thinks like that, Eagleflight. There's plenty that resent the fact that there's a boss or foreman over them telling 'em what to do. They figure when the boss's back is turned, it's time to loaf or start putting in half effort. It's downright rare when you meet a man who knows his own true value. When I meet one, I want him working for me."

"You figure I'm a man like that?"

"I been watching you."

"And?"

"You think you are?" asked Zeke.

"I can work," replied Jeremiah.

"That's why I figure you're the kind of man I keep an eye out for."

"Two dollars, huh?"

"Plus room and board."

"I'll talk to Lars."

The clanging of the iron signaling lunch sounded from the house behind them.

"Stay and have lunch with us, Eagleflight," said Simmons, cocking his head toward the triangle still echoing its tone. "Try out some of my wife's beef stew. Might make your decision easier!"

"That's hardly an invitation I'm likely to turn down," replied Jeremiah.

They turned and headed toward the house, joined by the two men from the barn.

"Your wagon's all loaded, Eagleflight," said the foreman.

"You see what I mean?" said Zeke. "My men know how to work, and they get the job done pronto!"

23

AROUND THE TABLE
AT THE BAR S

Inside the large, open-beamed dining room of the ranch

house, Jeremiah sat down at one end of a long bench next

to Simmons's foreman, a muscular cowboy of some forty years

by the name of Dirk Heyes.

Six others walked in after them, for a total of nine men

around the large plank table.

Zeke introduced Jeremiah to the others, while a very

robust woman of forty-five or so years that Jeremiah took to be Zeke's wife brought in a large steaming pot of stew, followed by a young lady bearing two trays of brown sliced bread, also steaming.

"Fresh this morning, men—eat up!" called out the older of the two women.

"Jody, this here's Jeremiah Eagleflight," said Zeke to his wife. "He's working at the livery in town right now, but Heyes'll have to clean out a bunk for him any day now—it's my hope he'll be joining us here real soon!"

"Consider yourself welcome, Mr. Eagleflight," said Mrs. Simmons. "And meet—"

But Jeremiah had suddenly ceased listening to any further words of introduction. None were necessary. Suddenly he recalled Millen's words at the hotel, which had hardly registered at the time.

He had noticed her as she entered the room. He had even glanced quickly at her face, though without pausing to give it a second look.

But as she set down one of the trays of bread almost in front of him, she glanced toward his face. He felt the pull of the gaze and looked up.

Their eyes met.

Suddenly recognition exploded in Jeremiah's disbelieving brain. His mouth fell open in amazed surprise.

Sister Mercy's face reddened, and she looked quickly away, moving to set down the other tray at the opposite end.

"—Miss Randolph," continued the rancher's wife.

"Uh . . . yes," stammered Jeremiah, "Miss, uh . . . Miss Randolph and I have already met."

"Oh, I see," said Mrs. Simmons, "in town?"

"Yes, ma'am."

"That's nice. So, if you decide to go to work for my husband, you'll already have a friend here."

"Uh . . . yes, ma'am," said Jeremiah, reaching for a slice of bread and stuffing one end of it quickly into his mouth.

Once everything had been served, Mrs. Simmons and Sister Mercy took seats at the far end of the table. Zeke's wife entered fully into conversation with all the men, though Sister Mercy said not a word, then excused herself and returned to the kitchen.

A minute or two later she returned with another tray of bread, then disappeared once more. Jeremiah did not see her again.

He could hardly believe his eyes!

The transformation was so thorough that he literally had not recognized her. She wore no bonnet, and her light brown hair flowed in wide curls down onto her shoulders. Now that he thought about it, he wasn't sure he'd even paid enough attention before now to notice what color her hair was!

And those eyes! A deep green, as if in some hidden recess inside her head she was thinking of the crystal clear emerald lakes he and Jess had seen high in the Rockies and her eyes conformed to the color of her imaginings. When she had cast that glance up from the tray of bread, his own eyes felt like they were melting into hers.

He had known her face was a pretty one. Even surrounded by an unfashionable black bonnet, and filled as it was with timidity and uncertainty, the attractiveness of her features could not be hidden.

Now the outdated black dress was gone. In its place, a colorful green plaid gingham shirt—matching her emerald eyes to perfection!—and *blue dungarees!* What a contrasting picture from a few days before.

Suddenly, not the face only—with its high prominent cheekbones, its undersized but perfect nose, and a mouth of not great width but straight across with pleasant smile revealing white medium-sized teeth—but indeed her entire countenance radiated with color and beauty.

This was a young lady who would turn the head of any man, thought Jeremiah.

Despite Eagleflight's observations, however, most of Mercy Randolph's beauty still existed unformed in the idea of its potential. It had begun to come awake, it was true, but the full vibrant expressiveness of *life* yet lay dormant beneath the surface.

Unknown even to herself, however, the shell had begun to crack.

When the new life of its deepest regions began to emerge and flower and bear fruit, even the admiring eyes of Jeremiah Eagleflight would scarcely recognize the butterfly as it flew from the cocoon from which it had already begun its gradual metamorphosis.

24

A PENSIVE WALK

Sister Mercy, meanwhile, was filled with her own thoughts after walking out of the kitchen, a tray of the bread she herself had baked in each hand. So unexpected were the words *Jeremiah Eagleflight* that she had nearly dropped the trays on the floor.

Something inside her had wanted to shout out, "Hello, Jeremiah! It's so wonderful to see you again!"

Yet the moment she caught a glimpse of his face amongst the roomful of men, she had glanced timidly away. As she moved nearer to set down the bread, she felt his nearness in the very pulse beating beneath her skin. She tried not to look at him for fear her eyes would betray her.

But alas! The pull of his presence was too strong. That one look into his eyes had nearly undone her. She had almost stumbled over Mr. Simmons's boot beside his chair.

Now evening had come, and the light of day settled into dusk as Sister Mercy walked slowly along. She took a deep breath and then exhaled slowly as she remembered the incident from earlier in the day and then continued her walk along the ridge overlooking the ranch.

The remainder of the day had been interminably long. As much as she had already grown to love Mrs. Simmons, she had not been able to keep her mind on her work or pay much attention to conversation with her employer. It had taken every ounce of her concentration and presence of mind to keep from saying something that would betray the inner turmoil prompted in her mind by their unannounced lunch guest.

She was glad when supper was at last over and her chores completed. What she needed was just some time alone.

Mercy looked down at the little valley where the Simmons ranch was located, peaceful now from a distance in the quiet and cooling light of evening. It had only been seven days since she had first walked out here from Sweetriver to meet Jody Simmons.

It seemed like seven weeks!

So quickly had the depressing cloud of her recent past faded in the radiance of Mrs. Simmons's warm and loving acceptance. In the strengthening purpose of working hard for her own daily bread, both Brother Joseph and her own foolhardiness at being such an easy dupe for his schemes had already begun to sink into distant memory.

Unfortunately, Brother Joseph was not the only unpleasantness in her recent past she had been trying to put behind her! After today, suddenly Jeremiah Eagleflight had become more difficult to forget than ever.

His face, his voice—how could she forget those!—and the painful and straightforward words he had spoken to her!

She had said to herself back in the hotel room that she would not think about what he'd said anymore—not then, not at that moment when all of life seemed falling about her ears.

Perhaps it had not been a wise resolve to make. In any case, she had made it and had stuck by it—until today.

The moment she came again face-to-face with Jeremiah Eagleflight, she knew the day of reckoning had arrived. She could ignore his words no longer. She had to face them, think about them, find out if there was any truth in them.

For the first time in her life, Mercy Randolph had to find out what she really did believe.

25

DEEPER QUESTIONS

As Mercy walked along, deep down she realized she had probably been thinking about what Jeremiah had said all along. She had only tried to pretend she wasn't thinking about it, hoping perhaps it would go away.

But it hadn't. And it wouldn't. His words had been gnawing away inside her for almost two weeks now.

Do you really believe all those things you say?

She had been so hasty to answer yes. The very eagerness of her defensive reply only confirmed what he'd said next, that she had a ready answer prepared for everything.

Everything she'd answered in reply came back into her memory. *Don't you think I'm a Christian? I studied at the Young Women's Missionary College. I dedicated my life to being a minister of the gospel. . . .*

But she'd never answered his question.

He'd said, *I don't doubt any of that. But do you really believe it all?*

All she'd been able to say was, *How could I not?*

That was hardly an adequate response. She hadn't given him a full straight answer to his question, she realized at last, for the plain and simple reason that she didn't know!

If she was honest with herself, she had to admit that his assessment of her was exactly correct.

She *had* been learning the right answers all her life, from her mother and father and all the hours and hours she'd spent in church listening to Rev. Walton, all the way to Evansville and the Young Women's Missionary College. She'd learned all the answers so she could recite them, just like he said.

And recite them she did, traveling across the country with the supposed evangelist Reverend Joseph Mertree, singing the songs and giving out the messages, and all the while she was blind to the reality of what was actually going on.

The truth was terrible to admit.

Jeremiah *was* right.

For every question he asked her—it was so plain now!— she pulled out an answer from the stockpile of everything she had been taught. But not from what she believed.

She'd taken offense when he'd meant no offense. She'd jumped to conclusions about *his* own beliefs with no foundation other than his desire to know what *she* believed. She'd misjudged him, one of the most serious of all sins!

She hadn't been a real person at all. What had she been these past months but Brother Joseph's spiritual puppet — singing the songs and saying the words and giving the memorized testimonials? She had thought she was answering the Lord's call. Looking back now, however, suddenly it seemed shallow and hollow and empty.

Even in the midst of her present doubts, she felt more *real* and alive, now that her brain was finally working, than she had a month ago!

The dreadful sermon she had tried to preach in the hotel to her congregation of one came back to her. She'd quoted from the Old Testament Jeremiah about truth, about truth-seeking men and about searching for God with all of one's heart.

It was all so clear now!

The Jeremiah she knew — Jeremiah Eagleflight, the man she had been so quick to judge as a heathen and unbeliever — *he* had actually been looking for truth. Or at least some answers to his questions that rang with truth. He had asked *her* to help him understand what she now saw were *honest,* rather than mocking, questions.

Not only had she been unable to help, she had turned his questions back on him, even angrily, during their first conversation. She had treated him as if his expressions of curiosity had been hostile threats, not sincere attempts to understand.

She had had no truth to give him, only the stale formulas she had long ago learned to apply in such circumstances. Rote words — just like he said — but no living food, any more than Brother Joseph had had any true spiritual food to offer Bart Wood and Shifty Snyder!

The prophet had said that God had commanded him to run through the streets looking for men of honest judgment who sought the truth. She had read the very words, right to Jeremiah Eagleflight himself! To him alone!

How could she have been so blind? She was not doing what the Lord commanded—looking for seekers of the truth. Worse, she had closed her eyes to the very one God had placed right in front of her nose! The Word of God had said, "Run ye to and fro through the streets . . . and see . . . if ye can find a man, if there be any . . . that seeketh the truth."

Any man . . . a single one.

She *had* found one. Or, more truthfully, he had found *her*. He had helped her, befriended her, given her money, spoken respectfully to her, and even come to the service she had tried to hold. But she had not had eyes to see that his heart was sincere.

It was Jeremiah who was the truth seeker, not her.

Her own words from out of the prophet came straight against her once more. "And ye shall seek me, and find me, when ye shall search for me with all your heart."

They had learned this passage at Evansville. "Always quote it in the company of the heathen," she had been taught. How could it be of much benefit to the unsaved *if the saved didn't know what it meant!*

What could it mean to one's listeners if the believers who quoted it never applied it to themselves or had never done the very thing so vital to faith—sought and searched with the whole heart?

She had never in her whole life sought God with her *whole* heart, thought Mercy. Was it any wonder she had not found him?

She had been taught by her parents, by teachers, by

pastors, by all the good people in Evansville. She had
grown up familiar with all the precepts. She had just
assumed her own faith in God instead of *searching* for it,
seeking it. She had never even stopped to think much about
it, until now.

Mercy walked on, breathing deeply of the peaceful
evening air. Dusk was settling over the Pawnee Valley and
that portion of it where the Sweet River ran slowly through
the vast acreage of Zeke and Jody Simmons's Bar S ranch.

It was odd, she thought to herself. There were no tears
tonight. She had cried enough in the last two weeks to last
her a year—after hearing Brother Joseph's deception at the
livery stable, in her hotel room, after her two conversations
with Jeremiah, and following the miserable failure of a
church service.

However, there were no tears tonight. She felt a deep seri-
ousness, a heavy sense of importance about the things that
were twisting and wrestling and jarring themselves against
one another in her brain.

But no sadness.

Even in the midst of what might have seemed like faith-
destroying questions and bitterly painful revelations of her
own superficial life till now. She actually felt a sense of
strength slowly growing inside.

She was *thinking*—thinking for herself, exercising the
muscles of her brain in new ways.

She could not deny that it felt good! She was gradually
discovering that she *was* a real person, that her brain and
heart were capable of activity.

If it meant she had to plunge down to the bottom of her
being to find out what she *wasn't* made of and what she
hadn't been and what she *didn't* believe in order then to climb

back out and discover *who* she was and *what* she was made of and what she *did* believe . . . then she would do it!

The exploration into the inner regions of her being would be worth it, even if—as Jeremiah himself had ventured to do—she had to ask some probing questions of herself that she had never considered before.

So she did not weep as she walked.

Her heart was heavy, it is true, with remorse for many things about the past, but not with regret for the present. She even felt a certain quiet contentment with regard to the future.

The days of feeling sorry for herself had come and gone. Learning to live was now the business at hand.

The shell so long surrounding her had split.

Now it was time for the shining new creation known as Mercy Randolph to emerge. The moment had come to step into the fullness of womanhood purposed for her by her Father from the beginning.

A NEW AND
EXTRAORDINARY
PRAYER

It was nearly dark now. Mercy turned to retrace her

steps back to the ranch house that was, for now, her home.

As she went, from out of the reservoir of past teaching,

the words of the Scriptures came into her mind. She

thought they were probably from Psalms, though she

couldn't remember exactly whether they were from the

same passage or two different ones. She only knew she had
memorized the words as a young girl.

*Create in me a clean heart, O God; and renew a right spirit within
me. Search me, O God, and know my heart: try me, and know my
thoughts: And see if there be any wicked way in me, and lead me in
the way everlasting.*

The words kept coming over and over . . . *search me . . .
search me . . . know my heart . . . try me . . . know my thoughts*.

What had been going on within her during the last two
weeks but a probing, searching, digging about in the deep
recesses of her being?

Perhaps God had been doing this very thing, knowing
what she needed even before she had known she needed to
pray for it!

The thought was new and powerful.

Mercy stopped walking momentarily, hands clasped to
her cheeks, eyes wide open — not seeing ahead into the dusk
but rather peering inward. Her mind reeled. The thought
was so extraordinary!

Might it be God himself who had had a hand in everything
that had happened — her discovery of the evangelistic hypoc-
risy in which she had been involved, her being left penniless
so far from home? Might God even have sent Jeremiah to
ask all those hurtful questions? What if God's hand had even
been in her failed sermon in the hotel lobby — all for the purpose of carrying out this inward search of her heart?

She could hardly take in the idea that all the seeming failure might have been in answer to a prayer — a prayer she
had not even prayed yet but that God knew she needed to
pray!

Then Mercy did something she had never done before in
all her life.

Slowly she sank to her knees.

And there, in the summer twilight of the Kansas prairie, where no human eye could see her and no human ear could hear the words that came softly from her lips, Mercy Randolph bowed her head and lifted her voice to her heavenly Father.

She prayed for the first time ever that God would direct the searchlight of his probing spirit toward *her*.

"Oh, God," she whispered, "even if you have been answering this prayer before I prayed it, I want to pray it now. I *want* you to keep searching into those places inside me where I thought I knew the right spiritual answers but maybe didn't know as much as I thought I did. I *want* you to try me and test me, like it says, and if there is wickedness in me, or if there's the kind of shallowness in me that Jeremiah said, I suppose I have to know . . . I *want* to know, and so I ask you to show me whatever you need to about myself.

"Help me, God, to seek for you and search for you! I don't even know how to. I'm so sorry for talking and preaching about it when I had no right to. I want to know you with my whole heart. But I don't even know how to do that. So I need your help.

"God, please, create a clean heart within me!

"I want to believe, God. Maybe I don't yet. I don't know — but I want to. If that's something I need to repent of and ask your forgiveness for, talking like I believed when all I was doing was saying everything I'd been taught, then I am sorry.

"I never meant to do wrong, God. I just never stopped to think about whether I really believed everything I said — that is, until Jeremiah started talking to me and asking me questions. I'm sorry I didn't have answers to give him, God. I'm asking you to give me something to say to him.

"And I pray for Jeremiah too, that you would do all these same things inside him—search him inside out like you're doing me, so that he can know the truth like he says he wants to.

"Show me what it means to believe, all the way deep down in my heart. I *want* to believe in a new and deeper and more personal way. When I talk to somebody about being a Christian, I want it to be more than just what I've been taught to say. So help me, please, God—help me to really *believe!*"

She continued to pray for some time, audibly and inaudibly, pouring out the thoughts and questions of her mind and the newfound longings of her heart.

When she rose thirty minutes later, it was dark, though a quarter-moon had risen just above the horizon, casting a pale glow over the silent prairie. Its thin light revealed the glistening traces of tears on Mercy's cheeks as she made her way down the hill to the house. These were no tears of sadness, but rather of quiet joy.

For—uncluttered by teaching and church, by books and ideas, by parents and brothers and sisters—she had at last met her Father face-to-face in the deepest regions of her heart.

27

BY CREEKSIDE

A scorching midafternoon sun beat down on the back of Jeremiah Eagleflight.

After two days of digging posts and yanking barbed wire around the ranch, he wasn't at all sure this was better than the livery stable in town. Harder work it was for sure. But then Zeke had promised him that. He'd known what he was getting himself in for.

He only wished he could look in on Jess once in a while. But there'd been no change, and Doc Haggerty promised he'd send word out to the Bar S if there was, or the minute Jess regained consciousness.

He pulled a strand of wire tight, then wound it around the post and looped it back over on top of itself. Still holding it with one hand, he set the staple in place over the two strands, holding it tight with two fingers and tapping it slightly with the hammer he had in his right hand to set its sharp points into the wood. Then two quick motions of his wrist drove the staple tight into the hard oak, squeezing the wire tight underneath it.

Jeremiah stood back, relaxing his grip on the wire, then set and pounded in two more staples, clipped the end of the wire, picked up the roll, and sloshed into the creek.

He paused for a moment, stooped down, scooped up a handful of water, and threw it at his face. He repeated the motion several times until his hair was dripping, then went on across to start the same process with wire, oak, and staples along the other side.

Nothing had been found out about One Eye Jackson. Not that it mattered. Revenge had never been something Jeremiah had put much stock in. Watching One Eye swing from the end of a rope wouldn't help his partner.

If Jess died, he didn't know what he'd do.

Neither of them had ever said much about what they thought of one another. Men didn't do that kind of thing.

But they were more than just uncle and nephew, more than just riding partners and poker buddies. They were friends.

And not *mere* friends, but good friends, the kind of friends that would live—or die—for each other, the kind of friends

that didn't come along very often. Most men, thought
Jeremiah, probably never knew the kind of camaraderie he
and Jess took for granted.

He *loved* Jess, if the truth were known. He wouldn't go
saying a thing like that in a saloon full of tough gambling
and drinking men. He'd never tell Jess to his face either.
But he did, just the same.

They'd been together since Jess had left home—what
would it be, going on eleven years now. If he died, it'd
change everything for Jeremiah. He wasn't sure what he'd
do, but life sure wouldn't be much fun anymore.

Jeremiah sighed in the hot sun, wiped his forehead,
already hot again in spite of the dousing from the creek, and
began to set the leading end of the barbed wire into the first
post.

Glancing up, however, he halted after the first staple. A
figure approached along the path following the creekbed.
He set down the roll of wire and waited.

The newcomer arrived and paused. The next moment or
two were awkward. He looked at the wire, she down
toward the creek.

"They told me I'd find you out here," said Mercy timidly,
glancing up.

"Lotta wire to string," replied Jeremiah.

"I saw the posts as I came."

"Set them in place yesterday."

"I knew you'd come to work, like Mr. Simmons said you
might. When did you start?"

"Day before yesterday."

"I'd been hoping to see you sometime besides around the
dinner table."

"Yeah, me too," said Jeremiah, "but Heyes got me out

here right away both mornings finishing these holes and hauling the posts."

There was a slight pause.

"I was surprised to see you at lunch the other day," said Mercy at length.

"Not half as surprised as I was to see you—in pants and a shirt and new boots! You looked like a regular cowgirl, Sister Mercy."

She laughed. Gradually the ice began to break. "How's your friend Jess?" she asked.

"You heard about him, huh?"

"Word about those kinds of things travels fast."

"Yeah, well, he's just the same. No change."

"I'm sorry. I hope he pulls through."

Jeremiah sighed slowly, nodded, then asked, "Heyes tells me you been working for Mrs. Simmons quite a while now?"

"Not all that long. About a week and a half, I suppose."

"You like it?"

"She's been wonderful to me, Jeremiah. I owe her almost as much . . . as I do you."

"Me! What are you talking about?"

"You watched out for me back in town, fed me, talked to me. You even came to my church service!" She smiled as the last words came out of her mouth.

"I would have done it for anyone," he replied. "You needed help."

"Maybe you would have, but you did it for me, though I guess I didn't show you much appreciation at the time. I'm sorry."

"Aw, don't worry about it. You did fine. I wasn't looking for appreciation."

"Do you think I did a *fine* job of preaching that Sunday

morning at the hotel?" As she asked, there was a hint of humor in Mercy's eye.

"You did all right," replied Jeremiah seriously.

"I did nothing of the kind! It was dreadful, and you know it. You knew it at the time too, though you were too considerate to say anything when you followed me out of town — and I was so rude to you."

"You had a lot on your mind, Sister Mercy," said Jeremiah sincerely, his left arm slung around the fence post and still holding the hammer in his right. "You didn't need me saying anything more to hurt you right then. I'd already said probably more to you than I ought to have."

"That's another thing I have to thank you for."

"What?"

"Everything else you said to me."

"Now I'm a little confused, Sister Mercy. I don't guess I know what you mean."

"All of what you said to me that day after you bought me lunch at the hotel — you can't have forgotten?"

"No, I haven't forgotten," he replied sheepishly.

"No one has ever said that kind of thing to me," she went on. "Nobody ever had the courage to make me look at it, until you. You made me look at myself, Jeremiah. I needed to do just that. You weren't afraid to say hard things to me, even though you knew I'd probably take it wrong. I did take it wrong too, at first. But now that I've had the chance to think about it, I see that you only wanted to help. You did it because you cared about me, cared about the person I was, even though you said yourself you didn't know who I really was."

"It wasn't that I really meant—"

"It's all right, Jeremiah," she interrupted. "You were absolutely right in everything you said. And now I want to thank you—thank you for caring about me and for having the courage to make me stop and think and look at myself. So, thank you, Jeremiah Eagleflight!" She held out her hand.

Jeremiah finally glanced up and looked into her emerald green eyes. "Do you really mean all that?" he said.

She smiled and nodded as he took her hand and shook it.

"You asked me before if I really meant what I said. Well, this is one time I can answer with confidence. I do. Yes, I really mean it—thank you for all you said to me."

"Didn't it hurt you pretty deep?"

"Sure it did. But I will grow out of it, and I will grow *from* it too."

"Well, I'm glad then, Sister Mercy. I'm glad you told me. That makes me feel a lot better. I have to tell you, I was a little worried."

"Worried! Why should you be worried? You were just speaking the truth, weren't you?"

"I was trying to."

"Then you had nothing to be worried about. If I didn't want to listen, then I'd be the one to suffer for it, not you."

"I suppose, but I honestly didn't want to hurt you."

"I know, Jeremiah. Besides, the fact is I did listen." She paused. "Well, not at first," she added. "But I've been think-ing about every word you said since, and that's why now I'm thankful for it."

Again they fell silent momentarily.

"One of the first changes I want you to make," Mercy went on brightly, "is in what you call me. From now on, I'd like you to just use my name. No *Sister*—just Mercy."

"Mind if I ask why?"

"Because I want to just be who I am—like you said. If I'm going to find out who that real person down inside is, then I ought to start with the name my mother and father gave me — Mercy Carter Randolph."

"Where's the Carter from?"

"My mother's name before she married my father."

"And so you figure dropping the *Sister* gets you closer to the real you, is that it?"

"There was so much you said that day, Jeremiah, that is all so clear to me now. I don't know how it took so long for me to see it myself. The names and labels weren't any different than the words I was using and the hollow replies I gave back to everything you said. *Reverend* and *Evangelist* and *Brother* and *Sister* — they were all just labels to make us look spiritual and pious, just like the answers I learned at the college in Evansville for things I didn't know if I even believed. I don't want to even think of being called *Sister* now, as if I were a special and more spiritual person than someone else. I'm not. I never was, and the very thought of how long I pretended to be makes me sorry."

"All right then, from now on you're just plain Mercy to me."

"Thank you."

"So tell me, just plain Mercy, have you discovered the answer to my question yet?" asked Jeremiah.

"You mean about whether I believe everything I used to say?"

"Or maybe just whether you believe or not, period?"

Mercy was silent, this time for a long time.

"No, Jeremiah, I haven't," she said at length. "I can't say I know I believe *everything*. If I'm going to be honest from now on, then I have to honestly admit that."

"You don't seem anxious or worried about it. You seem happier than I've ever seen you."

"I am! I am wonderfully happy. Don't you see, it's

because I've shed all the old clothes I was trying to wear all those years—the old clothes of spiritual words and answers and labels without reality underneath them, which I now see, thanks to you. I am for the first time in my life actually *thinking* for myself. It does reel so good, even though I don't know where it will lead yet."

"I hope it leads you where you want to go."

"It can't help but do that. Anyone who's honest in their thinking—honest with themselves—can't help but find the truth in the end, right?"

"I don't think I've thought about that one yet," laughed Jeremiah.

"There is *one* thing I am sure of," said Mercy.

"What's that?"

"I know that I now *want* to believe. There's no doubt about that. So I'm determined to search and seek and ask and pray until I do find out for myself."

Jeremiah nodded thoughtfully.

The change in the young lady he had known as Sister Mercy had already gone far beyond just clothes and circumstances. Though she might not have known it yet, this was a different young lady standing before him.

"But I've already kept you far too long from your work!" she exclaimed, suddenly realizing that the sun was beginning its afternoon descent toward the horizon.

"I'll just work until dark to make up for it," joked Jeremiah. "But why did you come all the way out here? What about your chores? And what's in that basket under the towel?" he added with a wink.

"Oh, I forgot! I asked if I could bring you some nourishment. Mrs. Simmons thought it was a great idea. It's fresh bread!"

Mercy removed the towel. Jeremiah's eyes lit up at the three thick slices, generously slabbed over with butter.

"Thank you!" he exclaimed, dropping his hammer to the ground and reaching for one. "Made by . . . ?"

"By me, of course!"

"Then I'll enjoy every bite twice as much!"

As Mercy walked away from the creek a few minutes later, she heard Jeremiah softly whistling a familiar tune, intermingling with blows from his hammer.

She smiled as she went. It was the tune to "What a Friend We Have in Jesus."

28

A REQUEST

The thought had been in Mercy's mind since the

moment she had come awake. It was so early and the idea

so strong that it had probably been what had roused her out

of a sound sleep.

She glanced toward the window. It was still dark. Dawn

was probably an hour away, but more sleep was out of the

question. Even if her body was still tired, her brain was behaving like it was high noon!

She lay in bed thinking. There was nothing she could do about it until morning anyway. The hours between now and then would give her time to decide whether or not to go through with it.

The very notion of doing something that reminded her of traveling with Brother Joseph repelled her at first. How could she step back into all that? What would people think, especially if nothing came of it? There was already talk amongst some of the townspeople, or so she had heard, about her presence in Sweetriver and why she had left Reverend Mertree. Rumors were floating about that the whole thing had been a sham. How could they not hold lingering suspicions toward her part in it?

She couldn't blame them. She didn't blame them. The rumors were true! She *had* been a part of the duplicity, even though she had been taken in herself along with the rest, and she could therefore not keep from taking a share of the guilt upon her own shoulders.

Most of all, she realized, the question on her mind was what would Jeremiah think?

Would it look like nothing more than the same old hollow religiosity? Would he think she was doing it again, trying to cover something over with holy words?

Was she doing that?

No. The thought had come to her completely unsought. She didn't even *want* to do it! There could hardly be any danger of trying to impress people with pious proclamations.

She would rather stay right where she was, on the Simmons ranch, and keep to herself. If there was one thing she *didn't* want to do right now, it was to appear to have some motive of gain.

And yet she couldn't escape the strong sense that she was *supposed* to do it. It was unlike anything she had felt before.

Was God telling her to? She'd never felt God telling her to do anything before. Was this what it felt like?

She didn't know. As much as she knew *about* the Christian life, she was coming to realize she knew very little in a practical way about actually *living* it, putting it into practice — doing it. She'd been a Christian all her life — well, at least she'd been what she thought was a Christian — and now here she was realizing she didn't know what it was really like when God told you to do something.

Whether God was telling her to do it or not, she couldn't escape the strong feeling that she was *supposed* to do it, whatever people might think — no matter if she looked like a religious fool again, and no matter if nothing came of it, even despite what Jeremiah might think.

Mercy sighed. She *had* to do it. The urging was just too strong to ignore.

By the time the sun squinted over the eastern horizon with its piercing red orange arrows of light, she was already dressed and busy with her day's chores. As breakfast approached, she watched for Jeremiah. When she finally saw him walking from the bunkhouse toward the house, he was laughing and talking with Mr. Simmons and Dirk Heyes.

Mercy went to the door and greeted them.

"Jeremiah," she said, "may I . . . have a word with you . . . alone?"

"You bet — I'll see you fellas inside," he added to the owner and foreman.

"What's on your mind, Mercy?" asked Jeremiah as they walked slowly away from the porch.

"I have a favor to ask you," she replied.

"Sure, anything," he said. "Anything I can do, that is!"

"Would you take me into town this morning?" she asked. "I already asked Mrs. Simmons."

"If Zeke'll let me go, sure. There's some things we need to deliver to Lars at the livery. I could take care of that at the same time—a couple of ponies he's buying and a young bull-calf."

"That's not quite all," added Mercy. "There's one more thing."

"Name it."

"I'd like to ask if it would be all right with you—," she began, then hesitated, reddening slightly.

"What is it—go ahead and ask."

"I'd like to know if you'd mind if I went and prayed for your friend?"

"Jess?"

Mercy nodded.

Jeremiah looked at her as if to say, "What possible objection would I have to that?"

"Uh . . . sure," he responded. "That'd be great! Poor Jess needs all the help he can get."

"I just wasn't sure what you'd think, you know."

"What *would* I think?"

"After Brother Joseph and all that happened and everything you said, I didn't know if maybe you didn't think too highly of prayer."

"There you go jumping to conclusions about me and what I think again, Mercy," said Jeremiah with a grin.

"I'm sorry."

"Just so long as you're not planning to put on a healing sideshow there at the doc's or anything like that."

"Of course not."

"What are you going to go there and pray, for him to get healed, like a faith-healer does?"

"I don't know, Jeremiah—but not like a faith-healer does. I just want to go there and pray for him."

"Well, it's sure all right by me!"

29

JESS FORBES

Mercy and Jeremiah entered Doc Haggerty's office and small house while it was still early in the morning.

"You're calling a mite early today, Eagleflight," said Doc. "I'm barely up and dressed yet."

"We wanted to get our business in town done before it gets too hot," replied Jeremiah. "Doc, meet Mercy Randolph. She's Mrs. Simmons's helper out at the Bar S."

"My pleasure, ma'am," said the doctor to Mercy. "I think I already know you. Where've I seen—it was at the revival meeting!" he said, his face brightening at once in remembrance.

"Yes, sir, I'm afraid it was," answered Mercy. "I take it you were there?"

"All three meetings, ma'am. My ma raised me a God-fearing man."

"I'm happy to hear that, Dr. Haggerty," said Mercy. "So did mine, though I'm only just now starting to realize the truth in half the things she taught me."

"I'm not sure I quite understand you, Miss Randolph."

"It's a long story, Dr. Haggerty," replied Mercy. "Perhaps after I know how it ends, I can tell you about it."

"I'll look forward to it!"

"Come on, Doc," put in Jeremiah impatiently. "We're here to see Jess. How is he?"

"No change, Eagleflight. Sleeping like a baby, but showing no sign of waking. If he doesn't come to before long, he's going to waste away. If the wound doesn't kill him, he'll die of starvation."

"You getting water in him?"

"Some. I still got the tube down his throat. Every once in a while it looks like his muscles are trying to swallow. But it's going to be too late if we can't get some food inside him pretty soon."

Doc Haggerty led the way into a small room where the unmoving form of Jeremiah's partner lay beneath a single white sheet.

Jeremiah walked to the bedside and stood quietly a moment, gazing into the pale unconscious face. From where she stood, Mercy could see the emotion in Jeremiah's eyes.

She watched as he stood silently gazing upon the form of his nephew, wondering what was going through his mind. No one uttered a word. It was clear the man lying there was far more to Jeremiah than just a partner. The look of caring of a man for his friend shone in his eyes.

After a moment, Jeremiah turned and looked back at her. He gave a slight nod, as if to indicate that now it was her turn, then stepped back and away from the bed.

Mercy stepped forward. She hadn't stopped to think about what she would actually say or do when the moment came. Now here it was, and she knew both Doc Haggerty and Jeremiah Eagleflight's eyes were upon her.

She stood at the edge of the bed a moment, gazing upon the face of the young man she hardly knew. Her only connection with him was that he was Jeremiah's nephew and friend. That alone gave her compassion for him. His eyes were closed, his mouth expressionless. The stubbled face was pale, though not white. She had never seen a corpse before. Had she not known he was alive she might have taken this for the face of a dead man, though every once in a while the faintest hint of movement in his nostrils betrayed that he still breathed.

Slowly she stretched out her hand and rested it gently on Jess's shoulder. After a moment she lifted it and placed it, with trembling fingers, on the rugged white skin of his forehead. She had expected the clammy cold of a cadaver and was surprised when the warmth of dormant life met her touch.

She held her hand there a minute, as if checking a child for a fever, then began to pray in a soft whisper.

"God, I ask you to take care of this young man, Jess Forbes. Whatever you've got in mind for his life and how long you want it to go and what you want to accomplish in it, well it's all in your hands, but I pray for him anyway. If you want to take him, then I know you know best."

She paused and took a breath. "Right now I don't know," she went on, "if it's proper for me to pray for healing. But if it is, then I ask you to heal his broken body and to fix up the place where he was wounded. Make his body whole again, God. I pray for Doctor Haggerty. Show him what to do to help Jess. Amen."

Her lips fell silent. There was nothing more to say. She had prayed what was inside her to pray, and—with the memory of Brother Joseph so fresh in her memory—was not about to embellish her prayers with excess words. There were many things she had recently discovered she did not know, but she *did* know that God required no convincing with moving speeches.

Jeremiah had heard very little of what Mercy had said. Her voice had been barely audible. It was obvious to him, however, that he had never seen anyone pray for another quite like this before.

When they left Doc Haggerty's office a few minutes later, both Mercy and Jeremiah were somber and silent. Something had happened to each of them inside as they stood at Jess's bedside, though neither yet knew exactly what it was.

30

DAWNING
OF LIGHT

Throughout the ride home in the wagon as Jeremiah
and Mercy sat beside one another, the quiet between them
continued.

Both had longed for an opportunity to talk again after

their meeting at the creekside a few days earlier. Now that

the chance presented itself, both remained pensive, alone

with their own thoughts.

Yet even though scarcely five words passed between them, there was no place either would rather have been, nor any other either of them would have chosen to share this time of reflection with than the other. The lack of words was not because there was nothing to say. On the contrary, the silence was rather too full for words to be capable of expressing all it contained.

The morning's events, though unpretentious and devoid of the exhibition displayed in the Mertree Tent of Meeting and Healing, had been anything but simple. The impact would be felt by these two young truth-seekers for the rest of their lives.

Well, I did it, Mercy thought, *come of it what may.*

But what was Jeremiah thinking?

She cast him a sidelong glance. Both men had watched her without saying anything—Doc with an open and hopeful mind she thought, Jeremiah silent and with what she assumed was skeptical curiosity.

It had only been a few whispered words, followed by an *Amen.* It was the way her own father would have prayed, but not Brother Joseph. She wondered at that. When it came time to really obey God, it was her father's example, not all the teaching at the missionary college, that felt like what God would have her follow.

What was going through Jeremiah's mind as he sat there at her side, guiding the team as they clattered along the dirt road back to the ranch? Had he expected something more than had happened?

All Mercy had ever known about healing was the flashy showmanship of Brother Joseph and others like him. She had seen him write down his eloquent prayers in preparation for a service. Praying for Jess had been so different she could hardly even think of it in the same light. She had not

even considered her words ahead of time. They had just
come out of her. She almost had the sensation that they
weren't her words at all.

Mercy took a deep breath. The feeling she had had since
before dawn, the urgency of needing to pray for Jess
Forbes, was gone now. She felt relaxed and calm.

She glanced around the countryside. Everything seemed
so clear and fresh and vibrant. Nothing had changed since
their ride into Sweetriver only two hours before.

But something *had* changed.

She couldn't put her finger on it, but everything looked different. Looked different, perhaps, to her inner eyes. A clarity,
a focus seemed to gather about her brain as they rode.

So many of the questions she had had, the doubts, all the
wondering about what she believed, about whether the
things she'd been taught were true—gradually they began to
look less worrisome and foreboding.

Thoughts tumbled one after the other. The confusion of a
week ago began adjusting and aligning into a new order that
made sense. One by one she found herself understanding
things that had been muddled and unclear.

What connection there could possibly be she didn't know,
but somehow the moment she touched Jess Forbes's forehead and cheek, feeling the faintest tingle in her nervous fingers as she did, at that moment it was as though she sensed
the confusion in her spirit beginning to unfog.

And now as they rode silently along, she felt as though
a gauze of haze had been removed from her eyes. It was
as if obeying the sense God gave her was more important
than understanding it. It almost made understanding it
unnecessary.

Words she had heard one of the men in Evansville say

came back to her. He had discovered a book in the college library, he said, that was unlike anything he had ever read in all his life. "It makes life with God so practical and real," she recalled his telling a small group of women. It had been all but meaningless back then. Now it returned to her memory as if it had been yesterday.

How or why she remembered these words from among all that he had told them, she couldn't imagine. How could her brain possibly even recall the specific words so clearly? It had been two years ago!

Yet suddenly the words from the book the fellow had been holding in his hand reverberated in her mind. "Obedience is the opener of eyes," he had read to them. "Upon obedience must our energy be spent; understanding will follow."

That's what she felt—that her eyes were suddenly being opened!

She felt she was at last beginning to understand many things about what faith in God meant.

Why now, why *right now*, as they rode back to the Bar S after she had prayed for Jess Forbes?

Then came back to her the feeling she had had lying awake in bed several hours before—the feeling that she needed to go into town and pray for Jess, the sense that she was supposed to, that she *had* to.

Perhaps it *had* been God prompting her.

Was that how God spoke to people, through their thoughts? Did he urge people to do things by making them feel like they were *supposed* to do something? It was all so new!

She was not accustomed to thinking of God as so close and personal, as being right inside every thought and feeling. Her mother and father spoke of such things. They had taught her and her brother and sister that very thing, that God's Spirit was inside every tiniest breath. She had heard the words. But not until right now, not until this very moment, did she really *understand* what they had meant in a personal way—for her.

Suddenly she knew what her mother and father had tried to convey all those years as they had shared from the depths of their own hearts and experience.

Then came the words again: "Obedience is the opener of eyes. . . . Understanding will follow."

Was she now seeing clearly and understanding so many things suddenly in a dawning new light because she had . . . *obeyed?*

Had she obeyed something she was supposed to do, done something God had wanted her to do? Was this the result?

Her eyes *were* being opened, she could not deny that. Understanding *was* coming to her! Had the simple act of praying for Jess Forbes been an act of *obedience*—obedience to God?

If so, then it meant that God had spoken to her!

If that was true, if God had actually spoken to *her*, Mercy Randolph, then that changed everything!

It meant that he was more real and alive and personal than she had ever dreamed!

31

REVELATION

The sense of focus and clarity did not leave her the rest of

the morning.

As she worked with Mrs. Simmons, Mercy was able to

keep her mind on the tasks before her, but down inside, the

events of the past two or three weeks played themselves

over in her mind—from her first encounter with Jeremiah

and Jess on the way to Sweetriver, to the revival, her over-

167

hearing Brother Joseph at the livery stable, remaining behind, the lonely days in the hotel, trying to hold a church service, and most of all the things Jeremiah had said to her and asked her.

She had been thinking about it all ever since. She had come to see that there was indeed a great deal of truth in the things Jeremiah had challenged her to think about. The only conclusion she had reached in the last week beyond that, however, was that she realized now that she *wanted* to believe.

Over and over, Jeremiah's words from that day in the hotel dining room continued to echo through her memory.

Do you really believe all those spiritual-sounding words you say . . . do you really believe everything you're talking about . . . do you really believe it all . . . I want to know if it means something down deeper in your heart. . . .

Just to recall the words was painful! But she *had* recalled them, many times. She had thought about them, even tried to pray about them.

But now, today, beginning almost immediately after leaving Doc's office, something built to a new climax within her.

Later that afternoon, Mrs. Simmons sent Mercy to the south pasture, away from both stream and river, where her husband and most of the men were rounding up and corralling a half-dozen of the orneriest bulls on the entire Bar S spread. Once they had them inside the pen, they would have to reinforce the corral with an additional rail all the way around the top, a job that would take all the rest of the day.

"Have Mercy ride out and bring us some water and something to eat," Zeke said to his wife as he left. "I don't want to stop till we're done, and if we don't get 'em in and those rails reinforced by nightfall, them bulls will have the whole thing torn down by daybreak."

Mrs. Simmons helped her hitch up the buckboard, and Mercy took off on the two-mile drive over the hill toward the plain to the south. As she went, she was reminded of her talk with Jeremiah beside the creek. He'd asked her the question again. She'd come far enough in her inner search to be able to say that she *wanted* to know the answer and was determined to find it.

Was she at last ready to take that search a step further?

She delivered the rolls, meat pies, and barrel of water, doing her best to keep up her end of the visiting that went on with the men. But a feeling of quietude was upon her, and she was anxious to be on her way once more.

About halfway back, a sudden pang smote Mercy's heart.

It was not a pang of pain, neither of happiness nor sadness nor any other human emotion. It was a stab of awareness, a revelation of a truth she had known for some time but just this moment suddenly *realized* she knew.

She pulled back on the reins and stopped the small buggy. She sat motionless in the seat, staring straight ahead across the fields yet seeing nothing, her entire consciousness possessed with an electric tingle of sudden discovery.

The sensation was one of awakening from a long sleep and, while still lying in bed, gradually becoming aware that she was awake — and had been awake for some time.

For the revelation had silently exploded within her: *Yes — yes, I do believe!*

That it was a quiet explosion took nothing from its import. She turned and looked about. There were the same fields. Behind her the men were still at work. The house still sat a mile ahead of her. There was the horse, fidgeting nervously with his feet and wondering when they would be off again.

Nothing had changed. But everything had changed!

That she hadn't lived the principles of the Christian life as she should, or that Brother Joseph had been a fraud, or that she had allowed herself to be part of a deception, or even that she hadn't understood so much of it and hadn't been able to give Jeremiah a ready answer to his probing questions—none of that kept it from being *true!*

Brother Joseph could be a bold-faced hypocrite—that didn't mean it couldn't still be true!

She could be as shallow and unreal as maybe Jeremiah thought she was—that couldn't prevent it from being true!

She might have uttered all kinds of spiritual-sounding things in her life without deep convictions within her to back them up—but that didn't mean the things she'd said were false, only that her own life was lacking.

At last she saw it all so clearly! The Christian faith of her parents that she had tried to make her own without really thinking it through for herself—*it was true!*

Everything she had thought she believed that had been shaken by Jeremiah's challenging questions, everything she had been taught, the truths the Bible pointed to—it had been true all along! Her childhood training, the example of her mother and father, what she had learned through the years in church and more recently at the college—now it all made sense and fit together.

Why now? Because, Mercy realized, she had made it her *own.* She had faced adversity, she had been challenged, she had been brought up short by her own immaturity. She had struggled through a crisis and decided that she *wanted* to believe more deeply. And suddenly she realized that her desire had been answered.

At last Mercy Randolph believed and knew that she believed!

She flipped the reins and the horse pranced into motion. She found herself singing again.

Now she would learn to live it too.

32

A RIDER

Mercy reached the ranch house at almost the same moment a rider crested the ridge at full gallop. Followed by a trailing cloud of dust, the great hooves thundered down the incline toward the ranch.

"Where's Eagleflight?" called out the rider even before he had slowed his horse. "You seen Eagleflight, lady?" he said, reining in the foamy roan in a great whinnying commotion of hooves and legs and stirrups and dust.

Mercy pointed in the direction from which she had just come and gave the man brief directions to where the ranch crew was working. She was only about halfway through before he was off again, disappearing out of sight to the south in what seemed only a matter of seconds. Mercy walked back into the house.

Ten minutes later she again heard the sound of galloping horses. She ran to the front door, just in time to see the same rider disappearing again over the ridge toward town as fast as he had come. Jeremiah Eagleflight was at his side, lashing his horse on its rump, flying like the wind. In two more seconds they were over the rise and disappeared from sight.

She could hardly concentrate on her work all the rest of the day. But all the men were gone, and neither she nor Mrs. Simmons had any idea what had been the message borne by the rider from town. Try as she would to think the best, Mercy's heart was filled with dark forebodings.

About suppertime, Zeke Simmons rode in from the work site, tied up his horse, and walked to the house.

"What's it all about, Zeke?" his wife asked.

"Oh, it's going fine. We got the bulls in and the rails half done. Figure on the boys being back for supper in about an hour."

"No, not that. The man who rode in so fast asking for Jeremiah?"

"Oh, that. Dangdest thing you ever saw. The man came flying in, shouting out Eagleflight's name, yelling at him that his friend had woke up at the doc's. Man, I never saw a guy mount a horse so fast! Why, Eagleflight's feet hardly touched the stirrups before he was long gone and following the fella back to town. He didn't even stop to ask me if he could go!" laughed Zeke.

"I imagine his friend means more to him than working for you," added his wife.

"Did the man say anything else?" asked Mercy.

"Nope, only that the Forbes kid was asking for his partner."

Mercy closed her eyes and breathed out a sigh of relief.

It was two hours after supper, and dusk had almost completely given way to darkness when Mercy heard a lone rider approaching slowly on horseback.

She was in her room and still dressed. Though all the men were in the bunkhouse and Mr. and Mrs. Simmons had retired to their room, she had kept her clothes on, sitting quietly by the window keeping watch. She knew it was Jeremiah as the dark figure of horse and rider passed into view, stopping at the barn.

She saw him tie up his horse, but then instead of taking the horse inside, Jeremiah turned and walked slowly toward the house.

Mercy's heart began to pound in her chest. She rose and quickly moved away from the window so that he wouldn't see her peeking at him through the curtains.

Two minutes later a knock came to her bedroom door.

It was Mrs. Simmons, dressed in her robe. "Mr. Eagleflight is at the door, Mercy," she said. "He apologizes for the lateness of the hour, but he would like to speak with you."

The news did nothing to still the pounding of Mercy's heart. Her hand unconsciously went to her cheek. "Would it be all right, do you think?" she asked.

"I think so, Mercy," replied Jody with a motherly smile.

"Mr. Eagleflight is a gentleman. I am certain he only wants to tell you whatever he has learned about his friend."

"Thank you," said Mercy, then followed her from the room.

33

A LATE
CONVERSATION

Mercy found Jeremiah waiting on the porch. She went out to meet him.

"Jess came to this afternoon," he said.

"I heard," replied Mercy. "Jeremiah, I'm so happy for you."

Jeremiah nodded his thanks, but no words came from his mouth as he stared down at the floor awkwardly. He seemed to be struggling to say something, but he couldn't find the words.

"Do you remember when you said you owed me thanks for what I did for you and the things I asked you?" he finally said, speaking slowly and hesitating a little over the words.

"Yes," replied Mercy. "I remember."

"I reckon now it's my turn."

"Whatever do you mean?"

"It's my turn to thank you—for what you did for Jess."

"I didn't do anything, Jeremiah."

"You prayed for him, and it must have done something, 'cause all of a sudden he's awake and hungry."

Now it was Mercy's turn to fall silent.

The night was black. They could see one another's forms in the dim glow from the lantern inside but no details of features. The moon that had risen over the prairie was but a thin line and gave off no light to the earth, only to itself.

The evening was silent, save for the crickets in the oaks up on the ridge overlooking the house. From the stables and fields an occasional sound of equine or bovine settling for the night could be heard. Then all quieted again.

She had been desperately anxious about Jess ever since watching the two riders disappear toward town.

She was full of relief and joy—for so many reasons! Because of Jess and because of all that had changed for *her*. After her own insight of the day, suddenly Mercy had so much to tell Jeremiah.

He was so much a part of it, she could hardly separate him from it. A month ago she would have thought such a thing impossible—that an unbeliever could have been so important an instrument in God's hand. Yet because of him

she had discovered a whole new region of belief inside herself.

She had been awaiting his return all evening so she could
tell him. But now it all grew pale in light of the wonderful
news about his partner.

Oh, how she longed for an hour or two—a whole day . . .
a week!—to pour out all her thoughts and feelings to Jeremiah—whether he was a believer or not!

In spite of all his peculiar views about the Bible and poker
and dice and drinking, she knew he would understand
everything probably better than anyone in the world right
now. He would understand because she knew he had *felt* the
dilemmas of her mind along with her. Suddenly his view-
points didn't matter half so much since she knew he cared
and knew that he would understand.

Now here they were alone, but silence was the only thing
flowing between them! Why couldn't she find her tongue!

Oh, this is so awful, thought Mercy. *I feel just like a little girl
again!*

It was Jeremiah's voice that sounded again in the night as
they both stood awkwardly on the porch. He spoke softly, yet
coming out of such stillness, the sound startled them both.

"I really mean what I said," he said. "I'm more grateful
than you can know that you cared about Jess and took
enough of an interest in him to want to pray for him."

Mercy nodded, though Jeremiah could barely make out
the motion of her head in the darkness.

She wanted to tell him about being woken up with the
feeling that God was telling her to do it. She wanted Jeremiah to know that God cared about Jess. She wanted to tell
him that she finally knew that God was real and that if Jess
was going to live, it was *God* who had healed him.

178

She wanted to tell him that it didn't matter whether Brother Joseph or Mercy Randolph—or Jeremiah Eagleflight for that matter—understood God's ways or lived by his principles. God was still God in spite of them, and he could give life to whomever he wanted—Jess Forbes or either of the two of them standing there on the porch of the Simmons ranch house, or even the man who had shot Jess, if that was what God wanted to do.

Why couldn't she overcome her reservations and just tell him? There was so much to say.

Mercy could feel her lungs moving in shorter and shorter breaths. Her heart began to quicken. She could feel herself flooded with—what it was she didn't know—strange new sensations rising up from inside, making her throat tight, a feeling of—

It wasn't only Jess, it wasn't only the things she'd suddenly realized about God and what she believed, it wasn't even all they had talked about in town and the questions he had raised.

The feelings struggling to find expression within her had more to do with—

Her thoughts were suddenly interrupted.

"Mercy," said Jeremiah.

She felt herself jump in her boots right where she stood! His voice had so startled her and sounded so loud in the night.

"There's—there's something I've been wanting to say," he said.

Mercy was afraid to look at him.

She snuck a glance out of the corner of her eye. Jeremiah was looking down at the porch, hat held between his hands as he fidgeted with its brim between his fingers, shuffling his feet nervously back and forth.

She turned her eyes away again.

"I . . . I don't exactly know how to say—that is, ever since that day when I found you preaching on the sidewalk—and then, well, after we talked and I said all those things to you . . ."

He took a deep breath and sighed. He was laboring over the words and speaking slowly and haltingly.

Mercy stood silently, her heart pounding in her ears.

"Well, ever since then," he went on, summoning another breath and doing his best to continue, "I've been thinking, and you . . . well, I've—"

He stopped again. "Shoot, Mercy, I don't know how to say it!" he added all at once.

Unconsciously, Mercy looked up.

Jeremiah's face had turned toward her. Though it was dark, she knew his eyes were looking straight into hers. She tried to hold his gaze in the darkness, feeling the warmth rising up the back of her neck. Her heart was pounding so loud she was afraid it would wake up the whole ranch.

All the things she had wanted to say to him vanished. She stood transfixed by eyes that she could not see gazing into hers out of the night.

"Aw, doggone," he muttered in frustration, looking away again. "I can't do it!"

Quickly he turned. "Good night, Mercy," he said, then strode quickly off the porch and through the darkness toward the bunkhouse.

Mercy stood unmoving, watching him go.

Then slowly she drew in a deep sigh to settle her still-beating heart and turned and walked back into the house to her room.

34

THE
NEXT MORNING

*An hour later Mercy still lay in her bed, wide awake
in the darkness.*

This day had begun before dawn, and now it was

approaching midnight. However, she felt not even the begin-

nings of sleepiness. Rather than fatigue, all over she tingled

with feelings and thoughts she could not have described.

What a day it had been!

Waking up before dawn feeling an urgency upon her. Then praying for Jess. The revelation of knowing she believed—in a practical way—in God and his Son, Jesus, and the reality of their work in her life. Jess waking up at Doc Haggerty's. And finally, the moments alone with Jeremiah on the porch.

As she lay silently reliving the day, her thoughts could not keep from gathering most heavily on the recent portion of it. The words Jeremiah had spoken, as broken and incomplete as they were, repeated themselves over and over in her brain.

Oh, Jeremiah, Jeremiah, she thought to herself. *What was it you were going to say? Why didn't you try a little harder to get it out?*

She turned over, burying her head in her pillow, with a warm dreamy smile on her face, the smile of Jeremiah Eagleflight's mouth lodged in her brain as she had seen him laughing with the men at lunch that day. She pulled the single blanket up around her shoulders. . . .

Jeremiah . . . Jeremiah Eagleflight . . .

When next Mercy Randolph became aware of herself, it was with the touch of Mrs. Simmons's hand on her shoulder and the ranch lady's gentle voice sounding in her ear.

"Mercy, Mercy dear," the voice said. "Mercy, it's morning. . . . It's time to be up."

Slowly Mercy's eyes opened. Sunlight streamed through the window.

"Oh my! I overslept. I'm sorry!" she exclaimed, throwing off the coverlet and scrambling out of bed. "What time is it?"

"Seven-fifteen. I've taken care of the ham and biscuits, but the men will be coming in soon. We still must fetch the eggs and fry them up."

"Oh, Mrs. Simmons — I'm sorry."

"Don't worry, dear, you were up late last night."

Mercy blushed.

"I know how it can be with a young man sometimes. I was young once too, you know."

"I . . . uh . . ." stammered Mercy.

"Don't worry, Mercy. My Zeke was nearly as handsome as young Mr. Eagleflight!" Mrs. Simmons smiled knowingly, leaving an astonished and embarrassed Mercy alone to dress.

Meanwhile in the bunkhouse, the hired hands of the Bar S buttoned up their shirts and pulled on their boots, getting ready to head across to breakfast. As they walked outside, one of the men sidled up to the foreman.

"Hey, Dirk, what do you say you fix me up with that pretty little filly working in the house?"

"Mrs. Simmons's helper?"

"That's her. The boss and his wife trust you, and you could put in a word for me."

"I don't know, Yancy. That ain't the kind of thing they pay me for."

"She's a fine-looking one! I'd like to —"

"She don't hardly seem your type, Yancy," put in another of the hands as he ambled toward the door.

"Why do you say that?"

"She used to be a preacher lady. I thought you went for those gals at the Silver Ox."

"I ain't none too particular," said Yancy with an unhealthy smile. "Besides, she's such a gorgeous little thing, I don't believe you."

"The man's right," said Heyes. "She came to town with that evangelist."

183

"It don't look to me like she's a preacher lady now," said Yancy, winking with a grin of significance at the other two.

Jeremiah walked up and fell into stride with them as they left the bunkhouse and made their way past the barn to their left. He heard the end of the conversation.

"Look, Yancy," he said, "you keep your thoughts about Mercy Randolph to yourself. That goes for all the rest of you too."

"What's it to you, Eagleflight?" Yancy barked back.

"It's my own business, that's what it is. I'm just telling you, keep away from her, and I don't want to hear you talking about her again, you hear?"

"If I do?" said Yancy menacingly.

"Then you'll have to deal with me."

"That'll suit me just fine," growled Yancy, who was known around the Bar S for his hot temper. "Look, Eagleflight, when I see a woman I want, I take her. If I got me a mind to take a fancy to the young kid the boss's wife has working for her, then I figure that's *my* business."

"Well, I'm making anything to do with her my business," replied Eagleflight, looking Yancy seriously in the face.

"Come on, come on, you guys," said Heyes. "You two get into a scrap and Zeke'll chew *me* out. You're all my responsibility, and you know how he wants it around here—peace and goodwill and all that. So I don't want no more of that kind of talk."

"Fine by me, Dirk," said Jeremiah. "But nobody will lay a finger on her or speak an uncivil word about her—and even you and Zeke can't do anything that'll keep me from backing up my words."

"Fine, fine, Eagleflight. None of us knew the trail led in

that direction. We'll be more careful now that we know you got *your* eye on her, won't we, Yancy?"

Yancy did not reply.

The next moment they were joined by two more of the men and continued on into the house for breakfast.

35

AN UNSETTLING
TALK WITH THE
SIMMONSES

That same morning Zeke rode into town. He had

several people to see and was gone about three hours.

He returned about thirty minutes before lunch, tied up

his horse, and walked into the house. Jody and Mercy were

in the kitchen preparing lunch. He walked in, grabbed a

high-back chair, turned it around, then sat down on it back-

wards, arms crossed over its back.

"Cup of coffee, Zeke?" asked Jody.

"Got some?"

"It's almost ready—we just put on the pot for lunch."

"What's cooking? Sure smells good."

"A ham hock with beans and molasses," answered Mercy cheerfully.

"Corn bread?"

"Just put it in the oven."

"My, but the Lord is smiling on me today!" the rancher exclaimed. The words struck Mercy's ears oddly. She had never heard Zeke say anything about God, though by now she well knew Jody to be a woman of deep, though soft-spoken faith.

"Anything new in town, Zeke?" Jody asked her husband.

"Now that you mention it, I reckon there is," he replied. "And it's got to do with your new helper here."

Mercy looked up in surprise.

"What do you mean?" asked Jody.

"With her and Eagleflight's friend, I should say. I was by Doc's."

"What did he have to say?"

"Why, the kid's up walking around Haggerty's place. Doc can't believe it. He's telling everybody. Why the whole town's talking about it."

"Talking about what—Mr. Forbes recovering?" asked Mercy.

"No, about you—about how you came in and prayed for him and then his getting better right afterward. Doc says it wasn't more than a couple hours."

"I don't understand what you mean, Mr. Simmons," Mercy fumbled. "Why are they talking about me?"

"'Cause folks have been wondering about you, wondering

who you are, why you're here. Pretty young lady like you comes to town, people take notice. Your coming out here to work for us didn't stop folks' curiosity."

Mercy could feel the embarrassment rising within her.

"There've been some people wondering why you left Brother Joseph," added Jody. "A few of the women have asked me about you, but I tell them it's none of my affair. If they want to know something, they ought to come straight to you, and that's exactly what I say."

"Don't you see, young lady?" said Zeke. "There couldn't help but be questions."

"Questions?"

"Folks are curious about you. After what happened with the Forbes kid, why, they're more curious than ever."

Mercy's face showed a bewildered concern.

"Believe me, dear," said Jody compassionately, "It's nothing to worry about. I have no doubt it is something God will put to great use in time."

"My wife's right, Mercy," added Zeke in a tone of fatherly wisdom she had never heard from him before. "The Almighty has ways of doing things that sometimes catch us by surprise. Something tells me your coming to Sweetriver is going to be one of those turning points that you always look back to and say everything changed after that."

Again Mercy was surprised by the ease with which the rancher spoke as if God was his personal friend.

"Certainly for me," she said thoughtfully.

"That I'm sure of," rejoined Zeke, "but I meant for everybody else—for us, surely for that Eagleflight kid—"

Mercy blushed and looked away at the mention of Jeremiah's name.

"—It can't be a secret even to you that he's some taken with you, now can it?" added the rancher.

Mercy didn't answer.

"What I was trying to say, though," added Zeke, "was that your coming changes things for more folks than just you. Wouldn't surprise me if the whole town of Sweetriver changes from it in time."

"How could that be?" asked Mercy.

"How God does things, only he knows," replied Jody. "I agree with my husband. I have the feeling that many things are going to be different for a lot of people. I can't say why, I just have the sense that your leaving Brother Joseph and remaining here, and our crossing paths with you—well, that we've only seen the start of what the Father intends to do."

"The Forbes kid, why that's only the beginning," added Zeke. "Of what, I can't say. But God's up to something, that I'm sure of."

His wife nodded. "That's exactly my feeling too."

"I reckon the doc said it best," added Zeke. "He told me just this morning, 'I didn't know quite what I thought of that Mertree fellow. Little too smooth a customer to please my taste in spiritual things. But you give me a simple, plain-speaking lady like that Sister Mercy, who prays for somebody who's fixing to die, and then he starts to get well and the next day is eating and getting up out of bed, now that's the kind of religion that'll make folks stand up and take notice!'"

Mercy flinched inwardly at the words. If there was one thing she didn't want right now, it was people talking about her spirituality! She was just trying to get it figured out for herself.

"I don't know what to even think about that," she said. "I don't know if it makes me feel altogether comfortable."

"Well, I reckon the doc's right, young lady," said Zeke with a smile as he rose from the table, "so you might ought to get used to it."

36

COFFEE IN
THE BUNKHOUSE

Two days passed.

Mercy saw nothing of Jeremiah except at mealtimes. She
tried not to look at him but could not help it. Most of the
time she found his eyes already upon her, and she had to
glance quickly away.

If the others at the table chanced to see them looking at

191

one another, everyone would know the state of her emotions in an instant.

Her heart was merry and her step light. She went about her work with a smile, unconsciously breaking into song without warning. Mrs. Simmons smiled inside to observe the new young friend who was already like a daughter to her. She well recognized the unmistakable signs, but said nothing. She did not want Mercy to know that her heart was easier to read than a book.

The following morning, Mercy woke once again with a sense of something she was supposed to do. This time, however, she hadn't an idea what it was, only that there was something she must attend to.

A late-summer thunderstorm blew in quickly that afternoon from the west. The men came riding in from the range moments before the downpour, galloping their mounted horses through the high, open double doors of the barn just in time to dismount and hear the crackle of lightning and boom of thunder behind them. The sky was dark as dusk, though it was still half an afternoon till suppertime.

"Take the rest of the afternoon off," Zeke told his men. "You been working hard, and this one's not going to let up before tonight."

Within an hour of the storm's appearance on the horizon, the entire Pawnee Valley lay drenched. Zeke feared a flash flood could rise in some of the washes to the west.

He entered the house while the men unsaddled their horses and retired to the bunkhouse. "Make up some coffee, Jody," he said. "The men are in for the rest of the day."

"What are they going to do?"

"Sleep, play poker—I gave 'em the rest of the day off. Too wet to get anything done."

Mercy listened, thinking immediately of Jeremiah, wondering what *he* would do with the time. All at once she knew what had been puzzling her all day.

When the coffee had been made, she asked Jody if she might take it to the bunkhouse.

"Certainly, dear."

"After that, might you be able to spare me for an hour?"

"Of course."

"I'd like to go out to the barn for a while."

"Then bundle up—it's pouring outside."

"I don't mind," replied Mercy. "I've always liked being out when it's raining, as long as there's a dry place to curl up."

Ten minutes later Mercy appeared at the bunkhouse door—well-bundled against the rain, thanks to Jody—and carrying a large pot of steaming coffee.

"Look what the lady brought us!" exclaimed the foreman, jumping from the table where a game of five-card draw was just getting under way. "Here, let me give you a hand with that," said Heyes, taking the coffee from her.

"Thank you," said Mercy. "It was heavier than I realized."

"The boys will all appreciate it," rejoined Heyes. "Right, boys?"

A round of further thanks rang around the cabin.

Mercy scanned the room for Jeremiah. Once relieved of the burden of the coffee, she walked timidly in his direction, hoping Heyes's emptying the coffee into the men's waiting tins would be distraction enough to keep their brief conversation from being noticed.

"Might I talk to you this afternoon," she said softly, "if you have the time?"

"I'm not doing a thing," replied Jeremiah.

"You're not going to join the game?"

"Me . . . play poker—don't you know it's a sinful game?" His eyes contained the sparkle of fun, but Mercy didn't see it.

"Please, Jeremiah, don't tease me. I would like to talk to you."

"Of course," he said softly, seeing that he had hurt her. "I didn't mean anything—uh, now?" he added. "You want me to come to the house?"

"I'll be in the barn," Mercy said, glancing around to make sure none of the other men were listening. Then she opened the bunkhouse door, pulled the large coat she had borrowed tightly around her shoulders, and dashed out into the rain.

Yancy lay on his bunk, observing the proceedings out of the corner of his eye. He had heard nothing, but he had carefully watched the whole exchange.

37 .

CONFESSION
AND CHALLENGE

Dark as it was under the cloud outside, when Jeremiah

entered the barn it was darker still. It took a minute or two

before his eyes accustomed themselves to the dim light.

"Mercy—Mercy, you in there?" he said.

"I'm over here, by the hay bales," her voice replied out of

the darkness.

Jeremiah walked toward her. He saw her form seated above him on a stack of hay several bales high.

"What are you doing way up there?" he asked cheerfully.

"I like high places," she replied lightly.

"Well I like to feel the ground under my feet, so I'll just sit on this bale down here. You can address me like you're up in a pulpit again!"

The silence that met his ears told him his attempt at humor had gone into her crooked again.

"I'm sorry," he said. "Sometimes I say things without thinking. Just making a joke. I meant nothing by it—forgive me."

"I'm sorry too," she replied. "I suppose I'm too sensitive about those kinds of things—like the poker."

"I'm sorry about that too. But I have been thinking about what you said. I haven't played since then."

"Why—because of what I said?"

"Not only 'cause you said it but because of what it was you said. If it *is* wrong, then I don't want any part of it."

"But I had no right to say what I did back then. You can't have forgotten what *you* said to *me.*"

"It doesn't matter whether you had a right to say it or not. If it was true, then I've got to pay attention to it, regardless. The truth, remember?"

The silence that followed lasted several minutes.

"That's just what I wanted to talk to you about, Jeremiah," said Mercy at length.

"What?"

"Everything you said to me that day."

He waited for her to continue.

"I've been wanting to tell you this for several days," she went on, "but with the news about Jess and everything else, there just hasn't been time."

196

"Zeke's been working us pretty hard."

"I've been busy in the house too. When I heard you weren't going back out this afternoon, I . . . I suppose it was pretty bold of me to talk to you like that—in front of the other men. I didn't mean to put you in an awkward—"

"Nah," interrupted Jeremiah, "didn't bother me a straw! So, here I am—what have you been trying to tell me?"

"All right," replied Mercy. She took a deep breath. "I've been thinking about everything you said to me, just like you said you have been about what I said," she began. "I remember every word—well, *almost* every word," she added with a light laugh. "I have to tell you, at first it was anything but pleasant. I cried a lot and said more than one angry thing to you in my mind."

"I'm glad you didn't say them to my face!" laughed Jeremiah.

"I wanted to! But finally I realized what a favor you'd done me, like I told you that day you were stringing wire by the creek."

"I remember."

"Do you also remember what I said when you asked me if I'd found anything out?"

"You said you hadn't yet."

"But I said I knew that I *wanted* to believe. Do you remember that?"

"Yeah. It stuck mighty deep inside my brain. I'd never heard someone say that before. I couldn't stop thinking about your words. When you said it, it seemed like *wanting* was just about as good as real believing."

"I don't know if that's true or not. But I do know that wanting to has kept me searching high and low in all the places inside me. I did that until finally I can say that I *have* found the answer to your first question, which was one of the things I knew I needed to tell you, one of the things I *wanted* to tell you, because you're the one who asked me the question."

She stopped briefly, then added, "So now I'm finally ready to give you an answer."

She paused again. Jeremiah looked up to where she sat on the bale, her booted feet dangling over the edge.

"I'm ready," he said.

"All right, Jeremiah Eagleflight, here's your answer," she said. "I know I'm a little late with it, but the wait's been worth it because I finally really *know* the answer. You asked me if I really believed what I was saying about God and spiritual things—well, now I can say, *Yes, I do believe it—I believe it with all my heart!*

"Back when you first asked me—I can't say I believed it *then*. I mean, I think I did believe in a shallow kind of way, maybe as much as I could. I don't think there was ever a time I *didn't* believe, but I just hadn't come all the way into real and full *believing*. I hope you understand what I'm trying to say. Back then, even though it was such a short time ago, when I look at it I feel like I was walking about in a fog, not seeing life as it really was."

As he sat there, Jeremiah realized he was listening to a different Mercy Randolph than he had first befriended back in Sweetriver.

She was a new person, it was true, but perhaps not as different as Jeremiah Eagleflight imagined. The seeds of life had lain dormant within her for years, planted and nurtured by godly parents, sending roots deep into the hearty soil of character. Yet all the while a portion of her being had remained asleep.

Struggling to find an identity of her own, Mercy had forced herself to live in what she deemed an acceptably "religious" manner, while the reality of such a life remained disconnected from her. The very unreality of it led further into the misconception that she must demonstrate external and vocal manifestations of spirituality. Thus began the desire to preach and save souls and talk *about* the very things of faith she herself did not yet possess.

As she began to recognize the emptiness of those attempts, however, and was faced with what she realized were the deficiencies in her own belief, the inner eyes of her self-awareness began to open and her spirit came awake.

There comes a moment when embryonic potential life—whether in root, in seed, in tiny acorn, or in solitary human heart—must decide to *live*. Thus does the seed or acorn or heart agree in its innermost being to fulfill its destiny in the Father's creation.

Will it *wake,* or will it wither and eventually die?

Will it fall in with the Father's final idea and become the flower only he is able to behold in the seed, the giant oak he visualizes in the acorn, or the completed person that is in the divine mind of the Creator at the moment of conception?

In Mercy Randolph, when the decision to enter into harmony with the divine plan awakened within her, sprouts of *personal* belief were at last free to shoot upward from out of the long-growing invisible root system of her upbringing.

Seemingly overnight, principles and truths built into her consciousness by her mother and father quickly sprouted into regions of light and air, sunshine and rain, sending forth new leaves and branches, flowering and blossoming as if she had walked with God for years. Though she had not realized it, he had, in truth, been at her side all the time.

"You were right about me!" Mercy went on. "I am so glad you weren't afraid to say what you did. You forced me to look into places I'd never looked before and might not have looked into if it hadn't been for you.

"I can never repay you, Jeremiah. I am so grateful because, whether you know it or not, I feel like I owe my newfound enthusiasm about God to you. I think God used you as his way of opening my eyes and waking me up!"

Jeremiah was quiet. The words were too much to take in. *God* . . . had used *him!* The very idea was more than he could grasp.

He sat on the thick-bound hay, staring at the floor of the barn, fiddling with the edge of the bale.

Mercy looked down at him, wondering what he was thinking. What she had to say next would be harder yet, but she could not stop now. She *had* to say it.

"Did you hear when I said a minute ago that I had two things to say to you?" she asked after a moment.

"Oh . . . yeah," Jeremiah mumbled, glancing up from being deep in thought.

"The second one's more difficult."

"Don't worry," said Jeremiah, attentive again, "I won't make a joke about anything."

Mercy drew in a breath and summoned up her courage.

"You weren't afraid to ask me a hard question," she said, "so now, Jeremiah Eagleflight, I'm going to ask *you* one. You have to know that it's only because I care about you that I would ask it, just like I now see that that is why you said what you did to me."

"Fair enough," he replied.

"All right, but first let me ask you something else. The very first time we talked, you told me you were a man who tries to do right. You said you wouldn't do anything you knew to be wrong. Is that right?"

"Yep. I think that's about what I said."

"Then later, when I asked if you were a believer, you wouldn't give me an answer."

"You assumed I wasn't."

"Which you corrected me for. But you never said you *were*."

"I suppose you got me there, Mercy," said Jeremiah with a smile.

This girl has learned to use her head! he thought. She hadn't had much to say the first couple times they'd talked, but now her brain was as sharp as the barbed wire he'd been stringing up all around the Bar S!

"Right after that, you told me you loved the truth," Mercy went on. "You said you didn't know all of what was true about God. I was moved by your honesty, Jeremiah. That's one of the reasons I listened to you. But it's what you said next that's stuck in my mind. You said, 'I believe in the truth, and I believe in living by what you know is true.'"

"You have quite a memory, Mercy!"

"I've heard that conversation we had over and over in my mind probably fifty times since!"

"I can see that."

"Were those your words?"

"Near as I recall."

"Is that what you believe?"

"I'd still say the same thing, that I believe in the truth, and I try to do right and believe in living by what you know to be true, and that I wouldn't do something I knew was wrong—yeah, I still would say all that."

"OK then, my question is this: If you believe in truth and

doing right, then *why* aren't you a Christian, Jeremiah? Maybe you are and just didn't want to say so. If that is the case, then *why* didn't you want to tell me?"

Mercy paused, then went on. "When you asked me what you did, you told me how I'd seemed to you—like I was repeating things out of a book and like there wasn't life inside me to go along with what I professed to believe. You were right. Now I want to tell you what I've observed about you. I hope you won't mind."

"Nope," said Jeremiah. His voice was thoughtful and low.

"Well, first of all, Jeremiah," Mercy went on, "it seems to me you are a man who knows himself pretty well. You are honest and forthright. You believe in living with integrity. You want to do right and avoid wrong. You say you love the truth.

"If that's so, unless there's something you haven't told me, then why haven't you set yourself to search for *truth* and to know what's *right* in the most important part of life there is? Why haven't you searched to find out if what Christians say about God is true? Why haven't you set yourself to live by what the Bible says is right and avoid what the Bible says is wrong, instead of just what *you* happen to think is right and wrong? For a man who loves the truth, it doesn't seem consistent for him not to want to find what the greatest truth of life is."

She stopped, suddenly realizing how much she'd said and hoping he would not be angry.

"I didn't mean to say all that!" she said, half embarrassed. "I hope you don't take offense, Jeremiah."

"Of course not," he replied. His voice was even softer than before, and he was still gazing down at the floor. "Those are all perfectly legitimate questions. And you're

202

right, Mercy—I don't claim to be a Christian. I wasn't holding anything back from you."

Another silence followed.

"Do you remember that church service in the hotel, if you
can even call it that?" she asked at length.

"I doubt either of us will ever forget it," he replied.

"For a long time, the very thought of that day positively
mortified me," Mercy went on. "I tried everything I could to
forget it! But then I began to remember the things I said
and the passage I read from the Bible, and it dawned on me
that perhaps it was just the perfect message for all those
attending the service."

"There *wasn't* anybody attending."

"Oh, but there was, Jeremiah. There were two people
there, two people who needed exactly those words from Scripture—you and me! There was never supposed to be anyone
else there but the two of us! As disappointed as I was to see
that hotel lobby empty, you were the only one besides me that
was *supposed* to be there! Do you remember what I read?"

"Probably not. I was feeling too sorry for you standing
there preaching to no one but me."

"I thought I was preaching to you, but I was preaching to
myself too. The verses I quoted were from Jeremiah the
prophet—you remember that, don't you?"

"Sure."

"Once I realized I was reading from Jeremiah to *you*, I
was embarrassed. But I couldn't stop because my brain was
so numb."

Jeremiah smiled to himself but said nothing.

"Part of the words," Mercy went on, "—and I've reread
them many times since—were, 'Run through the streets, and
see if you can find any man that seeks the truth.'

"That's why I've thought about them so much, Jeremiah. *You're* that kind of a man!" said Mercy with conviction. *"You* are a man that seeks the truth!

"But the second part of it, which was God speaking, said, 'Seek me, and you shall find me, when you search for me with all your heart.' Don't you see—that was the part of the Scripture about *me*. I had not done that, searched for God with all my heart. Though you hadn't either—neither of us ever had!

"I had said all kinds of things about spiritual matters and had even thought I was worthy to be called a minister of the gospel, but I had never sought God with all my heart. And you, Jeremiah, just like your namesake from the Old Testament, you are a man of truth, but you hadn't ever sought the Lord with all your heart either, even though that's the very first thing a man or woman of the truth ought to spend his or her energies doing.

"Neither of us really was living or loving the truth. You didn't *love* the truth as much as you thought you did. And I didn't *live* by the truth as much as I thought I did. Neither of us had searched for the Lord with all our hearts."

There was another long pause. The rain still beat on the roof of the huge barn, though neither of them had been aware of its sound since they had sat down. For the first time, the sound now found its way into Mercy's ears.

A feeling of contented calm and safety entered her breast. She gave the Father above thanks for sending the storm so that she might give confession to her newfound faith before men, and especially before this one particular man about whom she had grown to care so deeply.

"I believe, Jeremiah," she said, and now her voice reflected the calm that had come to reside in her spirit, "that in ways and for reasons perhaps we cannot completely see, that God planned to bring us together so that we each might be used in the other's life, to push us into that quest for truth and that search for faith.

"Why did your words penetrate so deeply, wounding me and yet exposing places that had been covered over with religious fog all my life? I don't know why it happened to be you, right here, right now. But *you* were the one God selected, and I am so thankful you were.

"Perhaps in the same way, I am now the one to ask questions that probe into places inside you and to challenge *you* to look at yourself more honestly, as you did me. I truly believe, Jeremiah, that God has been stirring about inside both our hearts. I don't know all the reasons. But I do know I am a different person than I was a month ago, thanks to your questions and God's helping me see things in whole new ways.

"I hope and pray that a month from now you will be able to look back on everything I have said today with as much gratefulness as I look back with on the two talks we had in Sweetriver."

Mercy stopped. She knew she had said all she was supposed to say. More words, on either side, were not called for just now.

A few moments more she sat, then quietly slipped down off her perch of hay, walked to the door, peered out into the still-falling rain, and ran across to the house, leaving Jeremiah where he sat, alone with his thoughts in the empty barn, rain that he still did not hear thundering down on the roof above him.

38

JEREMIAH'S CRUCIBLE

That same evening, Jeremiah's countenance was subdued

and quiet at supper. He said little and not once looked in

Mercy's direction.

Later that night he lay quiet and awake in his bunk long

after the snores of the other men echoed through the bunk-

house. But he heard none of them. His mind was on

other things.

The following morning, to his great relief, Zeke sent him into town for some things. He was glad for the chance to be alone and to see Jess again. His partner was upbeat and cheerful and talking about leaving the doc's for the hotel in a day or two.

Jeremiah was happy for him, he said, and delighted with the news. Except for the sling around his shoulder and arm and a remaining gauntness in his cheeks, Jess was nearly his old self again.

As he watched Jeremiah leave, however, Jess could not have said the same thing about his friend. Something was definitely wrong with Jeremiah. He had seen it the minute he'd set eyes on him. Sweetriver and that ranch where he was working didn't agree with him at all, thought Jess. As soon as he was well enough, he would get Jeremiah out of this place.

Riding back to the Bar S, Jeremiah continued to ponder everything Mercy had said. She had been right in the very first observation she had made. He *was* a man who knew himself pretty well.

A lesser man, a man who didn't know himself, a man who hadn't tried to live by what he considered right — such a man could easily dismiss Mercy's challenging words.

Bouncing slowly along, in no hurry to get back to the ranch, Jeremiah could not help smiling at the irony of it.

Most men would disregard everything she'd said. Ninety-five out of a hundred men he had ever met never thought about such things. Most men would laugh at all that religious stuff, he thought, especially the tough kind of men you found out west. But Jeremiah Eagleflight was not like most men.

Jeremiah laughed to himself. What was he saying?

Ninety-five! He couldn't think of a *single* man he had *ever* met who thought about things like he did!

That was the one real difference between him and Jess, the one area of life he couldn't share with his partner.

Who cared about truth, about doing what was right, about being consistent? Men who were tough didn't care about such things! They talked about being just and true to your word and maintaining a code of honor. But Jeremiah knew such talk was only a way of justifying looking out for oneself and doing so with high-sounding words to make it seem noble. Maybe it was his old grandfather's influence coming through causing *him* to think about those things.

Every man he'd ever met, deep down, was only out for himself. Nobody else.

A few men he met here and there *talked* about truth and right, but he'd never seen anybody really doing much about them when the chips were down.

The kind of men he'd known would either laugh at someone like Mercy or else argue with her and insist she was wrong. Or they would defend themselves to prove that what she'd said had nothing to do with them.

That's how men usually were—rough, unbending, unfeeling, unthinking, and unwilling to look at weakness within themselves.

Men were afraid to look down inside themselves, where feelings and thoughts were personal and sometimes fearsome. Instead they shielded themselves from a vulnerability to such things by putting on a thick skin of self-protection called masculine pride and then pretending it was the noble, the honorable, the "manly" way to conduct oneself.

But sometime back around when he was fifteen, he had determined that he was going to be different. Even if he was

the *only* man he ever met to do so, he was going to be one of
the rare men who didn't cover himself over with that tough
exterior called manliness, who set himself to live by right.

He *would* think. He *would* look into those regions that most
men avoided. He would *not* be afraid to examine his
thoughts and feelings.

He would do whatever it took to live by right and truth!
He would walk a different road even if he met no one else
while traveling it.

He had been a young man when he had made that decision. It had served him well . . . until yesterday.

Now suddenly he found himself face-to-face with the
unpleasant implications of his own resolve. He'd promised
himself that he would remain intellectually honest, willing to
look at anything and to live by right and truth. He'd always
thought it had to do with how he conducted himself toward
other people. Now all of a sudden it had to do with *him*.

How honest was he prepared to be now?

Did he love truth enough to look for it inside *himself*, not
just out in the world?

Did he want to live by right enough to search for it
instead of just taking what seemed right as it came along?

Now that he thought about it, all his talk about right and
truth didn't have any more depth than Mercy's spiritual
words of several weeks ago. She was absolutely right. He
hadn't *searched* for right and truth.

Mercy's words rang over and over in his ears: *For a man
who loves the truth, it doesn't seem consistent for him not to want to
find what the greatest truth of life is.*

Consistency. He'd never thought about whether he was
consistent. It had never mattered before. Now it mattered
more than anything.

Then came back into his mind Mercy's comment when they were talking by the creek. *I am for the first time in my life actually thinking for myself. . . . There is one thing I am sure of. I know that I now want to believe. . . . So I'm determined to search and seek and ask and pray until I do find out for myself.*

Was *he* prepared to follow Mercy's courageous footsteps?

Following into these regions of belief and faith required more backbone and fortitude than facing a charging bull or a drunk, crazed gunslinger. Those you could defeat with might and cunning and skill and brute strength.

To square off against your own innermost self, however, required something more, something no force of manhood could conquer. To follow such a lesser-trod path to its appointed end required a deeper kind of manhood, a more profound level of courage.

Was he prepared to go *that* far for the sake of *truth?*

Could he, like Mercy, say that he knew that he *wanted* to believe?

Did he really *want* to know the truth—all of it? No matter what it might mean, no matter what changes it might bring to his life or his future, no matter what truth might require of him?

As these and a hundred questions like them tumbled through Jeremiah Eagleflight's brain, he realized that he had come face-to-face with the greatest challenge a man could encounter. Somehow, though he could not trace the exact pathways his mind had journeyed to reach this conclusion, by the time he crested the ridge and began the final descent to the Simmons ranch, Jeremiah knew that he had come face-to-face with God himself, his Maker, the Creator of the universe.

Like Mercy before the revelation she had shared yesterday afternoon, he could not say that he *did* believe. The
answer to that question would take some time for him to
resolve.

But at last he knew without a doubt where the quest for
truth led and what the stakes were in what he realized was
no game of chance.

The road called truth led straight to the presence of God,
the Father of all men.

He knew in whose face he was now looking. What he was
prepared to do about it—of that he was not yet certain. Jeremiah had never been one to play games with important matters.

He knew what was at stake. It was not *a part* of life in
exchange for *some other*. It was not a matter of adopting the
Christian system of belief. The reality of the demand upon
whoever would live by the truth was total.

It was not even all or nothing.

It was simply *All.*

A TALK
WITH MERCY

How Jeremiah got through his chores and work for the

next several days was a mystery even he could not have

explained. The days' events blurred into a continuous haze

in which he could hardly distinguish one thing from another.

Inside, however, in the region of his person unseen by

men, his brain could not have been functioning with greater

clarity. Not only each day, but every *hour* of each day was filled with avenues of exploration and new places within himself he had never before opened to the gaze of his probing intellect.

He knew a choice lay before him.

There had been no question about that since the moment riding over the ridge when he had *known* himself to be in the presence of God.

Many men might have been able to ignore such an experience, allowing it to fade into memory without doing anything about it, only to gradually stop thinking about it at all.

But not Jeremiah Eagleflight.

He knew a decision was imperative. This was no Presence that could be ignored. God demanded a response and would not be put off.

By the third day Jeremiah was ready to make it.

It happened to be Sunday. A couple of the men were in the bunkhouse after breakfast. A few had gone into town.

Jeremiah walked slowly to the house. A weight of necessity lay upon his shoulders. Truth had borne itself down upon him. His own words to Mercy, his own resolve at fifteen—both had now come full circle and were performing their piercing surgery upon his soul.

It was not, therefore, with a light step of joy that he made his way up the porch and at last knocked on the door.

Mrs. Simmons answered.

"Is Mercy here?" Jeremiah asked.

"Yes, she is. Would you like to see her?"

"If you don't mind, ma'am."

A minute or two later Mercy appeared. She came outside and joined Jeremiah on the porch. He could not help noticing her bright yellow blouse and the pretty blue ribbon tied in her hair.

"I've been thinking about all you said in the barn," he said bluntly. "You were right. I reckon I could tell you what I thought about everything, but that's not important right now."

"I'd like to hear about it," said Mercy.

"Maybe sometime you can."

"I hope so."

"All I want now is to do what I got to do about it. I haven't had the schooling and training you had in spiritual things, Mercy. I know maybe for a while it wasn't all just right for you. But once you got on the road you'd been looking for, well, it seems you knew what to do and how to make sense of it all and how to get yourself moving. But I don't. I don't know what to do now."

"About what, Jeremiah?"

"About figuring out how to get started."

"Started—with what?"

"Believing . . . faith . . . what the Bible says—everything you told me I ought to be thinking about if I wanted to be the kind of man that lives by the truth. You can't have forgotten so soon?"

"No, I didn't forget. I just didn't know what you meant."

"So how do I get started? I figure I'm at just about the same place you were that day you brought me the bread out by the creek. You said you wanted to believe and that you were going to search until you did. That sounded like a pretty levelheaded way of going about it to me."

"You . . . *want* to believe, Jeremiah?"

"Yeah, I reckon I do."

"That's wonderful!"

"Maybe so, though I'm still not sure all of what I'm getting myself in for. But if I'm going to live by the truth and do what's right, then, like you said, I'd better start by doing

what the Bible says. Trouble is, I don't know what that is—
or at least, not what it says for *me* to do."

Mercy was quiet a long while, thinking. "Why don't you
go inside and ask Zeke?" she said at length.

"Zeke!" repeated Jeremiah. "Why would I ask him?"

"For one thing, he's a man, so he might understand what
you're thinking better than me. For another, I'm just starting to discover what faith means too."

"You're way ahead of me, Mercy," said Jeremiah.

"Not so far ahead, really. I don't even like to hear you say
that, Jeremiah."

"Isn't it true?"

"I don't know. I'm afraid if I told you something to do, it
might be just one of those things I *learned* to say."

Jeremiah was thoughtful a moment. "I see what you
mean."

"You were the one who told me I shouldn't just give back
the rote answers I'd learned. You were right."

"It's different now, though. I want to know some things I
don't, and I figure you do."

"I *could* probably answer some of your questions, but I'd
still rather you found the truth you're looking for on your
own. That's why I suggested Mr. Simmons."

"I still don't get it about Zeke."

"I think he just might surprise you, Jeremiah. He's way
ahead of us both in his understanding of God."

"I've never heard him say a word about God or religion or
anything!"

"You haven't forgotten Brother Joseph and *Sister* Mercy
so soon, have you?" asked Mercy. "I would think the last
thing you'd want would be someone who's always talking
about the things of faith."

"I reckon you're right."

"I've been watching Zeke," Mercy went on. "He's an extraordinary man. He doesn't let the spiritual side of himself show in words but in how he lives his life."

"He *is* different than any man I ever worked for. I don't suppose I ever stopped to ask myself why that might be."

"Then go talk to him. Tell him everything that's on your mind."

"All right, if that's what you think's best."

"I do. There's something about a man hearing it from another man."

"You know where he is?"

"He's in the house. He and Mrs. Simmons always spend Sunday morning reading the Bible together. I know he'll be happy to talk with you."

"Well, I'll be," mumbled Jeremiah in surprise as Mercy opened the door and led him inside.

"Mr. Simmons," she said, entering the living room where the rancher and his wife sat with open Bibles on their laps. "Jeremiah has something he would like to talk with you about."

SIGNING ON

An hour later Jeremiah and Zeke Simmons still sat together in the living room of the ranch house, talking quietly. As soon as she had discovered the nature of Jeremiah's request, Jody excused herself so the two men could be alone.

Most of the time Zeke listened attentively and prayer-fully. This latter activity, however, was carried out within his own inner closet and was unseen by the young, truth-seeking ranch hand.

"So tell me, Jeremiah," said Zeke at length, "do you want to move from *wanting* to believe to actually *believing?*"

"I reckon I do," replied Jeremiah. "But I don't see how a man can force himself to believe something. Seems like you either do or you don't."

"Like you either believe it's going to rain tomorrow or you don't?"

"Yeah, that's it. How can you make yourself believe something you don't?"

"You've hit upon the very reason why there are so few *believing* Christians in the world, Jeremiah. Belief in God is completely different than belief in ideas or belief in what is or isn't true. But most people don't know this difference."

"I don't get your meaning."

"People think that faith means believing certain things are true."

"Ain't that it?"

"The things of God *are* true. But *belief* in God—real Christian believing—is more than thinking them to be true. It's *living* the truth of them! That is something you can begin to do even before your brain is absolutely convinced."

"I'm afraid you lost me, Zeke."

"I asked you if you wanted to believe, and you said yes. But you weren't sure about some things, right?"

Jeremiah nodded.

"I'm saying that doesn't matter. You can live the truths of belief in God whether or not you're totally convinced about them yet. The *wanting* to is almost more important than the believing."

"I've never heard anything like that before."

"Most people get all confused about the ideas of religion. They think that's the main part of being a Christian."

"You mean the ideas?"

"Yep," said Zeke, nodding. "But they're not. You can start to be a Christian the way Jesus talked about in the Bible just by what you do, not by what your brain happens to be thinking."

"That's a new one."

"The question isn't what you may or may not believe in your head. The question is: Do you want to be a follower of Jesus? If you do, then follow him. It's a decision you make, Jeremiah, not just figuring out a lot of things to say you believe in."

"You mean it's *doing* something, not *believing* something?"

"Don't get me wrong. I'm not saying belief doesn't matter at all. But making that decision and then following him— that's what real *belief* is."

A long silence followed. Jeremiah was deep in thought, and Zeke allowed him plenty of time. He knew his own words were of far less importance than the gentle tugging of God's Spirit upon the heart of young Eagleflight.

"Do you know what Jesus said over and over to people in the Gospels?" asked Zeke at length.

Jeremiah looked up, waiting for the rancher to continue.

"He just said 'Follow me.' Then he told them what to do. No long sermons about what they had to believe first. He said 'Come along with me. As we go, here's what I want you to do.' It was a pretty simple message that preachers have been making more and more complicated ever since."

Still Jeremiah was silent, taking in every word. His eyes and ears were wide open.

"Let me give you an example, Jeremiah," Zeke went on. "When you came here, I made you an offer. I said, 'Look here, Eagleflight, I'll give you a job if you want it. I'll pay you so much a day, and I'll expect certain things. I'll give you a place to bunk down, a place to call home. You'll have to work hard, but I think you'll find me a fair man.' I made you that offer. Now, what did you have to do?"

"It was up to me to decide if I wanted to take you up on it, I reckon," answered Jeremiah.

"You see what I'm driving at? You had to make a decision whether you wanted to take me up on it or not."

"Yeah—makes sense."

"I couldn't make that decision for you," Zeke went on, "and neither could anybody else. You didn't know me, and you didn't know much about the Bar S, but you had to decide whether to say yes or no to me."

Jeremiah nodded, seeing the point Zeke was making.

"Once you decided, well then, you became a Bar S man. Nothing much about you had changed. You still didn't know much about what that meant. But from then on you were working for me. You weren't your own boss anymore. You had to do what I told you. That was the agreement. That was your decision. You chose to make me your boss, and from then on you had to find out what I wanted you to do and then do it.

"If I can say it like this, you had decided to 'follow' Zeke Simmons. You decided to make me your boss, to make the Bar S your home, to do what I told you, and in exchange you'd get your two dollars a day plus room and board."

"I reckon I see what you're getting at," said Jeremiah. "God's got a bigger spread than the Bar S, and he's hiring on new hands too."

Zeke laughed. "I couldn't have put it better!"

"And folks have to decide if they want to hire on, whether they're completely convinced in their brains or not?"

"Exactly! You didn't know beyond all doubt whether what I said was true about the Bar S. I said a lot of things about how it was on my ranch. But you couldn't know how true they all were until you hired on and could see things from the inside. But you decided to hire on anyway. You took my word for it."

"And I ain't been disappointed."

"That's something like what faith is. You see, God makes us an offer. Jesus says, 'Follow me. I want you to become one of my men. Then I want you to do things a certain way—the way I do. That's how people will know you're my follower.' But a lot of the things we don't understand about following him, we *can't* understand as long as we're standing on the outside watching.

"It's just like working here at the ranch, only bigger. When you go into town now, folks know you're a Bar S man. You're a follower of Zeke Simmons. You represent me. You do things a certain way, like Zeke wants you to. You work harder than most men. You're loyal to your boss and your fellow hands. You see, Jeremiah, there's a whole lot to being a Bar S man that you didn't realize when you hired on. But you made a decision, you took me up on my offer, and now you're one of my men."

He paused, thought a moment, then went on. "Do you know what the word *Christian* means, Jeremiah?" he asked.

Jeremiah shook his head.

"It just means someone who follows Christ. *Christian* is the label on folks who have hired on, who have taken Jesus up on his offer when he said, 'Follow me.' Being a Christian is nothing more than saying to God that you want to be a follower of Jesus, that you're taking him up on his offer, that you're putting your bedroll down in his bunkhouse for

221

keeps, and that you're going to call his spread your home from here on out. And believe me, he pays better than two dollars a day!"

A long silence followed. Zeke let these last words sink in. There was scarcely a sound, though in the distance an occasional cow's voice could be heard.

"That's all there is to it?" asked Jeremiah after some time, "bunking down in God's ranch and calling that your home?"

"In one way I suppose you could say that's all there is to it," replied Zeke. "But there's one thing more important than all the rest."

"What's that?"

"When you hire on, you've got to make him Boss."

"In other words, you can't hire on and not do the work of the ranch?" said Jeremiah.

"Yep. From that moment on, your life's not your own anymore. That's part of the agreement. He gives life—both eternal life later and a pretty great life here and now!—but we've got to lay down our allegiance and give it to him. That's what hiring on's all about. He's the Boss. We're working for him!

"And it's a fair enough exchange. When I hired you, I expected the same. I didn't want you working for the livery anymore. You could only have one boss."

The silence that followed this time was even longer. This was an offer, Jeremiah realized, that involved far more than Zeke's offering him a job at the Bar S. He knew he was staring into the face of a lifetime hitch on a spread he still didn't know too much about. He knew people said the Boss loved him and that he was good to work for. But he couldn't help being a little afraid too, because the commitment was for keeps.

41

FINDING OUT
WHAT THE BOSS
WANTS

At length Jeremiah drew in a long sigh, then exhaled

slowly.

"Well," he said carefully, "say that I *was* to sign on, and

say I wanted to be a follower of Jesus, what would I do

next?" he asked.

"The first thing," answered Zeke, "is you've got to tell him you've decided to hire on and take him up on his offer. You've got to tell him you've decided to be his follower."

"You mean . . . pray?"

"I don't much care what you call it," replied Zeke. "But if he's the Boss and you're joining the team, you'd better start talking to him, or else you'll never know what he wants you to do. Call it praying. Call it whatever you want. But if you're going to be his follower, then you've got to talk to him so you'll know where he's heading and where you're supposed to follow. The first thing to tell him is that you're signing on, just like you did me. You remember?"

Jeremiah nodded.

"You came to me, said you'd thought it over, said you wanted to accept my offer. We shook hands. Then I told you to bring your gear and we'd get you bunked down. That's how you became a Bar S man. Then you remember what happened the next day?"

"Sure. You sent me out digging them postholes."

"Right. You found out what I wanted you to do, then you went and did it. It's just the same when you decide to become a follower of Jesus. That's what you do next after telling him you've decided to hire on—you've got to find out what he wants you to do."

"How do you do that?" asked Jeremiah.

"Two ways. You ask him. And you find out what he's *already* told you to do and start right in doing that."

"What do you mean, *already* told me to do?"

"There are hundreds of things he's told his followers to do. They're the rules of the ranch. So that's where we start—doing those. I've got rules here too—no drinking on ranch property, working hard, showing respect to the women, no cussing. Everybody's got to comply with those things, even though I give the men different jobs from day to day.

"That's kind of the way it is on the Lord's ranch too. If we don't do the first things he's said about how folks on his spread are to behave, he's not going to show us anything else. When we do those, he'll show us other things to do."

"But I don't know what they are."

"Then you'll have to find out."

"How?"

"Read the four Gospels. You've heard of Matthew, Mark, Luke, and John?"

"Who hasn't?"

"They contain the rules of the ranch. So the minute you decide to hire on, you've got to start finding out what the Boss wants of you."

"Like not playing poker?"

Zeke smiled. "You haven't forgot where you and I first met so soon, have you, Jeremiah?"

"No, I reckon that's why I asked. Seems a mite confusing to me."

"That I play poker on occasion?"

Jeremiah nodded.

"Everybody's got to figure what God wants them to do about those kinds of things for themselves," said Zeke. "Me, I find a game of cards opens up opportunities for relationships with other men that I'll never have if I wait to meet those same men in church. Why, we don't even have a church in Sweetriver. So I've got to figure out some different way to spread the Word."

"But isn't gambling wrong?"

"I don't know. If it is, I'm sure God will get the message through to me. And it isn't so much gambling to me — I usually have something else I'm thinking about. Besides, I always manage to get whatever I win back into the hands of the fellow I won it from one way or another. I never keep my winnings."

"When you lose?"

"I don't worry about it. It's my way of assisting the local economy, you might say," laughed Zeke. "Sitting down at a table for me is about meeting and talking with men, not the money that changes hands."

"And you say you're not so worried about gambling?"

"Not so much. It's not the most worrisome of habits. It's not always what you do but whether it gets the upper hand. When it does, when you can't control it, then you got a problem that you've got to deal with."

"Hmm . . ."

"But we were talking about the rules of the ranch, remember? The rules of God's ranch are of an altogether different kind than most folks think."

"You mean like loving people and being nice?"

"You bet! First of all, repenting of our sin. We've all sinned. We're all sinners. But that sinfulness hasn't so much to do with things like gambling as it does with attitudes— things like pride and arrogance and selfishness and anger and bitterness. So before we can even be nice and kind, we've got to repent of all the wrong feelings we've kept inside all our lives. After that, we've got to fall in with the way the ranch is run, like putting others first and praying, like you said, and finding ways to be kind, and trusting God—a lot of things, Jeremiah. Jesus spent three years teaching folks how things on God's ranch are supposed to be. We that have decided to be his followers have to find out what those things are and then do what he said."

Jeremiah let out a long sigh.

"A lot to think about," he said.

"It's a big decision, all right—much more important than when you took this job from me."

Jeremiah rose. "Well, I thank you, Zeke," he said. "You've helped me understand it pretty clear, I think."

"You going to sign on, Jeremiah?" asked the rancher, rising too and giving Jeremiah his hand.

"I'll have to think about it," replied Jeremiah. "I've got to get out somewhere alone where I can meet up face-to-face with the Boss. If I give him my hand, it'll be for good. So I've got to know for sure it's *him* I've got a grip on."

42

DECISION

Most of the rest of the day Jeremiah spent alone.

Immediately after his talk with Zeke, he saddled his horse

and rode south. Far south. Lunchtime came and went, but

never once did he feel a pang of hunger. By the time he

came to himself, he was probably ten miles from the ranch.

He did not even realize how hard he had been riding. His

horse was sweating heavily under the late afternoon sun and was beginning to tire.

Jeremiah reined him in, then glanced all around the gently rising and falling prairie around him, taking stock of his surroundings.

He had not been trying to run or escape. He had been riding hard simply to burn off the mental energy that had been building within him all week. His brain was too full. All he knew to do to release the pent-up pressure was to ride.

Down inside he knew what he had to do, knew what he *wanted* to do.

He wanted it, yet still he knew it would not be easy. It would, in fact, be the hardest thing he had ever done.

Real courage was on the line. He knew he could not flinch, nor refuse to face it without being a coward. No one would know it but he himself. But if he backed down from *this* challenge, that's exactly what he would be—a coward.

He drew in a breath, then urged his mount forward. He had no destination. A steep hill lay ahead. That would be as good a place as any. Somehow it seemed fitting to be at the top, if not of a mountain, at least of the highest spot in the vicinity.

He recalled Mercy's words: *I like high places.* Well, he would follow her lead one more time. He rode on, up the hill.

Reaching the top, he dismounted, tied the reins to a tree, then walked slowly about, looking down on the prairie in all directions from the small summit. To the north, everything that met his eye belonged to Zeke Simmons and the Bar S. Farther south, far beyond his gaze, lay the Oklahoma Territory.

It was big country. Wide and free. This was exactly why

he and Jess rode throughout the West. There was always plenty of room.

He thought back to his conversation with Zeke of that very morning, imagining in his mind's eye what *God's* spread was like.

It was bigger than all this, bigger than everything his eyes could see, bigger than the whole West . . . the whole country! And he had been offered a place in it, a home in the biggest bunkhouse ever!

Jeremiah sat down on the dry ground.

"Well, God," he said aloud, "I reckon this is it. It's just me and you alone at last. I don't know if this is what is called praying, but like Zeke said, it doesn't matter what you call it, and I've got the feeling you're right here someplace and listening to me, so I'll just say what's on my mind. . . ."

He stopped, staring straight ahead.

"I don't reckon anything I've got to say will come as any surprise to you, 'cause I'm sure you know what I'm thinking. But I know I've got to say it, maybe for me more than for you. So I'm just going to say it and not beat around about it.

"What I got to say is this: I want to shake your hand and tell you that I'm deciding to be your follower. I'm joining up! I'm making myself one of your men, and I'm making you my Boss.

"I don't know a lot about what it's going to be like or what I'm supposed to do, but I promise you that I'll do what I know is right, and I'll try to find out more of what you want, and I hope you'll show me whatever you want me to do. I want to be a good hand, so I want to do what you tell me.

"One of the things Zeke said we all need to do is repent of being sinful. Well, I've seen lots of crying and wailing at the altar during revival meetings, and I guess that's what they call repenting. I don't myself feel like wailing or weeping. I figure you can hear me just fine like this.

"So I'll just tell you that I'm sorry for my sins and for not paying more attention to how you want your people to live. Mercy was right—I never thought much about you before and never bothered to find out what you might have wanted. I always prided myself on doing what was right, without asking your advice in the matter. That was wrong of me. I intend to listen to you better from now on."

Again Jeremiah paused. This time he glanced all around. A silence came over him, quieter, he thought, than he had ever heard. Not a sound was to be heard. He cocked his ear, listening, wondering if it was God answering him, speaking to him in the very absence of sound, telling him that he had heard Jeremiah's simple prayer of the heart.

"Well, God," he said at length, "I reckon that's about it. I'd just ask you one favor, and that's to help me be a good hand, to do what you want me to do. I'll try to talk to you, like Zeke said I needed to. But I'm going to need to have you talk to me too. And I'll promise you again that I'll do what you show me is right, and whenever I'm in doubt about what to do, if you'll just show me what you want, I'll try to do that too, figuring you know best."

He sat a few more minutes. A slight breeze began to blow, and with it the sounds of the prairie once more returned to Jeremiah's ears.

When he rose and returned to his horse ten minutes later, he felt that the fresh prairie breeze had blown straight up from the valley floor and into his soul.

He had done it.

He felt good. And he was glad.

43

THE PARTNERS

Jeremiah knew his life would not be the same after this.

It could not be the same — not if he meant what he had said.

He'd always been the kind of man who did things for

keeps. When he signed on to something, he saw it through

to the end.

There were two people he had to tell. He had *so* much to

say to Mercy. But he'd already flubbed it that night on the porch and hadn't mustered the gumption to try it again.

Now all this—the time would have to be just right, or he'd probably stumble all over his words again.

No, he'd tell Jess first.

Monday morning he told Zeke what he had done, then asked if he could go to town to see his partner.

"How's he doing?" asked the rancher.

"Just about healed up. But I've got to tell him about yesterday, about all you told me, and about what I did out there riding."

"I think that's a good idea, Jeremiah."

"A man's got to tell his partner something like that."

"Then you go on in. We'll look for you back at lunchtime."

"Thanks, Zeke, I appreciate it."

Jeremiah found Jess at the Silver Ox.

"Hey, Jeremiah, old buddy!" exclaimed his friend. "Come and join us. I'm already fifteen bucks ahead!"

Jeremiah walked forward and took the empty chair at the table.

"Deal you in, Eagleflight?" asked the man he knew as McGraw.

"No, thanks." Turning to his partner, he added, "Jess, I figured you'd have learned your lesson from last time."

"Aw, ain't nothing to worry about. One Eye Jackson's not been seen or heard from. Besides, McGraw here's been feeling so sorry for me since Slim laid me up, I figure I oughta take my money back from last time while his guard's down."

McGraw threw Jeremiah a wink and a grin, as if to say they both knew who would come out on top if the game lasted long enough.

"We'll I'm glad to see you're feeling good enough to play, but I came to town to talk to you."

"Can't it wait?" said Jess, picking up the hand he'd just been dealt and scanning the cards.

"A while. But I've got to be back by noon, so wrap it up as soon as you can, will you? I'll go see Doc and Lars down at the livery. Come and find me."

He turned and left the saloon.

The two partners met on the boardwalk fifteen minutes later as Jeremiah was walking back from the livery stable.

"Doc Haggerty says you're practically like new," said Jeremiah.

"Yep. I feel great! Moved outta his place Saturday and into the hotel."

"Living pretty high, aren't you, Jess?"

"I'm back in the dough, Jeremiah. Things are going my way again. Though I been thinking it's about time for us to head on."

They walked on a few steps. Jeremiah said nothing.

"Yeah, I figure another three or four days," Jess went on, "and I'll have us a good stake, and we can get outta here. I ain't at all sure this place agrees with you. Hey, where's your gun, you forget to put it on?"

"I didn't forget."

"Why ain't you packing it?"

"That's what I want to talk to you about, Jess," answered Jeremiah. "Come over here and sit down."

He led his nephew to the empty bench in front of the general store. The two men eased themselves down onto the bench and stretched their legs out across the wooden sidewalk.

"So, what you got on your mind?" asked Jess lightly. "Something happen to your gun?"

"No, nothing happened to my gun. It's sitting in its holster where I hung it over my bedpost. This ain't about my gun, Jess," he added, his voice growing quiet and thoughtful.

For the first time Jess detected his partner's serious tone. He looked over at him and waited.

"I made a decision yesterday, Jess," Jeremiah said at length. "A decision that's going to change things from now on."

"Uh . . . not to wear your gun no more?"

"Not exactly, though I suppose that's part of it. I took it off and hung it up last night. Somehow it just didn't seem right to have a gun strapped to my leg afterward."

"After what?"

"After I did what I did."

"You gonna get around to telling me what you did?" asked Jess.

"If you give me time! Sometimes it takes a guy a while to get his words pointed in the right direction, Jess."

"All right, all right! Take all the time you want."

"What it is I'm trying to tell you is that I decided to give myself to a new boss."

"You're quitting the Bar S?"

"There you go interrupting me again. No, I ain't quitting the Bar S."

"But you just said —"

"I know what I said. I said I decided to hitch up with a new boss, but I'm gonna keep working for Zeke Simmons too. Only now I'm throwing in with *his* boss too — the Boss that owns it all, Jess."

"You're talking in riddles! You're gonna work for two men?"

"I'm only going to *work* for one. That's Zeke. But I'm

throwing in with the other for everything else in life. I'm talking about God, Jess. I've decided I want to be a believer, a follower of his, a man that does what *God* wants me to do from now on instead of living my life independent and any way I want."

Jess stared back at his partner with a blank expression, as if he couldn't make sense of what he thought he'd heard. "You've gone and got religion?" he finally exclaimed in disbelief.

"I don't know as I'd say that. I just decided I wanted to be a follower of Jesus, that's all, to be counted as one of his men."

"Dang!" said Jess, slapping his leg with his hat. "I knew I should have kept you away from that preacher lady when you started getting soft on her!"

"I'm sorry you feel that way, Jess. I owe Mercy a lot. She's a straight shooter. I think you'll like her."

"I hope I don't have the chance to find out," he laughed.

"What do you mean by that?"

"Just that we'll be long gone before she gets the chance to preach at me!"

"You've got it all backwards, Jess."

"All I know is that I don't want to turn soft. Next thing I know you'll be trying to make me give up poker and whisky!"

"You think giving your life to God makes a man soft?"

"You ever seen a preacher that was every inch a man?"

"A few."

"They all come up a little short in my book."

"We're not talking about preachers, Jess, we're talking about me. You think I'm going soft?"

"I don't know, are you?"

236

"I hope not. Is that what you think Christians are like?"

"Religious fellas never seem quite as tough as the rest."

"Guess it depends on what you mean by tough and what kind of man you want to be."

"And that's the kind of man you want to be, Jeremiah—a religious kind of guy that other men laugh at? Or maybe a shyster like that Brother Joseph fella?"

"I want to be one of God's men, Jess. Nothing more, nothing less. Maybe a man like Zeke."

"Simmons?"

"Zeke can hold his own with any man I've ever seen, and he's a believer. Reads his Bible all the time. Runs his ranch by the Sermon on the Mount. Dangdest thing you ever saw. The men love him, work hard for him, and know better than to cross him. Nope, I don't think you'd call *him* soft."

Jess took in this new information with a look of modest interest and surprise.

"It takes guts to follow Jesus, Jess," Jeremiah went on. "It was the hardest decision I ever made, hardest thing I ever done. I'd have sooner faced ol' Jackson in a quick draw than to do what I did."

"Scary, huh?"

"Not scary—just took all the guts I had, that's all. Made me see just how soft I was. I'm looking for God to make a man of me!"

"You gonna try to reform *me?*"

"Don't plan to. Doubt I'd get very far anyway."

"Dang right you wouldn't," rejoined Jess.

"Reforming you's not why I decided to call myself a Christian. It's all got to do with me. I want to live by truth and do what's right, and being God's man is just about the only way I can see to do that."

"Well, I reckon it's all right by me then. You always were a mite serious about what you called the truth. It'll blow over anyway. If you ask me, you still got that preacher lady on your brain, and it's twisted up your thinking some. As soon as we get to Denver, you'll be back to your old self."

"Nothing'll make me go back on this decision, Jess. This one's for keeps."

"Yeah, well . . . whatever you say. In the meantime, you about ready to pack it up and head on outta here?"

"I'm afraid I'm not quite ready to leave Sweetriver, Jess."

"Why not?"

"I got obligations to Zeke."

"What kind of obligations?"

"I signed on. I can't just up and quit."

"Sure you can. We take jobs for a day or two, a week at the most, all the time. You quit fifty jobs like that before now."

"This one's different."

"I still don't see why."

"For one thing, Zeke only pays every two weeks, and you get nothing if you quit early."

"So when's the next payday?"

"I just got paid. So it's a week from Friday."

"Then we'll head west on the Saturday after that."

"I just don't think I can do that, Jess."

"Dad blame—what's got into you, Jeremiah?"

"I just can't up and leave, that's all."

"What's come over you, man? Two dang weeks more oughta be enough to get your obligations squared away."

"I've been trying to tell you, Jess—everything's changed."

"I can see that. I just ain't so sure I like it."

"Well, get used to it. The Jeremiah Eagleflight that rode

into Sweetriver isn't the same man as is sitting here today. I made a decision yesterday. I can't tell you everything that's going to come of it, but I do know that I'm not going back to the way I used to be."

Both men fell silent. For years they had seen almost everything eye to eye, and differences had been rare between them. Neither was altogether comfortable with the way the conversation had gone.

"You still ain't answered my question," Jess said at length.

"You mean about heading for Denver?"

Jess nodded.

"I'm just not ready to leave Sweetriver," said Jeremiah for the third or fourth time.

44

YANCY

Jeremiah rode back to the ranch, frustrated and irritated at himself.

He wanted to tell Jess everything in a way his nephew would understand. As it was, he'd only muddied the water and made it all the more difficult for Jess to grasp what he had done and why.

His thoughts turned to Mercy. He would talk to her once

and for all. He couldn't let what was in his mind go unsaid
any longer.

He crested the ridge feeling quiet and pensive, reflecting
on the change that had come upon him and thinking about
Mercy.

As he rode up to the ranch, he knew lunch had already
begun. He rode in, tied up his horse, walked into the empty
bunkhouse, then left and began the walk across to the house.

About halfway between his quarters and the house he
heard a stifled scream.

It sounded like Mercy!

He glanced around. There it was again. It came from the
barn!

He ran to the barn and burst through the closed door, just
in time to hear her scream in terror again.

"Shut up, you little vixen!" came a cruel voice, followed
by the sound of a slap and yet another scream, this time of
pain.

Jeremiah ran inside, just in time to see Yancy bend down
and grab Mercy's arm where she'd fallen and yank her force-
fully back to her feet.

"Please . . . please don't—," Mercy cried.

Her assailant had no time to reply.

"Yancy!" yelled Jeremiah from where he stood about ten
feet away. "Let her go!"

Yancy glanced up, still holding Mercy's twisted arm in the
viselike grip of his huge hand. "Get out of here, Eagleflight!"
he growled. "This ain't none of your affair! Me and the little
lady was just getting to know each other a little better."

"I told you before, anything to do with Miss Randolph is
my concern. Now, let her go, Yancy." Jeremiah's voice was
calm, though in his chest his heart pounded rapidly.

"If I don't?"

"You will, Yancy."

"Says who?"

"I say."

"You'll make me?"

"If I have to, Yancy. I hope it won't come to that."

A slow, devilish grin spread over Yancy's face.

"Jeremiah!" Mercy screamed at last. "He's been trying
to—"

"I told you to shut up, you little preaching tramp!" said
Yancy, glancing at Mercy and giving her arm a painful twist.

His evil words could not have been more ill chosen. The
next instant Yancy lay on his back on the floor, blood pouring out of his nose from a punishing blow by Jeremiah's fist.

Screaming again, Mercy leapt free and ran to Jeremiah.
She threw her arms around him, trembling in terror.

Yancy looked up at Jeremiah, standing over him with
fists still clenched. "You're a fool, Eagleflight! I'll kill you
for that!"

"Just you don't lay another finger on her, Yancy, or you'll
taste my fist again!"

Jeremiah turned and began to lead Mercy out of the barn.

Behind him, Yancy jumped to his feet and in a second had
grabbed Jeremiah from behind, torn him away from Mercy,
and thrown him to the ground.

"Jeremiah!" she screamed.

Jeremiah was just able to roll to one side before a pitch-
fork crashed into the wood planks where he had lain.

"Run, Mercy!" he cried as he jumped to his feet. "Get out
of here!"

"I can't leave you!"

"Get out of here!" he yelled again. This time she obeyed

the command, disappearing in a terrified run just as Yancy's
fist slammed into the side of Jeremiah's head.

Stunned, he staggered about, managing to keep his feet
but blinking back the sudden rush of liquid to his eyes. A
second blow, this time to his stomach, doubled him over
with loss of breath and was followed by a wicked, smashing
uppercut to the chin. Jeremiah toppled over backwards,
nearly unconscious.

"So, brave rescuer of ladies!" taunted Yancy, now with
the upper hand, wiping the blood from his nose with the
back of his hand. "You don't look so tough now! You look
like a miserable excuse of a man. You're nothing but a yellow coward, Eagleflight! But that ain't gonna stop me from
killing—"

Yancy's feet suddenly fell out from under him from a sideways kick against his knees from Jeremiah's right foot.
Obscenities filled the air.

But Yancy was on his feet the same moment Jeremiah's
legs were back under himself. The two squared off face-to-
face briefly, then Yancy charged. This time, however, Jeremiah was ready. He met Yancy's fist with the upward thrust
of his left forearm, knocking the blow sideways and following it with a well-aimed blow of his own into Yancy's chin.

Yancy stumbled back, swearing freely now, surprised at
the other man's strength. He had mistaken Jeremiah's soft-
spoken demeanor for timidity and cowardice and now realized his error.

The taunting smile was gone from his eyes now, and in its
place remained only the nefarious glare of a cunning villain.

He lunged forward.

Jeremiah stepped aside, trying again to kick Yancy's legs
out from under him as he came. Yancy staggered but held

his ground, turned back, and rushed forward again. This time his fist found its mark. A vicious cut above Jeremiah's eye burst open, and blood oozed down, obscuring his vision. A slam to his nose brought more blood.

Jeremiah jumped back to regain his bearings.

Yancy charged again. Jeremiah cocked his arm behind him and let his fist fly. It found its mark directly between Yancy's eyes.

He stumbled back and toppled over.

Sweating and panting heavily, Jeremiah stood where he was, hoping it was over at last.

Yancy lay on the floor about eight feet away from Jeremiah.

"You're a fool, Eagleflight!" he cursed. "No man does that to me and lives to tell about it!"

The next instant the revolver from the holster at Yancy's side was in his hand.

"Where's your gun, Eagleflight?"

"I'm not wearing one."

"You're a fool! Doesn't matter—you struck first. It will be self-defense. Say your prayers, you yellow coward!"

The hammer of Yancy's pistol cocked. At the same moment, another scream rang through the air.

Mercy flew forward.

"Jeremiah—no!" she yelled.

Jeremiah jumped toward her and threw her back. A sharp crack of gunfire rent the air, and Jeremiah fell to the floor, unconscious.

Mercy screamed in horror, fell to her knees at his side, and began ripping off his shirt. "Oh, God . . . God . . . no . . . please, God . . . ," she sobbed, frantically trying to find the wound.

A second shot exploded through the barn, this time from the door Mercy had thrown open ahead of the others.

Yancy's gun flew into the air and crashed onto the floor. He grabbed his hand and cried out in pain.

"Get up, Yancy!" said Dirk Heyes, walking slowly forward, his six-shooter still aimed down at Yancy.

"You shot me in the hand, Dirk!" cried Yancy, doing his best to hide the stinging wound.

"I could have shot you through the heart. You're through here, Yancy. Even if they don't string you up for this, you're fired!"

"You got no call," said Yancy, rising.

"You don't consider what you did call?" asked Heyes, nodding to where Jeremiah lay bleeding.

"He attacked me, Dirk. I was trying to protect the lady from him when he came after me."

"I don't believe you, Yancy," said Heyes, grabbing Yancy by the arm and roughly pushing him toward the door, gun at his back. "Here he is, Zeke. Tie the varmint up!"

Zeke, who was just approaching, took charge of Yancy, still cursing and swearing, while Heyes ran into the house to get Mrs. Simmons. Meanwhile, Zeke gave orders to one of the other men to ride into town for the doctor and the sheriff.

"Hurry!" he called after him. "And see if you can find his friend, the Forbes kid," he shouted after him. "He'll want to know too."

45

BEDSIDE

By the time Doc Haggerty arrived in his buggy, they

had carried Jeremiah's limp and bloody body into the house

and laid him in the only bed downstairs, which was

Mercy's. Mercy wiped off the blood and dirt on his face and

nose, while Mrs. Simmons cleaned the wound in his side.

When the doctor hurried in, both women quickly stepped aside.

Doc proceeded to examine the gash in Jeremiah's side, then turned and opened the black bag he had set on the side of the bed.

"The boy's lost some blood," he said, "but at first look I don't think it's too bad. Looks like the chunk of lead went clean through. What's with these two anyway?" he added, half to himself. "I haven't seen a gunshot wound in six months, then these two hit town and both manage to get themselves shot inside two weeks!"

He poured something out of a small bottle onto a clean white rag and dabbed at the raw, bleeding bullet hole in Jeremiah's side.

"Is he going to live, Doctor?" asked Mercy in a shaky voice. She was exerting every fiber within her to keep from showing her fear.

"Oh yeah, the kid'll live, all right. Might have broke the second rib from the bottom. Look, you see here —" He probed around with his fingers just above the raw flesh of the wound, trying to show Mercy the path the slug had taken, but she turned away with closed eyes. She had torn his shirt off in the barn and stuffed an end of it into the wound to keep Jeremiah from bleeding to death, without even thinking about what she was doing. But now, as he lay there unconscious, she could not force her eyes to look at the raw, torn flesh without her stomach rising into her throat.

" —the bullet ripped through his side, hit the rib, but then went on out his back. Not near so serious as the Forbes kid's wound."

Mercy sighed with relief.

"Couple inches either way though," Doc mused as he continued to clean the wound and then began applying some ointment. "Two inches to the left would have gone straight through his heart, and he'd have been dead in an instant. Two inches to the right would have missed him altogether."

He continued to dress the wound, then applied bandages, which he taped to Jeremiah's chest and back.

As he stretched on the last piece of tape, footsteps approached, then Jess half ran through the door into the room.

"Men with guns seem to follow you two like the plague, Forbes," said Doc Haggerty as Jess rushed up.

"He all right, Doc?"

"Yeah, he's fine."

"He don't look too good."

"He got himself pretty banged up before the crazy fool shot him. That reminds me, ladies," he said, turning again to Mercy and Jody, "get some ice or a slab of cold meat or something for the side of his head and that eye. They're going to swell up something fierce. Looks like he took a terrible pounding. You got any ice left in the icehouse, Jody?"

"Some, Doc."

"It won't take much. But I'll wager his head's going to hurt more than his side when he comes to."

As if in answer to his words, a thin groan sounded from the bed.

"Jeremiah—hey, Jeremiah, you there, buddy?" said Jess, stepping forward and leaning down toward Jeremiah's face.

"That you, Jess?" came a faint voice.

"I'm here. Don't you worry about a thing. Doc's got you all patched up—says you'll be on your feet in no time."

"What happened? One of Zeke's bulls stampede over my head?"

Mercy could hardly suppress her joy at hearing Jeremiah's voice, weak as it was, joking about his condition.

"I reckon I had it all wrong this morning," Jess went on. "I'm sorry, Jeremiah."

"What are you talking about?" Jeremiah whispered.

"Talking about you going soft and all that. Why, you're still one tough ornery cuss if you ask me. I had no right to say it."

The trace of a smile broke onto Jeremiah's lips. "Coming from you, Jess," he said, "I suppose I'll take that as high praise. . . . Where's—is Mercy here?"

He struggled to raise himself.

"You stay where you are, son," said Doc Haggerty, placing a restraining hand on Jeremiah's chest. "The little lady's right next to you. She tended you before I got here."

"I'm here, Jeremiah," said Mercy, laying her hand gently on top of his, where it lay limp at his side. Feeling her touch, he clasped her soft warm hand, gave it a squeeze, and continued to hold onto it for several moments, as if the touch itself restored vitality.

"Let the boy rest," said the doctor at length. "Let's all get ourselves out of here. Jody, you fetch some ice. Young lady," he added to Mercy, "you might make some broth. He's going to need you to keep as much as you can inside him while he's healing up so he doesn't waste away like his friend here almost did."

Mercy nodded and followed the other three from the room.

"Don't worry about Jeremiah, Mr. Forbes," said Mercy after they were outside. "We will take the best care of him in the world."

It was the first time Jess had laid eyes on Mercy since her

coming to the Simmons ranch, though he'd heard plenty about her praying for him—everyone he talked to in town brought it up. When he had walked into the bedroom where his partner lay, he had not recognized her. In fact, he hadn't had the slightest inkling who the pretty young lady was standing near Jeremiah's head with the other woman he took for the rancher's wife.

When Jeremiah had said her name, he was astonished to see the western-looking girl step forward and take his hand. The change that had come over her was unbelievable. And yet, as he had continued to stare at her, the dawn of recognition grew that this was indeed the same young woman who had come to town as a preaching evangelist.

"Uh . . . thank you—uh, miss," stuttered Jess. "You're, uh, Sister Mercy, I take it?"

"Just Mercy, Mr. Forbes," said Mercy, flashing him a pleasant smile as she walked him to the door.

"I didn't recognize you in there—you know, from before."

Again she smiled. "Think nothing of it," she said. "I hardly recognize myself from before either."

"Well, I'm . . . uh, much obliged for your helping Jeremiah."

"We'll have him back on his feet in no time. You come out and see him anytime."

"I will—I will, miss," said Jess, turning toward his horse, tied up at the rail ten yards away.

"Please, call me Mercy," said Mercy. "If I'm going to be Jeremiah's friend, I'd like to be yours too."

"Yes, ma'am—I'll try to do that."

Mercy smiled again, then turned back into the house to begin a pot of broth.

Jess strode to his horse and was beginning to mount

when Zeke approached and stopped him. They chatted quietly for a few moments, then Jess stepped up into the stirrup, threw his other leg across the saddle, and rode off toward Sweetriver.

46

A LETTER HOME

Sinclair Randolph usually made the post office the first stop of his weekly visit into Louisville. It was a habit he had formed long ago shortly after they had moved here. His new wife always accompanied him back in those days, and they rode into town every two or three days for the express purpose of checking the mail, on most occasions to find a letter waiting for them from his wife's mother in the nation's capital.

Now the city had grown to encompass them, and the mail came more frequently. But he still made the post office his first Monday errand.

Randolph smiled at the memory. His nervous mother-in-law had been so worried about her daughter moving so far away into the wilds of Kentucky. Now their own daughter was . . .

He did not allow himself to complete the thought. They didn't even know *where* she was, but it was certainly farther away than Louisville was from Washington!

He walked inside the brick building, went to the counter, and asked if he had any mail.

"That you do, Mr. Randolph," said the clerk a minute or two later, returning with something in his hand. "Why, you got a letter all the way from Kansas."

"Kansas!" repeated Randolph in surprise. "I don't know anyone in Kansas."

Before he had a chance to reflect upon the mystery further, the father saw whose hand had penned the words on the envelope—Sinclair and Ernestine Randolph, Louisville, Kentucky—and was bursting through the door and outside, fighting a blurring sensation in his eyes. He leapt upon the seat of his buggy and urged the horse standing at the front of his buggy into an immediate gallop. He had had a list of errands to do, but suddenly they were all far from his mind. He had to get this home to his wife without delay!

When Ernestine Randolph heard her husband clattering back after being gone less than an hour, she rushed to the window and looked out. He was shouting something as he came recklessly toward the house. A feeling of dread sweeping over her, she ran to the front door and out to meet him.

Already he was out of the buggy and racing toward her, leaving the lathered horse to its own devices.

Unable to speak, he thrust the envelope into his wife's hand. Their eyes met briefly. She glanced down at the letter. The next instant she was hastening back inside again to find a chair. This she would have to read sitting down!

She took in a long sigh, trying to steady her fluttering mother's heart, then tore open the envelope. She glanced at the handwriting on the page as a few tears began to flow, and she handed it to her husband, who had followed her into the room and now stood at her side.

"I can't," she said. "You read it to me."

He took the two pages from her, then drew in a deep breath and read aloud:

Dear Mother and Father,

I know it has been a long time since you heard from me. I am very sorry. I have no excuse other than my own pride, wanting to prove to myself that my decision to go west with Reverend Mertree had been the right one.

But it wasn't. He turned out to be all you suspected and worse. I feel like such a fool for not listening to you, Mother. You were entirely right, and I should never have left Evansville with him. Everything you said about independence is true, and I cannot imagine how my ears could have been so plugged that I couldn't hear the wisdom of your words. As you said, I was not as experienced as I thought. I hope I have learned some lessons that will help me grow and that I won't make such a mistake again.

It would be impossible in a letter to explain everything that has happened. The conclusion of it is simply this — last week I discovered Brother Joseph to be a charlatan who was out for nothing but financial gain. Oh, Mother and Daddy, I feel so stupid for being so gullible!

The poor man's voice cracked. He stopped, wiping at his eyes with the back of his free hand. Realizing he could not continue, he handed the second sheet to his wife. Though her eyes had filled with tears before he finished the first page, blinking several times, she did her best to continue where he had left off.

I immediately left his employ and now find myself in the middle of the western Kansas prairie, in a town called Sweetriver, without a penny to my name. I am all right. I am healthy and unharmed, except in pride. Though you are far away, believe it or not, I am learning a great many things from you right now. I should say I am remembering much, and I hope that is helping me grow.

I so long to see you! I would give anything to feel your arms around me again. Oh, to be a little girl in the safety of my father's house once more! I am going to try to conduct religious services here in Sweetriver, where there is no church, and hopefully will earn enough to pay for a ticket back to Louisville. I will let you know when to expect me, as soon as I am able to secure passage.

I love you both,

Mercy

When Mercy's mother and father managed to complete the letter through the tears they could not keep from running down their cheeks, a long silence fell between them. It was Mrs. Randolph who spoke first through her handkerchief.

"She is a good girl," she said.

Her husband nodded.

"What do you think we ought to do?" she asked.

"What do you mean?" replied Mr. Randolph. "What *can* we do?"

"You could take the train out there and try to find her."

"How would I find her?"

"How many Sweetrivers can there be in Kansas?"

"She might already be on her way back by then. Even if not, we don't know where she might be by the time I would get there. And even if I did find her, Ernestine, what would I do?" asked her husband.

"Bring her here—what else?"

"Do you not think that ought to be her decision?"

"She said she wants to come back."

"Yes, she did. She also said she has a plan for how to do it. It seems to me we should trust her to handle it just a little further—let the thing play itself out so that she can learn the full lesson God has for her."

"Aren't you being a little hard on her?"

"She did not ask us to come. I think she's growing up, Ernestine. It's just what we've been praying for."

"It sounds like she already has."

"She's starting to, all right. But it wouldn't surprise me if God has more yet to do, and I wouldn't want us to interfere. We've been praying for her every day. I have no doubt that God will make something good come of all this now that she's learned this lesson. If she were in danger that would be another thing, but it doesn't sound like she is."

"We ought to at least see if we can wire her some money."

"She didn't ask us to, Ernestine. It's not a good idea to step between a person and the consequences of her decisions. She'll come back to us when she's ready and be the stronger for it. We need to let that be her decision, just like it was her decision to leave Evansville and take up with that fellow Mertree."

"I don't know," sighed Mercy's mother. "I just feel so helpless."

"Are you not the one who has said over and over that praying is the best and most important thing we can do? Just look how the Lord has kept her safe and is now speaking more deeply to her."

"I know you're right. I just want to *do* something."

"She knows you and I love her. I think deep down she knows, too, that we would drop everything and come to help her in an instant or that we would send money if she asked. She knows that, but part of her still wants to work it out herself. Maybe she needs to see it all the way to the end in order to learn how to really depend on God for herself. We may find out later how God has brought a higher good than we can anticipate out of what looks bleak right now."

Mercy's father grew pensive for a moment.

"Don't misunderstand me, Ernestine," he said. "I am really proud of her. It takes guts to admit you are wrong and say you are sorry. I remember how hard it was for me to start saying it to my own folks. Not a lot of people ever learn how. I think the best thing for us to do is keep praying because it looks to me like the Lord is taking care of her for us."

"It'd be all right to write to her, don't you think, Sinclair?"

"Oh, of course. I just don't think we ought to send her money or plead with her to come home until she's ready. The Lord is doing a work in her life, and I don't think we ought to interfere."

47

A SURPRISE
VISITOR

Jeremiah remained in bed the rest of Monday and most of

Tuesday, sleeping on and off, putting up with the ice packs

as well as he could. At every opportunity, Mercy spoon-fed

him the hot soup she had made, almost giddily happy at his

recovery and for the chance to tend him with her own lov-

ing hands.

By Tuesday evening—pain everywhere, head throbbing,

broken rib screaming with every twist of his body, and the wound from Yancy's gun feeling like he had a bowie knife stuck into his gut—Jeremiah declared himself sick of bed.

"I am determined to get up and on my feet if it kills me!"

Staggering into the dining room amid welcoming cheers from his comrades, he attempted to join them for supper.

The effort, in fact, *did* nearly kill him. The wound began to bleed again, and he felt worse all day Wednesday for it. By Thursday the throbbing in his head had subsided, though the eye was still seriously black from Yancy's fist, and the ribs on the other side of his chest had begun to ache as well. On Friday, however, he again said he was determined to get his feet back under him, and this time the effort was successful. Saturday he was up and about for half the day, and on Sunday he returned to the bunkhouse to a cheerful and rousing welcome on the part of his fellow hands, who were, to a man, all glad to see Yancy gone.

On Mercy's part, though she tried to hide it, the Sunday of his departure was a day of depressing loneliness. It was no comfort to have her bed back and her room once more to herself. She had never been happier than during these past six days, sleeping on the couch in the living room by night and nursing and feeding and ministering to Jeremiah by day. Never had she felt so fulfilled. Never had love in her heart found more purposeful expression through her hands and fingers. Never had her heart been so full of song as she bounded and skipped through the house with light step and cheery smile.

This was *ministry,* she thought—caring for someone like Jeremiah!

It would still be some time before he could work. For several days following, Mercy made a dozen journeys a day back and forth between house and bunkhouse to do what she could for him, and gradually her spirits revived in service once more.

During midmorning on one of these days, a visitor arrived.

Mercy was in the kitchen making preparations for lunch when Jody came in from her workroom. "There's someone to see you, Mercy," she said.

Mercy glanced up, a look of question in her eyes. She had heard no horse ride in.

"I don't know who he is," Jody went on. "He's a bedraggled sort of man. I don't know him."

"He's asking for *me?*"

"Yes. I can send him away if you'd rather not—"

"No . . . no, I'll see him," said Mercy, wiping her hands and then following Jody to the front door where the visitor stood waiting on the porch.

Mercy opened the door, still with a look of question in her eyes. Quickly she took in the appearance of the man standing before her, hat in hand, looking, indeed, very slovenly and unkempt.

The man returned Mercy's questioning stare. "I . . . er . . . I wanted to see Sister Mercy," he said nervously.

"I'm Mercy Randolph."

"No, miss, ye see—I came to see *Sister* Mercy, the 'vangelist. I heerd she—"

"There's no mistake," said Mercy with a smile. "I used to be Sister Mercy."

Still the man looked her over uncertainly, not sure whether he recognized her or not.

"Ye're the 'vangelist?"

"I used to *call* myself an evangelist," replied Mercy. "Now

I go by just Mercy, and I call myself nothing more than a Christian."

The man continued to eye her skeptically. "If ye say so, miss," he said at length. "But tarnation, ye've changed a dang heap! I still can't quite get my eyes to figger out if ye're really who ye say ye be."

Slowly a hint of recognition began to filter into Mercy's consciousness.

"Could I talk to ye for a minute, ma'am?" the man asked.

"Of course . . . uh — Jody," she added, glancing back where the rancher's wife still stood just inside the door. "Would it be all right?"

"Of course, dear," answered Mrs. Simmons. "Bring him into the living room."

"Come in," Mercy said to the man, holding the door open, then leading him into the living room.

He followed, shuffling nervously, looking as if he had never been inside such a fine home before. He took the chair Mrs. Simmons offered him. She excused herself and returned to her work.

"I don't know if ye recollect seeing me afore, Sister," began the man, after fidgeting uneasily for a moment. "My name's Bart Wood."

Suddenly it all came back! Mercy's face flushed with anger as she recalled the conversation she had overheard outside the livery stable.

"Why . . . yes, Mr. Wood, now that you tell me your name, I know why I recognized your face!"

"Please, ma'am," he said, seeing the flame in Mercy's cheeks and eyes, "ye got every right to be sore at a no-account bum like me, but if ye'd jist hear me out, I'd be obliged to ye."

Mercy struggled to calm herself and sat silently.

"Well, ain't no use denyin' what I done, cuz I can see from yer face ye know well enough. But I tell ye God's truth, Sister, it ain't been sittin' too good on me. It's been a fire in my soul ever since. The Lord's been convictin' me mighty powerful about my sinful ways, and that's why when I heerd ye was still around town, I knew I had to come see ye, ma'am, and tell ye how sorry I am at the terrible thing I done."

Mercy still sat silently.

She watched as the man spoke, still cautious, wondering what angle he was trying to play now. Was he going to try to get more money out of her for this second grieving repentance?

An awkward silence followed. Wood was staring down at the hat still clutched between his short chunky fingers.

"Is there something you want me to do about it, Mr. Wood?" said Mercy tightly.

"Oh, no, ma'am—well, that is . . . I reckon there is, if ye wouldn't mind lending a helping hand to a man like me that once folks knowed only as the town drunk. I know there ain't no reason why ye should want to reach down and soil yer pretty clean hands with the likes of me. But . . . well, the fact is, Sister, I been mighty heartsick over what I done, and I'm telling ye the truth, that I ain't had a drop of whisky for going on two weeks now."

"I'm glad to hear it, Mr. Wood." Mercy's voice was still crisp and hard.

"And so, what I wish ye might do for me, Sister," Wood went on in his hesitating voice, "is to take back the money yer Brother Joseph give me. I don't want nothing more to do with it cuz it's burning a hole right in my soul."

Still Mercy sat, not quite sure what to make of what she had just heard. She watched as Bart Wood dug his hand into some hidden pocket of his person and then drew it out, clutching a handful of bills.

"Here's the twenty-five he give me. I ain't spent a dime of it."

He rose, shuffled to where Mercy sat, and handed the wad of money to her. Dumbfounded, she took it, still sitting silently as Wood sat back down.

"There's another five there too, Sister," he said. "Thirty dollars altogether."

"What . . . what's that for?" she asked, finally finding her voice.

"I reckon it's my way of giving the Lord back something. It's all the money I got to my name."

"But what do you want me to do with it, Mr. Wood?"

"I don't care, Sister. I can't keep it. It's the Lord's money, and I was wrong to take it."

"But—"

"Ye'll know how to use it for the Lord's work."

"I'm not in the Lord's work anymore, Mr. Wood," said Mercy, still unsure what to make of this dramatic turn of events and feeling guilty for misjudging the man upon first sight of him.

"From what they're saying in town, ye's still connected with the Almighty somehow, Sister. That's how I heerd ye was here. Folks are saying that when *ye* pray, it's different than with them shouting and ranting 'vangelists. Folks say ye pray soft so's no one can hardly hear ye, but that the Lord above hears and that he does what ye ask him."

The words hit against Mercy's ears with such force she sat as one stunned.

How could such things possibly be circulating about her! Everything about her newfound faith in God had been so private, so personal. Except for Jeremiah and Jody, she had said nothing to anyone, and both of them were here at the ranch. How was it that the town of Sweetriver could be talking about *her?*

"I tell ye, miss, there's more folks talking 'bout religion and God now than I ever seen in all my born days, and it's all on account of yer staying behind after that there crook Brother Joseph left, and then yer praying for the poker-playing Forbes kid."

"I . . . I just find that so difficult to understand, Mr. Wood. I haven't said a thing to make people think I know anything about spiritual matters. I'm only now discovering the truth for myself."

"It ain't what ye say, ma'am. Lots o' folks do a heap of talking 'bout religion. It's what a body does that counts more'n anything, and folks, I reckon, has been watching ye instead of listening. None of that matters anyhow, 'cause it's happening whether ye understand it or not. And now that I'm free of the bondage of that there money, I'm wondering if ye'd do jist one more favor for me, ma'am?"

"I'll try, Mr. Wood," said Mercy skeptically, suddenly on her guard again. Was he finally going to reveal what his real motive was for this little game of feigned repentance?

"Would ye pray for me, Sister?" he said in a soft voice.

"Pray for you? . . . Pray for what?"

"Pray for my soul, Sister."

"You mean, that God would forgive you for taking the money?"

"No, I already done that. I mean pray for my soul, Sister."

He paused, deep in thought and clearly struggling for words.

"Ye see, Sister," he went on, softly and in a noticeably humble and contrite tone, "that night when I went down on

my knees in that tent, when Brother Joseph was shouting
out his prayers above me . . . well, I knew the whole thing
was a sham 'cause he'd found me the first night after yer
wagon rolled into town and asked me if I'd like to make an
easy twenty dollars. So I knew he was a fake. But when I
went down on my knees like he told me to, something
inside, like a little fire, just started burning inside me, telling
me that I needed to repent and live a different kind of life
. . . that even if the blamed preacher was a fake and even if I
was a fake, that repentance weren't something a body faked
and that God was alive enough and that it was him setting
the little fire t' going inside me.

"That's what's been burning down there ever since, Sister,
that God wanted to get me to look at him and go down on
my knees for real this time and tell him I was ready to live a
different kind of life and be the kind of man he wanted me
to be."

He stopped and took in a deep breath, clearly feeling a tre-
mendous relief at voicing the burden that had been weigh-
ing on him.

"So I reckon that's what I'd like to ask ye to help me pray
for, Sister—that I could be one of God's men in spite of
everything I done."

Mercy's heart smote her. The false judgment that had
been in her heart toward this repentant man suddenly over-
whelmed her.

Her eyes filled with tears, and before she knew it she was
on her feet and walking toward him, an outpouring of love for
the simple and broken man welling up as a spring within her.

"Oh, Mr. Wood, I can't imagine anything it would give
me more pleasure to do!" she said as she knelt down beside
his chair.

Wood lurched forward with his heavy frame, then slipped to his knees on the hard oak floor as well, clasping his hands together and bowing his head.

"Oh, Father," prayed Mercy softly, "I thank you from the bottom of my heart for this precious and humble man who is courageous enough to come to you to ask forgiveness for his past and to ask you to make him clean. God, I do ask you to cleanse the heart of Bart Wood, just as you cleansed my heart. Forgive him for his past, for his sins, just as you forgave me. Oh, Father, and as you have given me such a new life in you, I ask you to bring Bart into fellowship with you. Make him your son, Father, so that you might make him your man. He and I are both in need of your restoring touch, Lord. We have not walked with you as we should, and now we want to with all our hearts. Help us, Lord. Help us walk with you all the rest of our lives."

By now Mercy was weeping softly and could pray no more.

"God, I appreciate yer taking the time to listen to one that ain't deserving of yer patience with me," prayed Bart, also softly and without the fervency he had displayed while in the employ of the Joseph Mertree evangelistic show. "Lord, I reckon ye know yerself I'm a miserable excuse of a man. I been nothing but a drunk most of my life. But if ye know that, Lord, I reckon ye also know that I want to mend my ways and live different from now on.

"So if ye want me, Lord, I'd like ye to have me. I ain't much, I reckon, but what there is left of me, it's yers, Lord, for whatever ye figger it's worth doing with. That fire ye put down in my heart at the meeting, well, I'd jist like ye to make it burn brighter and maybe burn out the way I used to be so I could be the kind of man that'd make ye proud to call me one of yer own. Well . . . that's about all I got on my mind. I'm all yers to do what you want with. Amen."

Bart's prayer had only increased the flow of Mercy's tears.

Both stood. Mercy laughed briefly, looking at her new brother through shining wet eyes.

"Well, ma'am," said Bart, "I sure do thank ye."

Mercy could not reply. The lump in her throat was too big, and the tears began once more.

Bart turned and headed toward the door.

"Mr. Wood . . . Bart—wait," said Mercy, at last finding her voice. "What will you do? Didn't you say that was the last of your money?"

"That it was, ma'am," he replied, turning around. "But I ain't worried. Ye can't believe how little a man can be worried about what's to become of him! Why, after what I been carrying around for weeks, why, Sister Mercy, I feel so good I could live a week without worrying about food! Besides, ain't that one of the first things a body's gotta learn that's fixing to hitch up with the Lord's wagon, that the Lord takes care of his folks?"

"Yes . . . yes, I suppose you are right," Mercy said with a smile.

"There, ye see—ain't a thing for me to worry about!" With those words, Bart Wood turned again and walked from the house, leaving Mercy still standing in the living room dealing with a fresh onrush of tears.

A moment later, she went farther into the house to find Mrs. Simmons. She had to tell Jody about this most extraordinary interview!

Mercy went from room to room, but Jody was nowhere to be found. Both the kitchen and her workroom were empty.

The rancher's wife, in fact, had slipped out the back door some minutes before from where she had been praying in the hallway. She had gone in search of her husband, who, she knew, would want to be apprised immediately of the eternal events then in progress in his own home.

By the time Mercy found her, Mrs. Simmons was returning toward the back of the house.

Even as the two women walked back to the kitchen, Zeke intercepted Bart in front as he approached his horse. Shaking his hand, Zeke asked if they might have a few words alone together. Wood complied, and the two men walked off slowly toward the fields side by side. Not another soul ever heard what they talked about, but it was a conversation Bart Wood remembered for the rest of his life.

An hour later, as the hands of the Bar S ranch gathered for lunch, it was with some surprise around the table that Zeke introduced their guest, adding that he had offered Yancy's job to Mr. Wood and that Bart had been kind enough to accept.

48

INVITATION

Summer drew to a close. Another thunderstorm blew in.

It was over in a day. Once more the sun came out clear.

But the rain and clouds seemed to have left some of their

wintry bluster behind.

The sun, which before had burned hot, now shone crisp

and cool. The next morning, leaving the house to fetch the

eggs from the chicken coop for breakfast, Mercy shivered

involuntarily and glanced about, as if wondering where the brief chill had come from.

The day warmed, though, nearly as hot as before. But the storm left a bit of itself in the trees and the grasses. Hints of yellow and orange began to show themselves.

Zeke sensed something too, sniffing the morning wind as he rode about his ranch. He knew the odor well. Somewhere in the far north of Canada, winter was already preparing to make its southern journey and was sending brief puffs of warning for all who would heed them.

Hints of autumn were in the wind, though it was yet but the second week of September and summer was still not past.

It had been almost two weeks since the shooting. Jeremiah was up and about every day now, though doing the most modest of chores. His side was still bandaged and his broken rib, though healing well, painfully restricted his movements.

More had been on his mind than his wounds and recovery, however. As frequently as he had seen Mercy these two weeks, and as tireless as had been her attention and ministry and service to him, there had been few opportunities for meaningful talk. Those there had been were awkward and strained.

He had to tell her of his Sunday ride the day before the shooting! She deserved to know. Everything had changed inside him, and she was such an instrumental part of it. Why was it so hard? Why couldn't he just say it, like he had to Jess?

There was more he had to say too. That was probably what made it so difficult. He knew that once he opened the door of his heart, *everything* was likely to tumble out all at once. That was more fearsome than Yancy's gun and what he had done that Sunday put together!

But he could not rest until he *did* tell her!

Every day it gnawed deeper and deeper into his gut. His sleep grew more and more fitful. He usually slept eight hours like a rock. Now it was six, sometimes four, and even those hours were spent tossing and turning. He woke each morning feeling more exhausted than the night before.

"Something wrong with you, Eagleflight?" Heyes asked.

"No, nothing."

"You need to see the doc?"

Jeremiah shook his head. "A cup of coffee is all I need," he said.

No amount of coffee helped. Zeke grew concerned. Everyone could see there was something on Jeremiah's mind. No one realized just what the trouble was.

Mercy took his growing silence upon herself, thinking him offended with her. She avoided his glances at the table. Jeremiah knew she didn't understand. *He* didn't understand!

At last the burden of his silence grew intolerable.

By Saturday afternoon he had reached a decision. He would wait no longer. Come of it what may, he had to get it out. He had tried and failed too many times. Tomorrow would be two weeks since his ride, and that was long enough.

He found Zeke in the barn. Could he borrow a rig tomorrow, he asked. Zeke agreed.

Jeremiah marched to the house and asked to see Mercy. Would she like to go for a ride with him tomorrow?

His brusque countenance didn't bode well, she thought. But if he was angry with her, she supposed she ought to find out. She nodded in agreement.

"For lunch?" he asked.

"You mean a picnic?" said Mercy.

272

"I reckon."

"That would be fun, Jeremiah. Shall I fix a basket?"

"If you like," he answered.

"All right," she said, a little confused again. "What time?"

"Noon, I reckon."

"I'll be ready."

He turned and walked back toward the bunkhouse without another word, leaving Mercy watching his retreat, not knowing whether to laugh or cry.

49

CONFESSION
OF ANOTHER KIND

Sunday came.

Jeremiah had slept hardly a wink that night, more agitated than he'd ever been in his life. Mercy fumbled through the morning, growing more and more afraid of what might be coming.

At noon, Jeremiah knocked on the door of the house.

Mercy answered.

"You ready?"

She nodded.

"Got the basket?"

"Yes, Jeremiah," she said. "I'll get it."

She disappeared inside and returned a moment later. He led her to the buggy, put the basket in back, helped her up, gingerly climbed up himself, flicked the reins, and headed southwest toward the Sweet River.

"It's a beautiful day," said Mercy after about five minutes.

"Yep."

"You can smell that summer's about over."

"Yep, reckon you can."

Mercy was silent. She hoped the whole afternoon wasn't going to be like this, no matter *what* was on Jeremiah's mind!

They rode on another ten minutes. Neither spoke a word.

"I'm sorry I'm so quiet," said Jeremiah at length.

"That's all right, Jeremiah."

"Ain't much of a way to have a picnic."

"I don't mind. I'm having fun."

"Well, I'm sorry anyway. Just got a lot on my mind, that's all."

"I understand. You don't have to say a word if you don't want to."

"I want to—it just ain't easy."

"I know."

"Thought we'd go to the river."

"That would be nice. I haven't seen the river yet."

"Kinda low this time of year. Smells good though. Lots of green grass around it."

"It sounds like the perfect place for a picnic."

"Yep. That's how I figured it."

They rode on, reaching the river without further dialogue. Jeremiah pulled up the horse, jumped down a little too hard, wincing slightly from his wound, tied the reins to the branch of a river willow, and then offered Mercy his hand. She took it, stepping down to the ground.

"Jeremiah!" she exclaimed. "It's the loveliest place I've seen in as long as I can remember."

"I thought you might like it," he said, hoisting down the picnic basket.

He led her to a patch of soft green grass about twenty yards up a gentle slope from the slowly meandering river. Mercy sat down, opened the top of the basket, pulled out a cloth spread, laid it on the grass, and began emptying the contents she had prepared onto it.

"I hope you're hungry!" she said enthusiastically. "I brought enough to feed the whole bunkhouse."

Jeremiah paced around, staring in the opposite direction at the flowing river. He didn't indicate that he had heard her. Mercy continued to prepare the picnic lunch.

"It's ready!" she called out.

Jeremiah turned, walked toward her, sat down, and began to eat silently. He had not smiled since the moment he had appeared on the porch yesterday.

Lunch progressed quietly.

"I'm sorry I'm so quiet," Jeremiah said again after some time.

"I told you, Jeremiah, I don't mind. Getting to be with you is enough. You don't have to tell me anything you don't want to."

"Don't want to, is that what you think?"

"I . . . I don't know. I didn't mean—"

"'Course I *want* to," he said. "That's why I brought you

out here, 'cause I want to. But, doggone, I just can't seem to get started with it!"

Mercy stared down at the checkered tablecloth lying on the ground.

"I was all set to tell you that day I came back from town and found you and Yancy in the barn. Then after that, well, I just ain't had much of a chance."

"I knew there was something on your mind, Jeremiah," Mercy said softly, still not looking up.

"You must have known I'd been thinking long and hard about what you told me in the barn that day."

"You told me that when you came to the house."

"Weren't you curious about what me and Zeke talked about?"

"Yes, I was interested, Jeremiah."

"Well, that's one of the things I've been wanting to say — to tell you about it. You wanna hear what Zeke told me?"

"If you'd like to tell me — yes, of course I would."

Jeremiah recounted their conversation. As she listened, Mercy's heart swelled with gratitude to God.

"Mr. Simmons is a wise man," she said when Jeremiah was through. "You see, I could never have made it all so understandable like that."

"Yeah, I reckon you knew what you were doing, telling me to talk to Zeke." Jeremiah looked around, took in a deep breath, then let it out slowly.

"Well, after I was through talking to Zeke, I went out for a long ride. I was gone most of the afternoon."

"I remember. I spent the whole time watching for you."

"You did?"

"I couldn't help wondering what was going on."

"What was going on was that I went out south, I don't

know, musta been ten miles, climbed to the top of a hill where you could see for miles all around, and then I just sat down and started talking to God. I don't know if you'd exactly call it praying, but whatever it was, I did it, and maybe it was praying, 'cause I could tell that God heard me."

"How could you tell, Jeremiah?" Mercy's inquisitive eyes were big and round.

"Just could, that's all. It got real quiet when I was done, and I just knew that silence was God letting me know he heard."

"What did you tell him?"

"I just told him that I wanted to be his man and that I'd decided to follow Jesus and that I was going to try to live by all the truth from now on, not just pieces of it here and there."

"Oh, Jeremiah, that's wonderful!" exclaimed Mercy.

Suddenly she jumped up from where she had been sitting, knelt beside him, and threw her arms around Jeremiah's broad shoulders.

Jeremiah winced sharply.

Realizing what she'd done, Mercy released him and stepped back.

Jeremiah tried to laugh, but unsuccessfully. Mercy thought the peculiar look on his face was from pain. He knew otherwise.

"I'm sorry," she said, mortified, "I forgot about your rib. . . . I . . . I was just so overcome with happiness!"

She sat back. Neither said a word for a minute or two.

"I've . . . I've been afraid you were angry with me," Mercy said at length.

"Angry—with *you?*" exclaimed Jeremiah, looking up. "Why would I ever be angry with you?"

"I didn't know. You've been so quiet, and I thought you didn't want to see me."

She started to cry and glanced away.

Jeremiah reached toward her and laid a gentle hand on the side of her arm.

"You've been taking such good care of me," he said softly. "I could never be angry with you! And besides that, if it wasn't for you—that is, what I've been trying to say ever since—well, that night when . . . it's just that I . . ."

Again he could not force the words out.

"I . . . I didn't know what you were thinking," she said, still looking down toward the ground. "You got so quiet. You quit smiling at me—I thought maybe you were upset about something I'd said."

Jeremiah withdrew his hand. His heart pounded inside him. The last thing he wanted was for Mercy to mistake what he thought of her!

Suddenly he leapt to his feet and strode toward the river, stopping at its bank, staring ahead into the gentle flow.

What a stupid fool he was! He had faced Yancy's gun. He had faced the God of the universe out alone on the prairie. He had faced the ridicule of his best friend by telling him he had decided to live his life for God. Why couldn't he face his own feelings like a man and just—

He felt a hand on the back of his shoulder. Startled, he spun around.

There stood Mercy less than a foot away. Her emerald green eyes gazed straight into his, a calm glow of radiant love flooding her whole face.

At last Jeremiah's tongue was loosed. "It ain't been just the talks we had, or praying," he said. "It ain't easy for a man to say it, Mercy, but, you see—it's *you* that my heart's been full of!

"That's what's got me so tied up in knots so that I can't

say what I'm thinking and so that I can't sleep right and so that sometimes I don't even know if I can think straight anymore—that's what I was trying to tell you that night on the porch. I've been spending some time in the Good Book I borrowed from Zeke, and I reckon it says it as well as can be said."

He stopped again.

"What does it say, Jeremiah?" asked Mercy. "What verse are you talking about?"

"It's in Proverbs. Seems like it was after a twenty-one. I memorized the words but not the numbers."

"What were they?"

"Well, it said this—'He that followeth after mercy findeth life,' . . . and I reckon that's what I'm doing, and dang if I haven't been trying to find a plain way to say it straight out—that, well, I'd be honored . . . that is—I've been wanting to ask . . . if you'd ever be able to consider . . . spending your life with me?"

By now Mercy's eyes were swimming in liquid joy and amazement.

Slowly she approached, still closer, and, gently this time, encircled him with her arms. Jeremiah returned the embrace, reaching his arms around her tiny shoulders, drawing her close. Mercy lay her head against his great chest, while Jeremiah rested his cheek atop the glistening hair that had haunted his dreams. The ten thousand words each wished they could utter required no tongue to be heard, for were not the deeper regions of their beings now one?

There they stood, hearts stilled at last, for what seemed an hour but could have been a minute, and though it seemed a minute, could have been an hour.

Then, by common consent, they turned and began walking slowly along the bank of the river, arm in arm.

Still there were no words. None seemed necessary.

When they returned to the buggy two hours later, however, both were laughing freely.

A NEW
PARTNERSHIP

*It was late afternoon before Mercy and Jeremiah
arrived back at the house.*

"That's Jess's horse," said Jeremiah as they pulled up in
front of the barn. "I wonder what he's doing here."

He tied up the buggy, helped Mercy down, and they
walked toward the house. Inside they found Jess deep in

conversation with Zeke in the living room. An open Bible lay in Zeke's lap.

"Howdy, Jess," said Jeremiah. "What are you up to?"

"I came out to get you," replied Jess.

"Since you weren't here," Zeke put in with a smile, "your partner and I got to talking. He told me what you told him about the decision you'd made and said he didn't understand it."

"I told him I thought maybe you'd gone loco, is what I said," added Jess.

"So I took the opportunity to explain it in a little more detail to him," said Zeke. "We've been having a very stimulating conversation ever since."

Just then Jody walked in from the kitchen. "More coffee, Mr. Forbes? — Oh, Mercy, Jeremiah . . . you're back!"

"None for me," said Jess, rising from his chair. "Well, you ready, Jeremiah?"

"Ready for what?"

"To get out of here — to leave."

"Leave! Are you crazy?"

"We talked about it plain enough. I said we'd leave after your payday."

"And I told you I wasn't ready to leave."

"Well, I lost the rest of my dough last night. I'm sick of this town, and I'm telling you it's time for us to hit the trail, man. I've had it with Sweetriver! So get your stuff, and let's get a move on to Denver."

Jess headed toward the door.

Jeremiah was silent. Was this finally it, the moment when he and his partner had to part ways?

"I can't go, Jess," he said at length.

"Why not, for dang sakes?"

"I, uh—I been laid up for two weeks. I owe Zeke here for all the time he's been paying me that I haven't done a stitch of work for him."

"Don't worry, Jeremiah," said Zeke. "You've given me more than a fair return on my money. If the trail's calling you, then you go on and don't think twice about me."

Looking down at the floor, Jeremiah did not see the quick wink Zeke cast his wife.

"There, you see!" said Jess.

"I tell you, I can't go," insisted Jeremiah.

"You're talking nonsense!"

"I like it here."

"Aw!"

"You don't believe me?"

"I don't know what to believe about you no more!"

"Well, I'm thinking straighter than I ever have."

"You're talking what sounds to me like nonsense!"

Across the room, Jody had seen the silent color rising in Mercy's cheeks, and, divining the truth, was now grinning in amusement with the heated exchange between partners.

"Maybe I'm thinking clear for once. You ever think that maybe we shouldn't just drift forever?" asked Jeremiah.

"No, I never thought that."

"Maybe we *ought* to think about it."

"The trail's an all right life."

"For a while. Not forever."

A sudden look of revelation came over Jess's face. "You're not talking about settling down!" he exclaimed in horrified shock.

"I'm talking about nothing, I tell you!" shot back Jeremiah.

"First you hang up your gun, now your saddle."

"Man's got a right to change."

"Come on, Jeremiah, what in tarnation's got into you?"

"What's got into me is that I found a lady I love, that's what!" thundered Jeremiah at last. *"And I ain't about to leave her!"*

Jess stood dumbfounded. He had heard the words, but he couldn't believe his ears. His partner talking about . . . *love!*

"Why you dang blind fool," Jeremiah added. "What do you think I been doing today but asking Mercy to marry me!"

If Jess still could not believe, the other two listeners in the room needed no further convincing. Zeke added his own cheers to Jody's exclamations of delight. He jumped from his chair and gave Jeremiah his hand and a rousing slap on the shoulder, all in one motion, while his wife ran and threw her arms around Mercy. The two women wept for joy in one another's arms.

"I'd say this calls for a celebration!" exclaimed Zeke. "Tonight we'll whoop it up here."

"I'll get started on a cake right away," put in Jody.

"You'll stay and join us, won't you, Mr. Forbes?" said Zeke.

Jess still stood in mute disbelief. He couldn't grasp the change that had suddenly crashed in upon his world. And a preacher lady besides!

"I'm calling a holiday for tomorrow," Zeke went on. "We'll butcher a calf, barbecue it, and invite the whole town out!"

As he spoke he ran to sound the iron triangle. The rest of the boys needed to hear the good news straight from Eagleflight's mouth!

A PRIVATE
INTERVIEW

A few hours after supper, when the cake was gone and

the laughing and happy partying in the large living room of

the ranch house was breaking up, Mercy stole quietly out

the back door. She knew she was the only one who had seen

Jess slip out. This was something only she could do. For her

future husband's sake, she hoped she would be successful.

With careful step she made her way around to the front of

the house, then across to the barn where several horses were tied in front. She walked quietly up behind the figure preparing to mount. "Leaving without saying good-bye?" she said.

Jess spun around in surprise and saw Mercy standing a couple yards away. He laughed nervously. "You know how it is, Sister Mercy. Times change, like Jeremiah said."

"I do know," she replied. "That doesn't mean friends should ride out of each other's lives without even a good-bye."

"I was just trying to spare you and Jeremiah the grief of having to feel sorry for me."

"You sure you're not feeling sorry for yourself, Jess?"

Jess looked down at the ground and shuffled back and forth a time or two. He wasn't used to being bored right in on like that. Jeremiah was right. She was a straight shooter.

"Just because times change," Mercy went on, "doesn't mean friends should ride out of each other's lives at all."

"Aw, come on, Sister Mercy—"

"I'm just Mercy now, remember?" Mercy interrupted. "I'm hoping you and I will become such good friends you'll get to know the *real* me without the label."

"Don't seem to matter much now anyway," Jess went on. "The fact is, you beat me, don't you see? You won. I had him for a good long spell, but you got him now."

"That's not at all how it is, Jess."

"You had the winning hand. I didn't fare so well at the saloon in this town, and I wound up losing my partner to boot."

"Jess—please!"

"Look, I'm man enough to take my losses on a poker

table. So I figure I can take this loss like a man too. I won't cry over it. You're a woman, and a pretty one at that. A man's got a right to a life with a woman if he finds one that loves him, and I'm glad for Jeremiah. I mean that. Sure, I'm gonna miss riding with him. But I want him to be happy. And so I figure the sooner he don't have to worry about me no more, the sooner he can get on with his life with you. I wish you both the best, Sister Mercy."

Jess stepped up, hooked his boot in the stirrup, then swung himself into the saddle.

"Don't you love him, Jess?" said Mercy, her eyes searching through the dusk to find those of Jess.

He glanced down, finding her penetrating gaze staring straight through him. "What kind of question is that?"

"Do you love him?'

"'Course I do."

"Say it."

"I love him," said Jess, shifting nervously in his saddle.

"Well so do I, Jess. I love him."

Mercy paused but did not take her gaze away from Jess's eyes. "Now I'm going to ask you another question, Jess Forbes, a question that will test how deeply you really do love your uncle. Do you love him enough to share him?"

"I reckon I do. I'm giving him to you and leaving you to love him all to yourself."

"I didn't say that. I asked if you loved him enough to share him, not leave him."

Jess sat silent.

"I do love him enough to share him, Jess. I *want* to share him . . . with you. It would kill Jeremiah for you to leave. I happen to know how deeply *he* loves *you*. I would never want to possess him so much that I took that away from him. I'm asking you to stay, Jess, and maybe try to find a place in your heart for me too—partners, and friends!"

"You sure you want that?" Jess asked after a long minute.

"Of course I want it. I know Jeremiah would want it. Remember, Jess, I'm the only one in that house back there that saw you leave. If I'd wanted you to just ride on out of our lives, I wouldn't have followed you out here and wouldn't have said what I did."

Jess nodded. "Yeah, I reckon that's so."

"What you've got to ask yourself, Jess, is whether you are leaving out of concern for Jeremiah, or whether it's because you're feeling sorry for *yourself*."

She paused.

"I think if you're honest," she added, "you and I both know which way Jeremiah would want it. So—how much do you love him, Jess?"

Without another word, Mercy turned and walked back through the twilight. Voices of laughter could be heard from a few of the men now moseying toward their quarters. Mercy did not approach the house, however. A half-moon had risen, and a dull glow settled over the prairie. She wanted to enjoy a peaceful quiet end to the wonderful day before returning inside. She needed to thank her Father before saying her good-nights to the man he had given her.

Jess sat unmoving in the saddle, watching her disappear in the thin light.

He sat a long time, staring in the direction he'd last seen her.

"Dang," he finally muttered to himself, "if that ain't some kind of woman Jeremiah's fixin' to hitch himself up with! He's one lucky cuss!"

No one saw Mercy the rest of the evening.

52

MISSING

The morning was half gone, and a few people were already starting to arrive from town for the day's celebration before Jeremiah realized he had not seen Mercy since the previous evening. He hadn't wanted to go back to the bunkhouse without saying good-night. But she wasn't in the room when the festivities broke up. It was late by then. He figured she must already be in her room and didn't want to make a fuss trying to see her again.

He walked over to the main house to find her.

"Hey, what do you have Mercy so busy about this morning?" he asked Mrs. Simmons cheerfully as he entered the kitchen.

"I don't have her busy about anything!" Jody laughed. "I thought she was with you."

"I haven't seen her all morning!" exclaimed Jeremiah.

"Neither have I," rejoined the rancher's wife in surprise.

A moment of silence followed. The initial lightness of the exchange quietly shifted to puzzlement, then concern. They gazed at one another a second longer with expressions of confusion mingled with just a hint of anxiety. Jeremiah turned and left the kitchen the way he had come. Mrs. Simmons set down the leg of beef she had been slicing, wiped her hands, and immediately set out to search the house.

The two met three minutes later, halfway between ranch house and barn. Both shook their heads in mounting confusion as they approached.

"She's nowhere in the house," said Mrs. Simmons, "and her bed hasn't been slept in."

"None of the men have seen her," said Eagleflight, exhaling a long breath of air to hide his rising concern.

"I'll get Zeke," said the rancher's wife. Even as she spoke, she was half running out toward the barbecue pit, where aromatic smoke already rose from the hot fire in preparation for thick steaks early in the afternoon.

Two minutes later the triangle sounded loudly from the ranch house of the Bar S. When all the men and the few guests who had arrived were assembled, Zeke explained the dilemma that had suddenly come up.

"Anyone seen her since last night?"

No one answered.

"All right, then. We gotta spread out and search every inch of this place. Any of the buggies missing?"

"I already checked," Jeremiah answered. "I thought she might have gone into town for something. But all three are here."

"Dirk, count the horses and saddles."

Heyes nodded.

"The rest of you fan out—she might be anywhere. Any of you folks from town seen her this morning, either in Sweetriver or between here and there?"

Shakes of the head were all that met Zeke's inquiry. The rancher fell silent and let out a sigh.

"Well, Eagleflight," he said at length, "what do you figure? One of us probably ought to ride into town, check the stores, ask around. No sense us getting all worked up if she's fine."

Suddenly the thought came burning into Jeremiah's brain like a hot coal: *What if she had changed her mind since yesterday?* What if she wasn't able to face him and had run off in the same way she had left that traveling evangelist?

Then he realized he hadn't seen Jess either since exactly the same time. *What if this was Jess's way of—*

What was he thinking? The idea was absurd. Jess would never do something so low to get his own way.

What if they had run off together?

That was even more ridiculous—Mercy and Jess!

"Yeah, yeah—you're right, Zeke," said Jeremiah, shaking off the negative thoughts. "I'll go. I'd rather be *doing* something than just sitting waiting like I'd have to here. You send somebody after me if she shows up."

Zeke nodded. Jeremiah turned and ran for the barn.

In three minutes the large doors flew open, and he galloped out, not even stopping to close them. Thirty seconds later he disappeared in a cloud of dust over the ridge, north toward town.

MESSENGER

Halfway to Sweetriver, a rider approached Jeremiah.

He raised his arm in signal. Jeremiah reined in alongside.

The fellow's appearance indicated he had come from a good distance. His question confirmed that he was a stranger.

"This the way to the Simmons place?" he asked.

"Straight ahead," replied Eagleflight, cocking his head behind him.

"How far?"

"'Bout a mile, mile and a half."

"Much obliged," said the man, giving the leather strips between his fingers a flick.

"Anything I can do for you?" added Jeremiah. "I'm one of Mr. Simmons's hands."

"Not unless your name's Eagleflight," replied the man, pulling back on his reins again.

"My name *is* Eagleflight," rejoined Jeremiah, suddenly sitting up straight in his saddle.

"Then this is my lucky day—you just saved me a couple miles' ride! I was coming out to give you this."

He stuck his hand inside his leather vest and removed an envelope from his shirt pocket. He extended his hand and held it out across the space between their two horses. Jeremiah leaned over in his saddle, reached out, and took the envelope. Along one side of it was written his name in a rough, uneven hand he did not recognize.

His heart began to pound. He tore at the envelope, nearly ripping the single sheet it contained as he fumbled to get the paper out. Reading the brief message took only a few seconds.

"Why you miserable—!" he cried in a rage, suddenly spurring his mount alongside that of the deliveryman, and before the man could defend himself, Jeremiah had clutched the man's collar in his fist.

"Where is she?" he cried.

"Hey—whoa, mister!" exclaimed the man. "I don't know what you're talking about."

"You claim you don't know what's written here?"

"Not a word, mister. I was just sent to deliver it to you."

Calming, Jeremiah released him.

"If you're telling the truth," he said after a moment, "then you won't mind finishing that ride out to the Bar S and talking to me and my boss about it."

"But I gave you the letter. I don't see —"

"Look," interrupted Jeremiah, "unless you want me to take you straight to the sheriff about this, then I suggest you do as I say."

"All right, all right, mister. I ain't looking for no trouble."

"Then let's go!"

Jeremiah wheeled his horse around, slapped first the stranger's then his own horse on the rump, and took off in a brisk gallop back in the direction of the Bar S.

RANSOM

Jeremiah, Dirk Heyes, and Zeke and Jody Simmons

sat around the table in their kitchen with the stranger who

had identified himself as Clint Whitney.

On the table in front of them was the message from

Zeke's former hand, which they had all now read over two

or three times.

Eagleflight,

I hear yor havin a big party out there at the Simmons place. I heerd ya last night, course I had other business, so I didn't stop in to join yer fun. It's all round town bout you and the preacher lady. Only trouble is, Eagleflight, yor pretty little guest a honor's gonna be celabratin with me. Ha, ha! Ain't gonna be much celabratin without her, now is there? Yep, a real purty lady that any man'd take a fancy to, specially a lonely fella like me.

Now heres what you gotta do. If you ever wanna see this little lady alive agin, you come out to Jackson's place. I got her here. I reckon you fer her's a fair exchange. You an me's gonna finish what we started back there at Zeke's. By yorself, Eagleflight.

Yancy

"You say you saw nothing of the lady?" Heyes asked the man again.

The stranger shook his head.

"And he said nothing else?"

"I told you everything, mister," replied Whitney. "He rode up fast behind me, asked if I was going to Sweetriver. I said I was. He asked if I'd like to make me an easy five bucks. I said I sure would. He said all I had to do was take this letter to the Bar S, two miles south of town. I said I'd do it. He gave me the five dollars and then said he'd know if I did it or not, and if I tried to skip out on him he'd come after me and kill me. One look told me he meant it. He gave me the letter, and I brung it straight to you. You know the rest."

Again it was silent.

"How'd the rascal get loose?" Zeke asked at length. "I thought Sheriff Travers had him locked up."

"For a week," said Heyes. "Couldn't hold him no longer'n that."

"Well, I suppose we'd better ride in and see if he wants to go get him again," said Zeke.

"No sheriff. I'll take care of this myself," Jeremiah said, rising from the table.

"Nobody's seen Jackson since the Forbes shooting. The sheriff'll want to know."

"If Jackson's back in town and teamed up with Yancy," put in Heyes, "they'll outnumber you two to one. Them two ain't gonna fight fair, Eagleflight. You gotta let me and some of the others ride out there with you."

"Come on, Dirk," rejoined Jeremiah. "You saw the look in Yancy's eye when he left here. You figure he'd have any second thoughts about putting a bullet in Mercy's head just to get back at me?"

Heyes said nothing. Neither did Zeke. They'd both seen the look Jeremiah spoke of long before the incident of a few weeks earlier. Zeke knew he'd been mistaken to hire Yancy in the first place and had no doubts the man had killed before, probably several times. He'd thought about asking the sheriff to check his wanted files but had never gotten around to it. Now he wished he'd paid closer heed to his hunch.

Without awaiting a reply, Jeremiah left the kitchen and walked toward the bunkhouse. When he returned a few minutes later, he was in the process of strapping his holster onto his hip.

"There are other ways to go about this, Jeremiah," said Zeke quietly.

"None that I can see, Zeke. I don't reckon this is a time when prayin's gonna do much good."

"You can't ask us not to pray, Jeremiah," said Mrs. Simmons.

"You can do what you like, ma'am," returned Jeremiah. "But when I ride up there, I'd just as soon have my gun with me while I'm doing my praying. Now," he added, glancing first at Zeke, then toward Dirk. "Which way's Jackson's place?"

Zeke sighed and then reluctantly gave Jeremiah the directions.

Five minutes later, they heard the sound of Jeremiah's horse galloping up the ridge that would take him across the pasture, then east to the river and into the foothills some two or three miles from the Bar S.

The moment Jeremiah was gone, Zeke rose from the table.

"Dirk, you get into town and see if you can find the Forbes kid. He's gotta know. Then get out to Jackson's with the sheriff as soon as you can."

Heyes was already making for the door.

"Meantime," Zeke went on, "me and some of the boys'll head up through the wash. I don't figure they'll spot us coming from that direction. Of course, by the time we get there, Eagleflight may have already gotten himself killed."

The rancher glanced with a serious expression toward his wife. She knew what he was saying. She now rose as well.

55

TERROR

Mercy Randolph sat upright in a rickety wooden chair in the most filthy, run-down cabin she had ever laid eyes on. Her kidnappers had retied her hands and feet, but at least she was sitting up now, and that was some relief. The coming of daylight had also helped. She was still scared. Last night had been the most terrifying one of her existence. She was glad it was over, though today could well bring—

She couldn't think about *that*. She would just have to keep praying.

She had nearly died of fright to feel Yancy's cold clammy hands suddenly close around her mouth as he had grabbed her in the darkness only three or four minutes after she left Jess the previous evening.

"Don't you worry 'bout a thing, preacher lady," he said into her ear in an evil whisper. "Yor friend Yancy's come to rescue you from this no-good place."

A terrible low laugh followed, and Yancy's intent was unmistakable. Mercy felt herself being slowly dragged away, farther and farther from the house, happy voices and laughter fading into the night.

If only she could scream! They would all rush out in an instant.

And there was Jess, still sitting so close on his horse, . . . but she could not utter so much as a peep with the rough hand pressed against her mouth.

Yancy pulled her far enough away so as to be out of sight, then stopped and tied a bandana about her mouth. As he yanked it tight across her face, her teeth bit into her lip. She gave out a cry of pain.

"Quiet, you!" growled Yancy. "I'd rather not kill you. But if you make me, I'll think nothin' of it."

Frightened out of her wits, Mercy now felt herself hoisted onto a horse. Yancy jumped up behind, put his two strong arms around her, grabbed the reins, and led his animal slowly off through the darkness at a slow walk. All she could think was how bad he smelled and that with every step she was getting farther and farther from the safety of those she loved.

When all sounds had faded into silence behind them, he

gradually increased the pace. An hour later, having no idea where they were, except seeing in the moonlight that they had been climbing and that they had entered a lightly forested region, Yancy pulled back on the reins.

He jumped down, dragged her after him, and carried Mercy into a dimly lit cabin. One Eye Jackson sat inside. He and Yancy exchanged a few words. Then Yancy carried her into another room and tossed her onto a hard bed.

"I don't reckon anybody'll hear you now," he said, untying the bandana. "But just you mind yor manners, lady, or else I'll make it worse fer you than you even wanna think about."

"Please, Mr. Yancy, I—"

"Shut up! I don't wanna hear nothin from you. You just lay there till I say different. If you do everything I say, I just might let you live through this."

He disappeared into the other room for a minute, then returned carrying a long rope. Leaving her mouth free, he proceeded to tie her to the bed.

"You can sleep if you want, or you can lay there and pray like the good preacher lady you are," he said when the job was completed. "I don't much care. Just you don't try to get outta there, or you don't even wanna know what I'll do."

He turned and left the room, closing the door behind him.

Unable at last to prevent tears from rising into her eyes, Mercy struggled to look around her. It was nearly dark, but the thin light of the moon shone in through the single window. There was no back door. Even if she managed to squirm herself free, she would have to break the glass and climb up on something to get out. They would hear her long before she could clear enough glass away to keep from cutting herself dreadfully.

Even though she knew there was no chance of escape, Mercy wriggled a while, trying to loosen the cords around her hands. It was no use. Yancy was a strong man and had taken no chances with his knots.

Mercy dozed off and on fitfully, managing occasionally to sleep. Crying and praying, Mercy somehow made it through the horrible night.

Light and Yancy's rude fingers woke her. He untied the rope, took hold of her wrist, yanked her up out of the bed, and dragged her into the other room.

"Now that we got ourselves a woman about the place," he said, "I want you to rustle me and Jackson up some grub, preacher lady. You got flour over there and a coupla eggs. What ya say to some flapjacks, Slim?"

"OK by me," replied the other.

"You heard the man—git to it, preacher lady. Today's the big day when yor Eagleflight's gonna come rescue ya—ha, ha!"

At the sound of Jeremiah's name, Mercy's heart began to beat rapidly. Now she knew what Yancy's awful plan was.

If only she could find some way to warn Jeremiah!

>-+->-0-<-+-<

Several hours had now passed.

Yancy disappeared shortly after breakfast and had not yet returned. She sat tied in the chair where he had left her, hoping that the mean-looking man called One Eye Jackson didn't get it into his head to do anything to her while Yancy was gone.

The sound of a horse approached. Again her heart began to pound, but a minute later Yancy walked through the door.

"The trap's been set, little lady!" he said with a grin. "Yor

304

feller'll be on his way up here to git hisself killed within the hour, I reckon. Ha, ha! Hear that, Jackson—Eagleflight's gonna git hisself killed today!"

Mercy could not keep away the tears again.

"Please, Mr. Yancy," she said. "Whatever you want, I'll—"

A slap across Mercy's face silenced her, bringing a red welt to her cheek and sending her crashing sideways onto the floor. Still bound to the chair, she cried out in terror and pain as she hit the floor.

Slowly Yancy walked toward her and yanked body and chair up to a sitting position with one motion.

"I told you earlier to shut up!" he said. "I don't wanna have to remind you agin, you hear?"

"Yes," Mercy whimpered.

"I don't much care what happens to you, preacher lady. My quarrel's with Eagleflight. Soon as he's got what's comin' to him, if yor still alive, then you and me, we might just go away somewhere together. But I gotta settle things with him first, and if you git in the way then I'll cancel my plans with you once and for all."

Struggling not to cry, Mercy nodded and then sat still.

Yancy turned to occupy himself with One Eye. "You git up on the ridge," said Yancy. "You can see the plain from there. I wanna make sure he comes alone."

Slowly the minutes dragged on as Yancy endlessly polished his rifle, waiting for the trap to be sprung.

56

APPROACH

Jeremiah rode out northeast from the Bar S across the

pastureland between several ranches and the southern flow

of the Sweet River until he came to the bend of the river

back eastward. Without pausing, he dashed his horse

straight into the slow current. At this time of the year it was

barely past the animal's knees, and Jeremiah was able to

walk him through without swimming. A minute later he

urged him out the opposite side, up the bank, and into the trees.

—◦◦—◦◦—◦◦—

One Eye Jackson hurried down the hill behind his house as best he could without slipping, then around to the front of his cabin. He ran up the porch and into the house.

"He's coming," he said.

"What'd you see?" asked Yancy.

"A rider comin' this way, approaching the river."

"Just one?"

Jackson nodded.

Yancy smiled. "Then all we gotta do is wait."

He grabbed a chair, placed it facing the door, and sat down with a rifle across his lap.

—◦◦—◦◦—◦◦—

A mile after leaving the river, Jeremiah encountered the road leading to Jackson's, exactly as Zeke had described it.

He reined in and stopped.

Now, as he drew closer, he realized for the first time the recklessness of simply galloping straight in. Not only might they pick him off his saddle with a rifle before he was even in sight of the place — for they obviously expected him — but he also had Mercy's safety to think of.

If only he knew the lay of the land better. Well, it couldn't be helped.

Cautiously he urged his horse forward, at a walk now, doing his best to stay amongst the trees at the edge of the road. If they *were* waiting from some unknown vantage point ahead, he would rather not make their job any easier.

Slowly the terrain became more rugged and the climb steeper. Around a bend in the trail and through a clump of pine, Jeremiah now spotted a cabin. It could be none other than One Eye's place. It sat at the base of a steep rocky slope extending eastward.

He dismounted and tied his reins to a tree. They hadn't shot him yet. They must be waiting for him to come straight into their lair. He would leave the horse here and go the rest of the way on foot. Maybe he could get closer before they spotted him and maybe even find out where the two men were.

Creeping into the woods and on up the hill to his right and forward, slowly Jeremiah circled his way up the side of the incline until he drew even with the cabin. No one was visible in front. All was deathly still. One horse, saddled, was tied at the rail in front. They had to be waiting for him inside.

Taking each step gingerly so as not to snap a dry twig or set loose a rock and send it rolling down the steep slope, he continued on, steadily working his way around behind the small shack from above.

If only he could draw them both outside and then creep in the back door and snatch Mercy.

Jeremiah continued to work his way farther up and around the hillside. He could see the rear of the place now. There was no back door — only a small window. That might make things more difficult. If he could just get a look inside!

He crept down the hill now, very slowly and carefully, tiptoeing from tree to tree as he went. Any sound would betray him, and the rocks under his feet were loose and full of shale.

He was on the flat and in the clearing now . . . a few more steps. Jeremiah hurried forward to the house, then crouched down. He breathed a temporary sigh of relief, leaned his back against the wall of the cabin underneath the window, and slid down against one of the posts upon which the structure sat. For now at least he was out of sight.

He had to get a look inside.

Gradually he rose, inching his head up toward the dirty pane of glass. This would either get his head shot off, or tell him something more about what was going on inside the cabin.

Slowly he brought one eye, then the other, up over the sill, then squinted to peer inside. He looked into a small bedroom. It was empty except for a bed. No one was visible, and he could see nothing through the door into the front of the cabin.

He slumped back down to the ground to think. It was a long way back to his horse. If he tried to get back and make an approach from the front, he might easily give himself away before he got that far. He had been lucky to get here without being spotted. No, he thought, he would be better off making his move from right here.

He had to come up with a plan to lure Yancy and Jackson away from Mercy. *What would Jess do,* he thought to himself, *if this was a game of poker with a big pot, and he knew he had to out-bluff his opponents to have a chance of winning?*

There was only one door to the place, opening onto a small raised front porch on the opposite side from where he now sat. *That door's the key,* thought Jeremiah. All movement in or out had to proceed through that door.

He must find some way to get them *out* long enough for him to get *in* and get Mercy. *Jess, Jess, where are you when I need you? You always were the most cunning one in this partnership.*

A sound startled him.

He heard the front door open. Holding his breath, he hoped no one came around back. Someone was talking, but he could make out no words. Then the door closed, and it was silent again.

Jeremiah tried to think.

ATTEMPTED BLUFF

Inside, Mercy still sat where she was, face still red from
Yancy's blow, growing more anxious with every minute that
passed. Slowly the seconds crept by with agonizing uncertainty.

Suddenly the sound of breaking glass shattered the
silence, followed the next instant by a thud that shook the floor.

"Hey, what the — !" Yancy cried out, swearing. He leapt

to his feet and ran into the bedroom, where the disturbance had originated. He found nothing but a large rock in the middle of the floor, surrounded by broken glass.

"Eagleflight!" he yelled, spouting another curse as he turned back from the door. "He's out back!" he cried. "Jackson, come with me!"

"Jeremiah!" screamed Mercy.

Yancy spun around, rifle still in his hands, and pointed the barrel at Mercy's head. "Shut up!" he growled. "Another sound outta you and I'll end this for good!"

Trembling, Mercy bit her lip. *Oh God*, she prayed, *take care of Jeremiah!*

Yancy and Jackson rushed out the front door, rifle cocked and pistol drawn.

"You go that way!" said Yancy as he pointed to the right. "I'll go around to the left. He won't get by us. He's out behind the cabin somewhere."

They crept to the corners of the small house, inching around carefully. Then, with backs hugging the walls, they hurried to the cabin's rear corners. Again they paused, then looked around slowly and carefully once more. In less than a minute they met by the broken window in back. Neither had seen sign or heard whisper of their visitor.

"Eagleflight!" cried Yancy again, squinting out across the wooded hillside and up the ridge. "I know you're out there! Come and face me like a man. Otherwise your preacher lady's a goner."

Only silence met Yancy's challenge.

Slowly Yancy crept away from the house.

"You cover me," he said softly to Jackson. "He's out there, and I aim to find him. You see him, or if the lady makes a run for it, kill 'em!"

From where he had been listening on his belly in the cramped space underneath the house, Jeremiah now eased forward under the front porch. Glancing back, he could see Jackson's booted feet standing behind the cabin, where he himself had been only moments earlier. Inching out from the crawl space, he stood, then tiptoed, with agonizing care lest a board creak, up the three steps and inside the open door.

A gasp of terrified pleasure escaped Mercy's lips at the sight of him. A finger hastily pressed over his lips silenced any further outcry. Hurriedly Jeremiah assessed the situation. The next instant his knife shredded the cords that bound Mercy's hands and feet. He took her hand and helped her to her feet. For a second or two her knees wobbled on stiff cramped legs. Jeremiah steadied her. Silently he motioned her to follow.

They approached the door. Jeremiah drew his gun and eased around the edge of the opening, glancing quickly to the right and left. Seeing no one, he reached again for Mercy's hand and drew her after him onto the porch, then carefully and gingerly down the stairs.

A clearing of some twenty yards lay between the cabin and a clump of thick pines. If they could make it to the trees, they might put some distance between themselves and the cabin while the two kidnappers were still occupied in back.

Jeremiah turned and lowered his mouth to Mercy's ear.

"We've got to get to those trees," he whispered, pointing around in the direction of the woods. "I want you to walk as fast as you can without making a sound—"

"I won't leave you," interrupted Mercy with a frantic whisper before he could finish.

"I'll be right behind you," replied Jeremiah. "I'll walk backwards, keeping my eye on the cabin. If we're spotted,

I'll be in their line of fire so they won't be able to get a shot at you."

"Oh, Jeremiah—"

"Mercy," he said, cutting her off, "you've *got* to do as I say." He nodded his head toward the opposite side of the clearing with a look of command in his eyes. Without further objection, Mercy began slowly walking away from the porch. Jeremiah followed, inching backwards, gun drawn and eyes glued on the cabin for any sign of either Yancy's or Jackson's return from behind it.

>—+»—o—«+—<

High above the cabin on the eastward slope, Yancy paused.

Something was wrong, he thought. It was too quiet. Now that he thought of it, Eagleflight couldn't have thrown that stone through the cabin window from anything close to a distance like this.

Suddenly the truth dawned on him that the bait still sat back in the cabin—*alone*. He had broken the first rule of a successful kidnapping—never leave the victim unguarded! He had foolishly allowed himself to be lured away!

Spinning around, Yancy immediately broke into a run back down the side of the ridge.

He only took two or three steps. From the height he had climbed, and with the cabin below him, he now saw that his search had indeed been a wild-goose chase. For there on the other side of the cabin were Eagleflight and the girl making for the woods.

Yancy raised his rifle to his shoulder. An explosion of gunfire split the air, and then another.

"They're on the other side!" he cried out to his accomplice, breaking into a reckless downhill sprint. "After them, you fool!"

He paused and sent off a third shot, but it was too late to accomplish anything from this distance, and his prey was on the run.

▷─◁▷─◇─◁▷─◁

At the sound of Yancy's rifle, Mercy screamed. But both shots were nowhere close, for Yancy had let them go too hastily.

Jeremiah spun around briefly. "Run, Mercy!" he cried. "Run for the trees!"

She hesitated.

"Mercy!"

She needed no more exhortation and dashed forward.

Jeremiah sent two shots vaguely up the hill behind the cabin, where he now saw Yancy's form rushing toward them. He then turned and followed Mercy as fast as he could run. They reached the trees together. He grabbed her hand and pulled her some distance into the small wood.

More shots were fired behind them.

Jackson had run to the front of the cabin and was now shooting away wildly. A clump of bark exploded off a tree just beside them. Jeremiah threw Mercy behind the trunk of a large pine, then stopped himself and leaned against her to protect her, both of them breathing heavily.

They were momentarily invisible from the cabin. Echoes of gunfire died away.

Yancy now ran up from behind the cabin and joined One Eye. Together they peered ahead into the trees.

"Mercy, listen to me," whispered Jeremiah. "You must do exactly as I say."

She nodded with fear in her eyes.

"I want you to run from tree to tree, moving down the hill away from here. Stop at each tree to make sure you are still hidden. Keep each tree between yourself and the cabin. They won't be able to see you. You'll be safe after you get far enough into the woods. Keep yourself behind the trunks so they can't see you—do you understand?"

"Yes, but what will you—?"

"You can't worry about me. I'll follow as best I can. But you have to get away first. You have to obey me in this, or they will kill us both. Get through the woods and down the hill. If something goes wrong and I don't join you quickly—"

"Jeremiah," said Mercy, tears flooding her eyes.

"Mercy—you *have* to go. If you make it to the river, get across it. You'll be safe then. The Bar S is southwest from there. Now get going! I'll follow as soon as you're out of sight!"

Reluctantly, Mercy obeyed. She ran to the next tree Jeremiah had pointed to, stopping behind it briefly to catch her breath, and then made a dash for the next.

THE WINNING HAND

As Mercy ran into the woods, Jeremiah crept to the edge of the trunk hiding him, held his gun out around it, and let loose a volley of shots in the direction of the cabin.

In answer, three sharp reports sounded from Yancy's rifle, blasting off pieces of bark from the very tree behind which Jeremiah stood. He clearly had Jeremiah's position pin-pointed.

316

"Hey, Eagleflight!" called Yancy when the echoes from both of their guns had died away. "You can see I know where you are—or you want me to demonstrate agin?"

Only silence met his question.

Cracks sounded as two slugs shattered against the brittle pine bark, splintering bits flying against Jeremiah's face behind the trunk.

"You made your point, Yancy," Jeremiah finally called out.

"I didn't call you out here to have no shoot-out, Eagleflight," said Yancy. "This is civilized Sweetriver, after all, not Dodge City."

"It's your play, Yancy. Why'd you call me out then?"

"Like I told you—to finish what we started."

"How do you propose doing it?"

"Man-to-man, face-to-face—my fists agin yors, Eagleflight."

"You're the one who's got me pinned down with the rifle."

"All right—I'm dropping my weapon. Rumor has it that you done got yorself some religion too, Eagleflight. Pretty little preacher lady got you round her little finger, eh? Ha, ha! Well, I reckon we'll find out soon enough what kind of man or coward yor religion's made of you. You always were a mite yeller for me even afore the lady come along. But I don't figger yor religion'll take kindly to you shooting an unarmed man. So I'm tellin you I'm dropping my rifle, and you can come out and face me if yor man enough for it. Then we'll settle this thing man-to-man."

The sound of a rifle falling on the dirt followed.

Jeremiah waited a few seconds, then cautiously peered around the edge of the tree trunk. About halfway to the cabin in the middle of the clearing Yancy stood, calmly waiting, hands empty, a rifle on the ground about eight feet away. Jeremiah came the rest of the way into the open, warm pistol still in his hand. He stopped.

"Well, if it ain't my old friend Eagleflight!" said Yancy. "Come on over—you can see my rifle's on the ground and my hands is empty."

"There's still your friend there," said Jeremiah, motioning to One Eye Jackson, who stood motionless.

"Aw, he ain't gonna hurt you, Eagleflight. I told him me and you's gotta fight this out ourselves. He knows if he hurt you I'd have to kill him. Git back to the cabin, Jackson. Show Eagleflight there ain't nothin to be afeared of."

Jackson obeyed.

"Now put that gun away, Eagleflight. A religious man like you ain't gonna shoot nobody."

Keeping a wary eye on both men, Jeremiah slowly placed his gun back in his holster and took a few steps forward from amongst the trees. Yancy now began walking slowly forward, making no move toward his rifle. Behind him, Jackson untied Yancy's horse, then mounted and wheeled it around.

A sickening feeling came over Jeremiah, but it was too late. By holstering his gun, he'd given away his only advantage. When he heard the next words out of Yancy's mouth, he knew what was so dangerous about two-to-one odds.

"Go git the girl, Jackson," ordered Yancy without turning around, eyes glued on Jeremiah where he stood, powerless. "Go down the trail quarter mile or so, then cut into the woods. She'll be makin fer the river."

Jackson lashed the horse and galloped away from the cabin down the road, while Jeremiah watched in agony.

"Go ahead, Eagleflight," taunted Yancy. "Why don't you try to stop him. Pull yor gun and shoot him, Eagleflight!

Ha, ha! Yor a yeller coward, just like I figgered! Course, if you tried it, I'd whip out my pistol and kill you . . . and we'd get us the girl anyway. Ha, ha!"

Standing helpless, Jeremiah watched Jackson disappear. The echo of hooves gradually receded in the direction from which he himself had ridden twenty minutes earlier.

Once again the two men stood facing one another, hands down at their sides. All fell quiet. A slow evil grin spread over Yancy's face.

"You see, Eagleflight," he said, "yor religion and yor fallin all over that preacher lady's made a blamed fool outta you. Now you got yorself in a bad situation. You *gotta* fight me. It's the only chance yor little preachin' girlfriend has. You gotta get the best of me, Eagleflight, afore Jackson gits back with her. You gotta knock me out cold, so you can get the drop on him when he comes back. Ha, ha! So come on. Show me what yor made of, Eagleflight."

Yancy clenched his fists and raised them to fighting level, then slowly began to advance. The smile disappeared from his lips.

Jeremiah walked forward to meet him, slowly clenching and then raising his own hands.

When only about ten feet separated them, Yancy stopped. An evil glint came into his eye, and this time there was no mistaking the murderous gleam.

He loosened his fists and dropped his hands to his side. Beside his holster, the fingers of his right hand began to twitch in anticipation.

"I just wanted to see yor eyes up close, Eagleflight," he said in a menacing tone. "I wanted to see yor eyes the second you knew you was a dead man. You see, I got no intention of *fightin'* you. . . . I'm gonna *kill* you!"

With speed so lightning fast that Jeremiah scarcely saw the motion, Yancy's hand slapped his side and drew his gun.

Before his finger could find the trigger an explosion rang out from the hillside above the cabin. Blood spurted from Yancy's right shoulder, and he fell forward with a scream of pain. Jeremiah's pistol was out of its holster the next instant, covering the wounded man in case any thoughts entered his mind of picking up his gun where it lay beside him.

Several Bar S men now scrambled down the hillside.

A moment later, Zeke came running up. Alongside him was his wife, whose leather vest and chaps presented an altogether different picture than Jeremiah had observed since hiring on. In her hand, Jody carried the rifle that had saved his life.

With an expression of more astonishment than thanks, Jeremiah stood with his mouth gaping at the sight, then slowly nodded his bewildered appreciation while some of the other men checked Yancy's wound.

"We didn't want to put you in the position of trying to figure how the Lord's people ought to deal with somebody trying to kill them," said Zeke. "So we figured we'd better take care of Yancy for you."

"But . . . Mrs. Simmons—," stammered Jeremiah, still staring at the unlikely female marksman.

"Something I discovered about this lady after I married her," laughed Zeke. "She's the fastest draw and deadliest shot I've ever seen. When somebody's life's on the line—like yours was, 'cause Yancy's fast himself—I make sure Jody's with me."

"You're right about my life being on the line. I wouldn't have been able to do anything to save myself," replied Jeremiah. "He had me dead to rights."

"We had just cleared the ridge up there when I saw you both down here in front of the house," said Zeke. "I could see what was on Yancy's mind right off, and I knew we only had a few seconds."

"Zeke told me to kneel down and take aim," said Jody, "but not to fire unless he drew on you. About three seconds later that's exactly what he did."

"Well, I'm indebted to you both," said Jeremiah, at last finding his tongue. "I've never seen anything like it," he added, shaking his head.

"Get up, Yancy," said Zeke, stooping down to help his old ranch hand. "I did everything I could to try to help you. Why in tarnation wouldn't you pay attention to what was going on at the Bar S? You could have had a good life there. Now you're going to have to spend a little longer in Travers's jail than you did last time. Come on—we'd better get you patched up."

>─◆─○─◆─◁

From deep in the woods, Mercy heard the shot.

Unable to help herself, she cried out, then turned and ran terrified back toward the cabin, not pausing long enough to think what would happen to her if her worst fears were true and the bullet had indeed found Jeremiah's heart.

She had not gone far, however, before the sound of heavy booted feet lumbered toward her.

Mercy glanced toward the sound. It was the horrible One Eye Jackson!

She tried to run, but in a panic succeeded only in tripping over an exposed root and falling flat on her face. A moment later the cold grip of a strong hand laid hold of her shoulder.

"Ain't no way to treat yor ol' friend One Eye," said Jackson, "tryin to run away like that. Come with me, Lady Mercy. We's going back up t' my place."

He yanked her to her feet and pushed her rudely in front of him. But they had only gone a short distance when suddenly a voice sounded unexpectedly behind them.

"Let go of her, Jackson," it said, "and get your hands into the air."

Jackson turned around to see his old poker rival holding a gun pointed straight at his midsection.

"Jess!" cried Mercy, wriggling free from the grasp that held her and running to the safety of Jess's side. He placed his left arm around her while she wept on his shoulder in relief.

"You put a bullet into my gut once, Jackson," said Jess. "So I reckon I owe you the one in my pistol right now. But I don't want to shoot you in front of the lady. So you just march out of these trees the way you came."

Jackson swore under his breath. There was nothing he could do, and he knew it. He raised his hands and obeyed.

Jess momentarily stepped away from Mercy. He removed the Colt from Jackson's holster and stuck it into his own belt. Pistol outstretched in front of him, Jess Forbes then followed Jackson out of the woods and up the hill. As they walked, he steadied his partner's now faint and wobbly-legged lady.

When at last the cabin came into sight, Mercy suddenly found her strength. Weeping now for joy, she broke free and ran forward into Jeremiah's waiting arms.

59

ANOTHER LETTER

The letter that arrived at the Randolph home in Louis-

ville in the final week of October was not so unexpected as

Mercy's first from Kansas, though it was no less enthusiasti-

cally received by Sinclair and Ernestine Randolph.

Mercy had written twice to her parents in the meantime,

telling them about the Simmonses and of her newfound spiri-

tual discoveries. But she had only mentioned the name

Jeremiah Eagleflight in passing. Now it was time they knew more.

Dear Mother and Father,

Oh, so much has happened! I hardly know where to begin. We had a dangerous scare with a couple of really bad men. I don't want to alarm you, but it involved me. I am all right, though. Everything turned out fine, and I will tell you all about it when I see you.

I think I have spoken of a man named Jeremiah Eagleflight. He works here on the Simmons ranch too. He helped me so much after I left Reverend Mertree. He was not a Christian at the time, but he behaved like one and helped me to see spiritual truth in new ways. He was also the one who rescued me from the men I mentioned. He is like no one I have ever met. He is such a gentle and kind and considerate man. Even though he wears a gun and wasn't afraid for a second to fight for me when I was in danger, he is such a gentleman. He is a Christian now and isn't wearing his gun anymore.

Oh, there is so much to tell! But the long and the short of it is that he has asked me to marry him. Can you believe it? I never dreamed of such things as have happened to me! So you see, I *have* to talk to you—and soon. You must meet him too.

So I am coming home. I have saved a little money, and the Simmonses have agreed to help me with the rest. I am sorry this letter is so short, but I want to tell you everything myself when I get there! The Simmonses and Jeremiah will take me to Fort Hays, and I will catch the train from there to Kansas City and then on to Louisville.

I can't wait to see you. I should be home in less than a week after you receive this letter.

Mercy

The tears that fell from Mrs. Randolph's eyes this time were tears of quiet joy. Her daughter was coming home! Suddenly there was so much to do—she could be here any day!

60

PLANS

Mercy Randolph and Jeremiah Eagleflight walked

slowly away from the Simmonses' house toward the open

pastureland between the ranch and the Sweet River.

Sunset came earlier now that autumn was advancing

toward winter. They walked west toward the red and orange

and pink horizon, where the huge round globe of the sun was

now half gone behind the line of the prairie in the distance.

It was a spectacular display. As the sun steadily disappeared, the remnants of its glow stretched skyward, giving way now to darker shades of purple, deepening reds, and flaming oranges. About them all was calm and peaceful. Even the cattle scattered across the range seemed to sense the holiness of God's paintbrush and were still.

On they walked in the quiet dusk. Mercy clung tightly to Jeremiah's arm. A slight chill was in the air, but neither of them felt the cold. What was cold to such as they? Were they not in love, with their whole lives in front of them? What could a little cold matter alongside that?

"How soon will you come?" asked Mercy at length.

"As soon as you write to tell me I should," replied Jeremiah.

"Oh, I shall miss you," exclaimed Mercy. "I wish you could come with me, and we could go see my parents together."

"I think this is best. You need some time alone with them after what has happened. And who knows, you may get away from here and change your mind."

"Change my mind—about what?"

"About me."

"Jeremiah Eagleflight—don't you say such a thing! I will never change my mind about you!"

He laughed. "Just making sure," he said. "I promise I will be along soon. I need to have a talk with your father, and I don't want to wait any longer than I have to."

"You'll be able to celebrate Christmas in Louisville with us! It will be wonderful."

"If your family will have me—I have nowhere else to go."

"They will want you," assured Mercy. "I will make sure of it!"

"Do they know what a determined lady their daughter has become?" laughed Jeremiah.

"*Become?*—I'm afraid I always was."

Slowly they turned and began walking back toward the house. Inside, Zeke and Jody, along with Jess, were waiting for them.

"Well, young lady," said Zeke once they were all sitting down together, "we are all going to miss you around here."

"Me most of all," put in Jody. "I'll be the only woman again." She paused and a thoughtful look spread over her face. "I almost wish I could go with you," she added.

Suddenly a light came over Mercy's face. "Why *don't* you?" she exclaimed.

The words fell like an unexpected thunderclap. The room suddenly became silent.

"My mother would love to see you!" Mercy went on enthusiastically. "I told you what she said in her last letter— how appreciative she and my father were that you took me in, and how they wanted to meet you and Zeke someday."

Jody glanced at Zeke.

"Nothing wrong with the idea that I can see," the rancher said. "Maybe I'll join Eagleflight when it comes time for him to go. Then you and I can come home on the train together, maybe stop off in Kansas City for a few days."

"Oh, how exciting!" exclaimed Jody. "I can see some new fabrics and patterns. I'll get up on the latest fashions for Mrs. Dunakin. And who knows, maybe we'll just take in the wedding of a certain young couple while we're there."

"What about me?" put in Jess, with the tone of a child being left out of a game.

"Why, you have to stay here with Heyes to keep the ranch and the boys in line," rejoined Zeke. "Now that I put you on my payroll, you've got to earn your keep." The rancher threw a wink at Jess's partner.

"Dang—sounds like I'll miss out on all the fun."

"Don't worry, Jess," said Mercy. "As soon as there are any wedding plans, we'll send for you. After all, you're the only possible one who could stand alongside Jeremiah—isn't that right, Jeremiah?"

"That's right," replied Jeremiah. "He's my partner through thick and thin."

"Well, Mrs. Simmons," said Zeke, turning to his wife. "You better get yourself packed. We're leaving for Fort Hays with the sunrise!"

61

PARTINGS
AND PROMISES

The first day's wagon ride to Fort Hays to meet the

Union Pacific the next morning was lively.

A beautiful, crisp, sunny fall day had risen to meet the

Kansas travelers.

Jody and Zeke laughed with anticipation at the idea of

such a spur-of-the-moment trip.

"I threw things into my case so fast last night," said Jody, "I don't even know what's in it."

"Just an excuse," put in Zeke with a glance at Jeremiah, "so she can get there and then say she has to buy some new clothes."

"I may just do that very thing," rejoined Jody. "And why not? We haven't been to Kansas City in ages, Zeke. Could we stop off in the city on our way back?"

"If you're going to shop, I may just have to look for a new pair of boots."

"And take me out to dinner?"

Zeke nodded. "Why not? We'll spend a couple days in Kansas City on our way back—best steaks in the West."

"A second honeymoon!" exclaimed Mercy. "What fun you'll have."

The closer they came to their destination the following morning, the more subdued the mood became between Mercy and Jeremiah. No sooner had they discovered their love for one another than they had to part.

They arrived in Fort Hays shortly after noon. The eastbound was scheduled for departure at two-thirty.

"Let's go over to the hotel so the ladies can freshen up," suggested Zeke. "Then we can all have some lunch."

Zeke greeted the proprietor, an old friend. He and Jeremiah found a table near the street window and ordered four dinners while the ladies washed their faces and straightened their dresses and hair in the ladies' guest room. Jody seemed to be even more excited about the trip than Mercy, and by the time the two returned they were giggling like schoolgirls.

"They don't seem none too sad about leaving us, do they, Zeke?" said Jeremiah as they approached.

"Oh, Jeremiah," said Mercy, "I don't know what to feel. I'm excited about going home to Louisville and seeing my family again. But I want to stay here with you too. I don't think I could bear it if Jody weren't going with me."

"Did you see the photographer's booth set up there in the lobby?" asked Jeremiah.

"I didn't know that's what it was," replied Mercy.

"What do you say we go have our picture taken together?"

"Oh yes!" exclaimed Mercy. "Then I will be able to show you to my parents!"

"Let's go," said Zeke. "This I want to see. Maybe Jody and I will do the same."

All four rose from the table and walked into the lobby.

The photographer at the booth greeted his prospective customers warmly.

"Sit right down there in front of the camera," he said after the arrangements had been made. "A little closer, young lady . . . get your faces right together. Good—now hold it right there."

He stepped back, put his head under the camera's black cloth, focused the lens one final time, then *poof!* went the flash of powder.

"That's all there is to it," he said. "You can pick up the photograph tomorrow."

"Tomorrow—we'll all be gone by then," said Jeremiah.

"I can post it to you by mail."

"Is there any chance you could get it ready right now—today?" asked Jeremiah. "I'll pay you extra if I have to."

"Well . . . I don't know."

"The ladies have a train to catch."

"What time's the train?"

"Two-thirty."

"Hmm . . ." The man looked at his watch. "It's about ten till twelve. Yes . . . well, perhaps I could do it at that. Come back at two-fifteen, and I'll try to have it for you."

"Our turn now, Jody," said Zeke.

A few minutes later, laughing over the adventure, the four returned to their table, where their dinners were just arriving. The men consumed the stew, potatoes, biscuits, and coffee with the appetites of hardworking men. Mercy's stomach, however, was a little too queasy to swallow much of anything. Suddenly she realized that she was very, very sad in the midst of anticipating going home. She was being pulled in opposite directions at the same time, and her insides were caught right in the middle.

An hour later the men headed for the station, each with a suitcase in one hand and a pretty lady on the other arm. They boarded the train together. Zeke led the way inside, found two seats, and stowed the women's bags. The conductor strode down the aisle reminding the passengers to get settled.

Zeke looked at his watch. "I'll go fetch the photographs," he said.

He returned a few minutes later, handing the small framed oval to Mercy, who took it and smiled.

Eagleflight glanced over his shoulder and was just about to offer comment when the conductor's voice sounded.

"Ten minutes," he called as he went. "Train pulls out in ten minutes."

The four turned and left the coach.

Reaching the wooden platform again, Jeremiah spoke first to Jody. "You take good care of her, Mrs. Simmons," he said.

"Don't you worry about a thing, Jeremiah. And *you* take good care of my husband!"

Zeke laughed.

Mercy and Eagleflight now walked a short distance away
from the rancher and his wife, who were by now like father
and mother to them.

"You have the address," said Mercy, suddenly nervous.
"You will write, won't you?"

"I'm not much of a letter writer."

"You *must* write. I want to know everything that happens
at the ranch, and to you."

"I'm hoping you'll write and tell me to come."

Mercy nodded, then gazed up into his eyes. She could not
stop the tears that followed.

Jeremiah took her in his arms. They held one another for
a few moments.

"I love you, Mercy Randolph," whispered Jeremiah into
her ear.

"Jeremiah, I don't want to leave you!" said Mercy, melting
completely into his embrace. She felt his vest against her face.
She cried softly, her tears staining the rough brown leather.

"You gotta admit, though," said Jeremiah, "God's been
mighty good to us this far. You're the one who helped me
start realizing it. Now I figure we've both gotta trust him,
like you told me once, to see us through this, as hard as it is."

Silently Mercy nodded.

"'Board!" called out the conductor behind them.

A moment longer they stood. Then Mercy stepped back,
took in a deep breath, and did her best to smile. But her
eyes were full of tears, and her smile full of an aching heart.
There was so much to say, but she could not get out a single
word. She turned to rejoin Jody, streams now running
down her glistening cheeks.

Jeremiah walked over and stood beside Zeke. The two
women boarded the train, one a seasoned rancher's wife

who knew who she was and what she was about, the other a strong-spirited girl who was just learning.

A few chugs sounded from the engine in front, then slowly the train eased into motion. Unconsciously Jeremiah began walking across the platform alongside the window where Mercy sat, her hand against the pane toward him, their eyes locked upon one another.

The engine gradually picked up speed. Jeremiah increased his step. In half a minute he reached the end of the platform and could go no farther.

Within moments Mercy's face disappeared from view. Staring after her, eyes fixed on the receding window where he knew she sat gazing after him, he now raised his hand in one final farewell.

He held it aloft for another fifteen or twenty seconds until the last car of the train had disappeared from view, then slowly lowered it. Still he stood, alone, gazing down the now-empty track.

He drew in a couple of breaths to steady himself and wiped once or twice unconsciously at his eyes. At last Jeremiah Eagleflight turned and walked back toward Zeke on the station platform, where he had left him.

Everything in him wanted to jump on a horse and follow the train to Louisville! But he himself had told Mercy, "This is best, God's been good to us. . . . We gotta trust him."

Jeremiah sighed again. Hard as it was, they could be in no hurry. They had to give God time to carry out whatever might be his plans for them.

He and Zeke looked at one another with expressions that said more than would be possible with words. Zeke gave Jeremiah a fatherly pat on the back. Then the two men turned and left the station together.